倍斯特出版事業有限公司
Best Publishing Ltd.

◎著

*i*BT 新托福寫作 拿高分

獨立+
整合題型

Score High on iBT Writing Test!

最新具指標性的iBT新托福寫作書

只要跟著【超強範文】+【高分句型應用與解析】2大元素

輕鬆應戰 iBT 新托福寫作！

○ 最詳實擬真！
iBT新托福寫作範文、應用與解析：
→ 發展論點＋整合寫作＋聽力 同步快速提升
突破iBT 110⁺！

MP3

Author's Words
作者序

　　很高興能與倍斯特出版社合作，撰寫這本充滿創意的托福寫作書。在作者十餘年的英語教學經驗中，用過許多國內外出版的托福教材，比起大多數以模擬考為主的托福教材，本書可説是一項前所未有的創舉！是第一本結合電影、名人、軼事、時事，同時以學術風格撰寫，符合實際考題難度的托福教材。托福測驗是學術英文的測驗，但許多應考者往往不熟悉學術英文及口語化英文的差異，導致寫作時太過口語化，而無法提升分數，因此本書非常適合需要加強學術英文的考生。尤其在寫作部分，考生若能運用學術字彙、優美正確的文法、精準生動的例證及豐富的轉折語提高連貫性，要取得25分以上的分數應該不會太難，而上述四點也是ETS官方寫作評分標準所要求的。本書不但對以上四點做出詳細解析，而且在重要句型整理章節更整理、補充豐富的句型模板及例句。希望本書能導引讀者進入學術英文寫作的美麗世界。

莊琬君

Editor's Words
編者序

　　iBT新托福寫作考試旨在測驗考生是否能完整表達論述內容，以及上下文的連結是否符合邏輯，分有獨立型與整合型兩種類型，前者考驗考生是否能構思出自己的一套論點，以支持自己的想法；後者則考驗是否能抓住閱讀以及聽力的重點，並統合寫出符合考題的答案。

　　為了能夠讓考生自然而然累積論點，本書特別將時下英美電影，以及歐美名人故事將考試題目做結合，並引導讀者在隨後的高分範文中看到和電影情節、名人故事相關的論點，以及支持論點的細節，讓讀者不再抗拒寫作，而是能學著從日常生活的娛樂中，汲取、收集靈感，慢慢地累積自己的批判性能力，英文寫作也能有穩定的進步。

　　另外，全書也有句型整理、解析及應用的單元，這尤其對整合題型有幫助，如何在短時間累積句型，並依照考題的變化，做出不同的歸納方式，並不容易，但藉由本書的範例、整理，同時融入大眾較有興趣的電影與名人故事，我們相信準備iBT新托福寫作考試是可以不那麼單一、乏味的。

　　現在就跟著本書的電影畫面、名人故事結合寫作，加強寫作能力，在循序漸進中，無形中你也能有所啟發，發展出千變萬化的文字、句型與論點，絕對不能錯過！

編輯部敬上

CONTENTS 目次

PART ❶ 獨立題型篇

chapter 1 | 媒體與教育類題型

chapter 2 │ 環境與人生觀類題型

○題目："The world is losing lots of natural resources. Choose one resource that is disappearing and explain why it's urgent to save it." Use specific details and examples to support your viewpoint.

○題目："Developing an industry is more important than saving the environment for endangered animals." Do you agree or disagree with the statement? Use specific details and examples to support your viewpoint.

○題目："Some people believe human activities are harmful to the earth; others think human activities make the earth a better place. What is your opinion?" Use specific details and examples to support your viewpoint.

○題目："Only people who possess a large amount of wealth are successful". Do you agree or disagree with the statement? Use specific details and examples to support your viewpoint.

chapter 3 | 前十二個單元句型整理、解析及應用

Part ❷ 整合題型篇

chapter 4 ｜ 美國教育、歷史與文學類型

chapter 5 ｜ 西洋藝術與科學類型

chapter 6 │ 前十二個單元句型整理、解析及應用

使 · 用 · 說 · 明 · 與 · 學 · 習 · 特 · 色
INSTRUCTIONS

• Part 1 獨立題型的題目摸擬 ETS 官方公布的題庫裡，最普遍的四種題型：Agree/Disagree（同意與否題）、Stating Opinions（闡述意見題）、Comparison（比較題），及 Stating Preference（偏好題）。

• 即使讀者未看過範文引用的電影或名人例證，透過劇情簡述就能快速建立相關背景知識。

• 針對四種文類，搭配MP3，邊「聽」高分範文，邊熟悉高分寫法！

• Unit 1-12挑選範文的字彙，均針對不同類型題目，提供精準生動的相關字彙。在Unit 13-18句型整理中，掌握高分句型！

Unit 25 西洋藝術類

🎬 **塗鴉藝術及凱斯‧哈林 Graffiti Art and Keith Haring**

Unit 25 西洋藝術類：塗鴉藝術及凱斯‧哈林

with outlines. His themes involve sexuality, war, birth, and death, often mocking the mainstream society in caricatures.

As Haring's reputation grew, he took on larger projects. His most notable work is the public mural titled, "Crack is Wack", inspired by his studio assistant who was addicted to crack and addressing the deteriorating drug issue in New York. The mural is representative of Haring's broad concerns for the American society in the 1980s. He was a social activist as well, heavily involved in socio-political movements, in which he participated in charitable support for children and fought against racial discrimination. Before his death at age 31, he established the Keith Haring Foundation and the Pop Shop; both have continued his legacy till today.

請聽與短文相關的課堂內容 〔Track 25〕

Now listen to a lecture in an art class regarding graffiti.

(Professor) Graffiti has existed for as long as written words have existed, with examples traced back to Ancient Greece, Ancient Egypt, and the Roman Empire. In fact, the word graffiti came from the Roman Empire. Some even consider cave drawings by cavemen in the Neolithic Age the earliest form of graffiti, and thus make it the longest existent art form. Basically, graffiti refers to writing or drawings that have been scrawled, painted, or sprayed on surfaces in public in an illicit manner. The general functions of graffiti include

209

● Part 2 整合題型篇的單元主題皆呼應美國學術圈及主流媒體近年來的熱門話題，不但能增加專業知識，協助讀者累積至少相當於美國本土大一學生的英文程度，也引起讀者興趣。閱讀篇章及課堂講述也符合大一至大二大學教科書的難度（即托福考試的程度）。

Unit 31

美國教育類重要句型整理、

Unit 32

美國歷史類重要句型整理、解析及應用

將閱讀篇章的主要論點換句話說（Paraphrase）的重要句型、解析及應用

使用說明

Unit 21 的範文採取面對面結構，以及 Unit 22 的範文採取點對點結構，但不管是哪一個結構，主文都須要換句話說，所以句型重點都在 "Paraphrase 換句話說句型"。

解析 1

除了以類似字（synonyms）將主要論點重述，最佳的 paraphrase 應變化原句的結構，且保留大部分的原意。例如 although S+V 轉換為 despite N 或 in spite of N。

論點原句

Though hippies were sometimes criticized for their use of drugs, they indeed made significant contributions to the American society.
(Part 2 Unit 21)

雖然嬉皮有時因為使用毒品而被批評，他們的確對美國社會做出重要貢獻。
《節選自 Part 2 Unit 21》

264

● 每單元高分範文除有單句解析外，Unit 31-36 整理出必備主旨句及闡明閱讀篇章和課堂講述之間關係的整合句。針對不同題型，以不同的範文結構作答。

Unit 22 美國歷史類：美國內戰之後的重建時期

高分範文搶先看 〔Track 22〕

The lecture presents three arguments regarding the political, social and economic areas of the Reconstruction period to refute the arguments in the reading.

課堂講述呈現關於重建時期的政治、社會和經濟方面的三個論點，以反駁閱讀篇章的論點。閱讀篇章主張重建時期是最成功的，然而課堂講述的

Unit 22 美國歷史類：美國內戰之後的重建時期

高分範文解析

關鍵句 1

Whereas the reading argues for the successes of Reconstruction, the lecture contends otherwise.

解析

第一段的兩句都屬於此篇範文的主旨句（thesis statement）。此單元的閱讀篇章和課堂講述各提出三個相反的論點，而例句 1.更精簡地闡明兩者互相取代的關係。otherwise（adv.）意近 contrarily。

PART 1

獨立題型篇

　　各類英文檢定考試的寫作評分項目不離以下三點：第一、用字準確（accuracy)、第二、句型變化（variation）、第三、論點（concrete supporting ideas)，Part 1 獨立題型篇先用電影劇情或名人故事帶入常見的 iBT 寫作題目，並搶先看重要論點句做暖身。接著切入看中英對照的高分範文，進而學習深度應用，一邊建構論點，一邊讓學術寫作上的用字、論點又準、又好！

將看完的章節打個勾，提升寫作自信心！

Unit ❶ 媒體類

畫面過於聳動——搭配電影：《獨家腥聞》（*Nightcrawler*）

話說 iBT 新托福寫作題目與電影或名人故事
➡ 從以下題目為例，看題目與電影《獨家腥聞》
（*Nightcrawler*）間的關連

"The media today present too many provocative images; instead, the media should place more emphasis on the deeper meaning behind those images." Do you agree or disagree with the statement? Use specific details and examples to support your viewpoint.

「當今的媒體呈現太多聳動的畫面；反之，媒體應該放更多重心去探討那些畫面背後的深層意義。」你同意或不同意以上敘述？請使用精準的細節和例證支持你的論點。

劇情簡述

傑克‧葛倫霍（Jake Gyllenhaal）在《獨家腥聞》（*Nightcrawler*（又譯《夜行者》））扮演的路易斯‧布魯（Louis Bloom）是一位靠著販賣贓物維生的年輕人。一晚，他偶然撞見拍攝車禍現場血腥畫面的攝影師，決定效法並販賣血腥畫面給電視台。他視自己為充滿野心的企業家，而販賣車禍及犯罪現場的聳動畫面給電視台，的確替他賺進豐厚的收入。另一方面，新聞節目製作人尼娜因為收視率低迷，勉為其難地同意買下路易斯拍的畫面。對雙方而言，這是一場雙贏的決定。

此類題型重點句搶先看

❶ Presenting provocative images has evolved into one of the fastest ways to reach consumers, though occasionally ethical questions are raised.

呈現聳動的畫面已演變成打動消費者最快速的方式，雖然偶爾道德方面的問題會被提出來。

❷ News programs have no choice but to flow with the tide to boost ratings, and tabloids have to publish spine-tingling photos to increase sales.

新聞節目不得不隨波逐流地跟上這股趨勢，以提高收視率，而八卦媒體必須出版令人血脈噴張的照片，以提升銷售量。

高分範文搶先看 ▶ Track 01

Upon first glance, the statement seems like a justifiable critique, considering there's so much violence and **risqué**[1] content in the media nowadays. However, I concede that in a democratic society with limited **censorship**[2] of the media, it is rarely the duty of the media to probe further into the concepts behind those images, and that **provocative**[3] images are simply indicative of the vibrant competitions in the media.

First, all companies are pursuing the utmost profit, and those in the media are no exception. Besides, with the advent of the Internet, there has been an explosion of media resources, which leads to probably the fiercest competition in media history. Therefore, presenting provocative images has evolved into one of the fastest ways to reach consumers, though occasionally

乍看之下，敘述似乎是句正當的批評，考慮到當今媒體充斥著暴力和幾近傷風敗俗的內容。然而，我認為在民主社會有限的媒體審查制度之下，深入探討畫面背後的觀念並不是媒體的責任，而且聳動的畫面只是顯示媒體蓬勃的競爭現象。

首先，所有的公司都在追求最高利潤，媒體業也不例外。此外，隨著網路問世，媒體資源已呈爆炸性的發展，導致可能是媒體史上最激烈的競爭狀態。因此，呈現聳動的畫面已演變成打動消費者最快速的方式，雖然偶爾道德方面的問題會被提出來。例如，廣告常常運用辛辣刺激的畫面去吸引觀眾的注意。同理，新聞節

ethical questions are raised. For instance, advertisements often apply **piquant**[4] images to draw spectators' attention. By the same token, news programs have no choice but to flow with the tide to boost ratings, and tabloids have to publish **spine-tingling**[5] photos to increase sales. If ethical issues are disregarded, utilizing sensational images is merely an efficient marketing strategy.

Moreover, what constitutes such images is highly disputable, as various people hold divergent standards for them. I would argue that it is not the media's responsibility to provide deeper concepts. On the contrary, it is the viewers' responsibility to research further should they be interested. For example, as tabloids and melodrama **abound**[6], audience can turn to public television and education channels if they wish to

目不得不隨波逐流地跟上這股趨勢，以提高收視率，而八卦媒體必須出版令人血脈噴張的照片，以提升銷售量。暫時忽略道德議題的話，運用聳動的畫面只是個高效率的行銷策略。

而且，這種畫面的構成元素是高度可議的，因為不同的人對這些畫面抱持的標準有所差異。我主張提供更深層的觀念並不是媒體的責任。相反地，做出更深入的探討應該是觀眾的責任，萬一他們有興趣的話。例如，雖然八卦媒體和煽情戲劇節目到處充斥，如果觀眾想要獲取知識性的內容，他們可以轉向公共電視或教育頻道。也就是説，不須強制媒體去強調深層意義。

have access to intellectual discourse. In other words, it is not mandatory for the media to emphasize profound meaning.

In conclusion, I disagree with the statement because it **undermines**[7] the diversity of the media. It is not the media's job to **instill**[8] concepts into us; rather, it is the viewers' job to search for meaning.

總而言之，我不同意題目敘述，因為它輕忽了媒體的多樣性。灌輸觀念給我們並不是媒體的工作，反之，追尋意義應該是觀眾的工作。

高分範文解析

關鍵句 1 ▶

Besides, with the advent of the Internet, there has been an explosion of media resources, **which** leads to probably the fiercest competition in media history. （此外，隨著網路問世，媒體資源已呈爆炸性的發展，導致可能是媒體史上最激烈的競爭狀態。）

解析

1. 重點：利用形容詞子句及副詞片語增加句型的豐富度。形容詞子句中的關係代名詞 which 在此代替關代之前的主要子句，即 which 代替「媒體資源已呈爆炸性發展」。

2. with N. （副詞片語）表隨之發生的現象。例 1：With the accolades from movie critics, Gyllenhaal's performance might win him the Best Actor Award, which is predicted by some journalists. （隨著影評家的讚賞，葛倫霍的表演可能為他贏得最佳男主角獎，這已被一些記者預測。）

例 2：With the crowning of the Best Actress Award, Jennifer Lawrence elevated her status in Hollywood, which certainly will boost her income. （隨著最佳女主角獎的加冕，珍妮佛・羅倫斯提高她在好萊塢的地位，這當然會提高她的片酬。）

關鍵句 2

Moreover, what constitutes such images is highly disputable, as various people hold divergent standards for them. （而且，這種畫面的構成元素是高度可議的，因為不同的人對這些畫面抱持的標準有所差異。）

解析

1. 重點：名詞子句 what constitutes such images 當作第一個子句裡的主詞，視為單數，故主要動詞為 is。例：What marked a milestone in Gyllenhaal's acting career was his performance in *Nightcrawler*. （在葛倫霍的演藝生涯裡劃下里程碑的，是他在《獨家腥聞》裡的表演。）

重要字彙與例句

① risqué *adj.* 近乎色情的，傷風敗俗的

The party was filled with risqué banter and laughter.

那場派對充斥著不正經的玩笑話和笑聲。

② censorship *n.* 審查制度

The severity of censorship indicates the level of freedom of speech in a country.

在一個國家，審查制度的嚴厲暗示了言論自由的程度。

③ provocative *adj.* 聳動的

Applying provocative photos to boost the sales of magazines is no news nowadays.

今日，應用聳動的照片去提升雜誌的銷售量已經不是什麼新鮮事了。

④ piquant *adj.* 辛辣刺激的，聳動的

Celebrities with piquant language seem to be favored by the media currently.

當今言論辛辣的名人似乎比較受到媒體青睞。

⑤ spine-tingling *adj.* 令人感覺激動的

The movie provides spine-tingling sensations.

這部電影提供了令人激動的感官體驗。

⑥ **abound** *vi.* **豐富；富於**

The philanthropist abounds in charity.

這位慈善家廣行善事，多施賙濟。

⑦ **undermine** *vt.* **削弱；輕忽**

The king's influence was gradually undermined after he stepped down due to health reasons.

國王的影響力漸漸式微，在他因為健康因素退位之後。

⑧ **instill** *vt.* **灌輸**

It is not only parents' responsibility but also educators' to instill concepts of telling right from wrong into children.

灌輸孩子是非對錯的觀念不只是父母的責任，也是教育者的責任。

Unit ❷ 媒體類

藉由電影學習外國事物——搭配電影：《三個傻瓜》（*3 Idiots*）

話說 iBT 新托福寫作題目與電影或名人故事
➡ 從以下題目為例，看題目與電影《三個傻瓜》（*3 Idiots*）間的關連

> "Movies tell us a lot about the country where they were produced. Name a movie and explain what you have learned about the country by watching it." Use specific details and examples to support your choice.
>
> 「電影透露出電影製作國家的很多事物。指出一部電影，並闡述你從那部電影學到關於其國家的哪些事物。」請使用精準的細節和例證支持你的選擇。

劇情簡述

《三個傻瓜》（*3 Idiots*）的主要角色是三位工程系的學生。法罕一出生，他的父親就決定他將來要當工程師。對來自赤貧家庭的拉加而言，當上工程師才有希望拯救全家脫離貧窮。總愛挑戰權威的藍丘有個秘密——沒人知道他的真實身份。他其實不是藍丘，努力取得的第一名和文憑，最終都不屬於他。真實的他，一位失怙的僕人，其實是唸不起大學的。但他並不在乎社會看重的文憑或金錢，最終利用對知識的熱愛扭轉自我的命運。

此類題型重點句搶先看

❶ Inequality and traditions seem to be intertwined in India as two sides of the same coin, which can be analyzed in two aspects: gender roles and social hierarchy.

在印度，不平等現象和傳統似乎是密不可分，一體兩面的，這種關係可由兩方面分析：性別角色和社會階級。

❷ The movie conveys an important message that the younger generation in India can indeed break the shackles of traditions.

這部電影傳達一則重要的訊息，印度的年輕世代的確有可能打破傳統的枷鎖。

ch.1
媒體與教育類題型

ch.2

ch.3

高分範文搶先看　▶ Track 02

Movies certainly enlighten us in many ways, broadening our horizon and allowing us to learn about countries we have never been to. I would draw on the movie, "3 Idiots", to explain what I learned about current Indian society, particularly about inequality and the clash between traditions and new thoughts.

Inequality and traditions seem to be **intertwined**[1] in India as two sides of the same coin, which can be analyzed in two aspects: gender roles and social **hierarchy**[2]. First, regarding gender roles, the movie emphasizes that males and females carry **conventional**[3] expectations. Sons must pursue degrees that guarantee them **prestigious**[4] jobs, while daughters must honor their parents by marrying richer men. For instance, two of the three major

電影的確在很多方面啟發我們，拓展我們的視野，並讓我們學到關於未曾造訪的國家的事物。我將引用《三個傻瓜》這部電影闡述我從這部電影學到關於現代印度社會的某些現象，尤其是不平等現象及傳統與新思維的衝突。

在印度，不平等現象和傳統似乎是密不可分，一體兩面的，這種關係可由兩方面分析：性別角色和社會階級。首先，關於性別角色，電影強調兩性都背負著傳統期待。兒子必須追求能保障他們高聲望工作的學位，而女兒必須藉由跟富人結婚為家庭帶來榮耀。例如，三個主要男性角色裡，有兩位是因為父母的期待，才研讀工程學。然而，女性比男性面對更多不平等。如同電影

male characters study Engineering because of their parents' expectations. However, women face more inequality than men, as a female medical student in the film suggests that when it comes to marriage, family honor **precedes** a woman's individuality. Nonetheless, there is hope for the younger generation's **defiance**[6] against tradition, as the male characters insist on pursuing their dreams, and the female character flees from her own wedding.

Secondly, traditional social hierarchy, namely the caste system, still exerts enormous influence, as suggested by the story of the **protagonist**[7], Rancho, who conceals his true identity as an orphaned servant and is hired by his employer to acquire a degree in his son's name. Despite having devoted 4 years to attain the degree, he cannot claim the degree

裡一位醫學系女學生暗示的，當面對婚姻，家族名譽比女性個人意志重要多了。不過，年輕世代對傳統的抵抗是有希望的，如同男性角色堅持追求夢想，女性角色逃離她自己的婚禮。

第二，傳統社會階級，即種姓制度，仍發揮極大的影響力。由主角藍丘的故事可略知一二。他隱瞞真實的身分—失怙的僕人，被老闆僱用以他兒子的名義去取得學位。儘管花了四年取得學位，他無法以自己的真名宣稱擁有這文憑。幸運的是，藍丘的快樂結局教導我們處於社會劣勢的人，利用知識仍有可能翻轉命運。

under his real name. Fortunately, the happy ending for Rancho teaches us that the **underprivileged**[8] can turn the tables by utilizing their knowledge.

Undeniably, traditions might be difficult to break, but the contemporary Indian society is changing. The movie conveys an important message that the younger generation in India can indeed break the shackles of traditions.

不可否認地，傳統可能很難破除，但現代印度社會正在改變。這部電影傳達一則重要的訊息，印度的年輕世代的確有可能打破傳統的枷鎖。

高分範文解析

關鍵句 1

Movies certainly enlighten us in many ways, broadening our horizon and allowing us to learn about countries we have never been to. （電影的確在很多方面啟發我們，拓展我們的視野，並讓我們學到關於未曾造訪的國家的事物。）

解析

1.重點：利用分詞構句增加句型的豐富度。此句是分詞構句，也可還原成形容詞子句，如下：Movies certainly enlighten us in many ways, which broaden our horizon and allow us to learn about countries we have never been to. 例：Fictions expand our imaginary world, allowing us to immerse in fantasy temporarily. （小說拓展我們的想像世界，讓我們暫時沉浸在幻想裡。）

關鍵句 2

Despite having devoted 4 years to attain the degree, he cannot claim the degree under his real name. （儘管花了四年取得學位，他無法以自己的真名宣稱擁有這文憑。）

解析

1. 重點：Despite= In spite of，儘管，詞性是介系詞，注意其後只能搭配名詞或動名詞。若要接子句，despite 或 in spite of 之後必須先補上 the fact 兩字才能接子句。

2. 例 1：Despite female scientists' dedication, their research did not receive enough recognition. （儘管女性科學家有所貢獻，她們的研究沒受到足夠的認可。）

例 2：In spite of the fact that Leonardo Dicaprio has been known for his acting talent, he did not win the Academy Award for Best Actor until 2016. （儘管李奧納多 · 狄卡皮歐一直以演技才華出名，他直到 2016 年才贏得奧斯卡金像獎最佳男主角獎項。）

重要字彙與例句

① intertwine *vi., vt.* 互相交織；纏繞

The past and the present intertwine in this novel, making it a little incomprehensible for careless readers.

這本小說裡過去和現在兩段時間互相交織，對粗心的讀者而言，有點難理解。

② hierarchy *n.* 階級

For the nation with a vast population, social hierarchy is essential to maintain its stability.

對有眾多人口的國家而言，社會階級對維持其穩定是必要的。

③ conventional *adj.* 習俗的；傳統的

Conventional practices are usually tried and true, passed down from generation to generation.

習俗上的常例通常是歷久彌新，代代相傳。

④ prestigious *adj.* 高名望的

Donald Trump, a prestigious real-estate tycoon, took the public by surprise when he announced his decision to run for president.

當高聲望的房地產大亨，唐諾‧川普，宣佈他參選總統的決定時，大眾為之驚訝。

⑤ **precede** *vt.* **優先於；領先於**

One's health should always precedes his job, property, or ambition.

一個人的健康應該總是比他的工作，財產或野心重要。

⑥ **defiance** *n.* **違抗**

The university students held a rally to bid their defiance against the school authority.

這些大學生舉辦集會以表達對學校當局的抗議。

⑦ **protagonist** *n.* **主角**

The presentation of the protagonist varies according to different actors' acting techniques and temperament.

這個主角的呈現方式會隨著不同演員的演技和氣質而變化。

⑧ **underprivileged** *adj.* **處於社會劣勢的；因貧困而權益較少的**

Obamacare was initially designed to make medical assistance more accessible for the underprivileged.

歐巴馬健保制度最初的設計是讓貧困人民更容易取得醫療協助。

Unit **3** 媒體類

偏好電影還是小說——搭配電影：《科學怪人》（*Frankenstein*）與《瘋狂麥斯》（*Mad Max*）

話說 iBT 新托福寫作題目與電影或名人故事

➡ 從以下題目為例，看題目與電影《科學怪人》（*Frankenstein*）與《瘋狂麥斯》（*Mad Max*）間的關連

"Some people prefer watching movies, while others prefer reading novels. Which do you prefer?" Explain the reasons for your preference with specific examples and details.

「有些人偏好看電影，而有些人偏好讀小説。你偏好哪一個？」請使用精準的細節和例證解釋你偏好的理由。

劇情簡述

　　《科學怪人》（*Frankenstein*）是十九世紀的英國作家瑪麗・雪萊（Mary Shelley）所著的科幻經典小說。主要角色是一位名為弗蘭肯斯坦的瘋狂醫生及他利用科技創造出的人形怪物。至今這部小說在世界各國不斷翻拍成電影，加入不同文化的詮釋及當代新科學觀念。《瘋狂麥斯》系列電影（*Mad Max*）至 2015 年已累積四部作品。第一集於 1979 年上映，也推出小說版本，36 年間電影科技大躍進，第四部作品搭配 4DX 技術提供彷彿身歷其境的觀影響宴。

此類題型重點句搶先看

❶ Another example is that sci-fi novels, such as *Frankenstein* and *The Time Machine*, written in the 19th century encompass extraordinary vision far ahead of the authors' time. Yet, movie adaptations of those novels in the 21st century can provide more diverse angles by integrating new technologies and new scientific theories. 另一個例子是 19 世紀的科幻小說，例如《科學怪人》和《時光機器》，內含了超越作者那個時代的非凡視野。然而，在 21 世紀，改編自那些小說的電影能藉由融入新科技和新科學理論，提供更豐富的角度。

❷ With the advancement of 4DX technology, fictional elements are materialized in theaters, which cannot be achieved by reading novels. 隨著 4DX 科技的進步，虛構的元素能在電影院裡被具體化，這是讀小說不可能辦到的。

高分範文搶先看 `Track 03`

Both movies and novels have distinctive advantages. I prefer movies to novels because of the diversity of angles and technologies in movies.

The first reason for my preference is that elements in fiction are often limited by the writer's background, while movies incorporate contemporary viewpoints and various cultural dimensions, making them more **approachable**[1] to the audience. Likewise, the readers' comprehension of a novel is confined by their personal background, which can be broadened by watching movies. For instance, a reader who has never studied British literature would have difficulty visualizing the lifestyles and historical background in Jane Austen's novels. However, by watching movie adaptations, he can **perceive**[2] those elements instantly.

電影及小說都有各自獨特的優點。我偏好電影多於小說,理由是電影裡多樣化的角度和科技。

支持我的偏好的第一個理由是,小說裡的元素常常被作者的背景限制,然而電影能融入當代觀點和豐富的文化面向,使電影對觀眾而言更容易理解。同樣地,讀者對小說的理解能力也會受限於個人背景,但看電影可以拓展理解能力。例如,一位從未讀過英國文學的讀者在想像珍·奧斯汀小說裡的生活風格及歷史背景時,可能會遭遇困難。但是,藉由觀賞小說改編成的電影,他能立刻理解那些元素。另一個例子是 19 世紀的科幻小說,例如《科學怪人》和《時光機器》,內含了超越作者那個時代的非凡視野。然而,在

Another example is that sci-fi novels, such as *Frankenstein* and *The Time Machine*, written in the 19th century encompass extraordinary vision far ahead of the authors' time. Yet, movie adaptations of those novels in the 21st century can provide more diverse angles by integrating new technologies and new scientific theories.

The second reason concerns the advancement of technology. While the **genres**[3] of novels have not evolved dramatically over the past few centuries, movie technologies have gone through enormous **amelioration**[4] in merely one century. With the advancement of 4DX technology, fictional elements are materialized in theaters, which cannot be achieved by reading novels. We can now immerse ourselves in similar sensations to those movie characters experience. Imagine the

21 世紀，改編自那些小說的電影能藉由融入新科技和新科學理論，提供更豐富的角度。

第二個理由是關於科技的發達。小說的類型在過去幾個世紀沒有太明顯的演進，相對而言，電影科技僅在一個世紀內就經歷了巨大的進步。隨著 4DX 科技的進步，虛構的元素能在電影院裡被具體化，這是讀小說不可能辦到的。現在我們可以沉浸在類似電影角色經歷的感官體驗中。想像一下讀《瘋狂麥斯》的小說和在 4DX 戲院觀賞這部電影的差別，在戲院裡，我們能感受到椅子震動，風吹拂著，及霧氣對著我們噴灑；相反地，讀小說是靜

ch.**1** 媒體與教育類題型

ch.**2**

ch.**3**

discrepancy[5] between reading the **novelization**[6] "Mad Max" and watching it in a 4DX theater where we can feel the seats vibrating, wind blowing, and mist sprayed on us; contrarily, reading the novelization is **sedentary**[7].

In sum, movies bridge viewers from different backgrounds and add current perspectives, without requiring viewers to possess any relevant knowledge, as well as create more thrills with technologies, which explains my **propensity**[8] to choose movies over novels.

止不動的。

總而言之，電影縮短不同背景的觀眾間的距離，並加入當代觀點，不需要觀眾擁有相關知識，而且能運用科技創造更多刺激，以上解釋了為何我傾向偏好電影多於小説。

高分範文解析

關鍵句 1

The first reason for my preference is that elements in fiction are often limited by the writer's background, while movies incorporate contemporary viewpoints and various cultural dimensions, making them more approachable to the audience.（支持我的偏好的第一個理由是，小說裡的元素常常被作者的背景限制，然而電影能融入當代觀點和豐富的文化面向，使電影對觀眾而言更容易理解。）

解析

1.重點：名詞子句 that elements in fictions are ... to audience 是主詞 the first reason 的補語。此名詞子句包含兩個由 while 連接，意義相反的子句，而句尾的分詞片語 making them ... 是修飾先行詞 viewpoints 及 dimensions。例：The reason for Donald Trump's growing popularity is that his remarks cater to the media's preference, while the other candidates' remarks tend to be conservative, making them less featured in the media.（唐諾・川普越來越受到歡迎的原因是，他的發言迎合媒體的喜好，然而，其他候選人的發言傾向保守，使他們受到媒體比較少的關注。）

關鍵句 2

In sum, movies bridge viewers from different backgrounds and add current perspectives, without requiring viewers to possess any relevant knowledge, as well as create more thrills with technologies, which explains my **propensity** to choose movies over novels.（總而言之，電影縮短不同背景的觀眾間的距離，並加入當代觀點，不需要觀眾擁有相關知識，而且能運用科技創造更多刺激，以上解釋了為何我傾向偏好電影多於小說。）

解析

1. 重點：此完整句由一個主要子句及一個形容詞子句組合而成。主要子句裡一共有三個動詞，分別由 and，as well as 連接：bridge... and... add... as well as create。and 及 as well as 可在同一句並列。副詞片語 without requiring ... knowledge 修飾主要子句。例：Ang Lee studied movies in New York and developed his career there, without major breakthroughs in his early years, as well as took on various jobs. （李安在紐約學習電影，並在那裡發展他的事業，他早期沒有重大的突破，且從事各式各樣的工作。）

重要字彙與例句

① approachable *adj.* 容易接近的；容易理解的

The movie *Interstellar* has made the black hole theory more approachable.

《星際效應》這部電影讓黑洞理論更容易理解。

② perceive *vt.* 認知

We cannot perceive the predicament that refugees face.

我們無法認知難民面對的困境。

③ genre *n.* （文學、藝術的）類型

Artists are constantly pushing the boundaries of western art genres.

藝術家不斷地拓展西洋藝術類型的界線。

④ amelioration *n.* 進步；改善

Gene engineering technology has gone through significant amelioration in the past 30 years.

基因工程科技在過去三十年經歷了顯著的進步。

⑤ discrepancy *n.* 差異

The discrepancy between fantasy and reality is what makes fictions appealing.

讓小說有吸引力的正是幻想和實際的落差。

⑥ novelization *n.* 電影改編成的小說

Novelization is an essential part of the movie campaign.

電影改編成小說是電影行銷活動必要的一部分。

⑦ sedentary *adj.* 靜止的；久坐的

Sedentary lifestyle is definitely harmful to our health.

久坐的生活型態對我們的健康絕對是有害的。

⑧ propensity *n.* 傾向

More and more young girls have the propensity to choose science majors.

越來越多年輕女孩傾向選擇科學方面的主修。

Unit ❹ 教育類

大學教育在於培養價值觀，而不是為工作做準備──搭配電影：《蒙娜麗莎的微笑》（*Mona Lisa Smile*）

話說 iBT 新托福寫作題目與電影或名人故事
➡ 從以下題目為例，看題目與電影 《蒙娜麗莎的微笑》（*Mona Lisa Smile*）間的關連

"The purpose of university education is to help students form a set of values, not to prepare them for future jobs". Do you agree or disagree with the statement? Use specific details and examples to support your viewpoint.

「大學教育的目的是幫助學生建構價值觀，不是讓他們對未來的工作做準備。」你同意或不同意以上敘述？請使用精準的細節和例證支持你的論點。

劇情簡述

　　華森老師在 1953 年到衛斯理學院教藝術。當時的美國主流價值認為女性的最佳「工作」是家庭主婦，因此華森老師堅持追尋自我的價值觀引起不少爭議。其中一位學生結婚後漸漸發現主流的婚姻制度讓她感到窒息，最終決定離婚並追求自己的事業。而另一位學生曾考慮申請法學院，但在她的價值觀裡，家庭的重要性超越當上律師，因此她選擇當家庭主婦。這部電影傳遞一個訊息：不管我們選擇什麼工作，當我們依循自我價值觀，人生才會感到圓滿。

此類題型重點句搶先看

❶ University education should enable us to steer our lives with personal values.

大學教育應該賦予我們運用個人價值觀掌控人生方向的能力。

❷ No matter what jobs we choose, our individual values serve as an anchor for a meaningful life, which is why universities should assist students to construct value systems.

不管我們選擇什麼工作，個人價值觀能作為有意義的生活的精神支柱。

這就是為何大學應該協助學生建構價值觀。

高分範文搶先看 ▶ Track 04

Although the global recession has made most people feel that the purpose of university education should be to prepare students for jobs, I am **inclined**[1] to agree with the statement.

My major argument concerns the core functions of different educational institutions. In most western countries, there is a clear distinction between vocational colleges and universities. If one considers that his investment in education will solely lead to landing a job, studying in a vocational college seems a wiser choice. After all, the core function of vocational colleges is to equip students with practical skills to meet market demands. <u>On the contrary, universities are constituted by diversified departments, from sciences to humanities, indicating that the</u>

雖然全球經濟萎縮讓大部份人覺得大學教育的目的應該是使學生對工作做好準備，我仍傾向同意題目的敘述。

我的主要論點是關於不同教育機構的核心功能。在大部份的西方國家，職訓學院和大學之間有明顯的區別。如果有人認為他教育投資的目的只是找到工作，念職訓學院似乎是比較明智的選擇。畢竟，職訓學院的核心功能是讓學生準備好實用技能以因應市場需求。相反地，大學是由各式各樣的科系組合而成，包括各種科學和人文科系，也就意謂著學術環境提供的是文化及跨學科的交流；藉由這些交流，教授傳授他們的智慧，而學生能吸收這些智慧以協助發展自我的價值觀。

academic environment provides cultural and **interdisciplinary**[2] dialogues from which professors **impart**[3] their wisdom which students can **imbibe**[4] to help develop personal values.

Furthermore, university education should enable us to **steer**[5] our lives with personal values. Take two characters in the movie, *Mona Lisa Smile*, for example. One student followed mainstream expectations to become a housewife, an ideal "job" for women in the 1950s; on the other hand, another student gave up the opportunity to study in law school, choosing to be a housewife over being a lawyer. Conforming to the mainstream left the former feeling **enslaved**[6] in her marriage, while choosing her family over being a lawyer left the latter feeling fulfilled because she followed her own value system. No matter what jobs

此外，大學教育應該賦予我們運用個人價值觀掌控人生方向的能力。以電影《蒙娜麗莎的微笑》的兩個角色為例，一位學生遵守主流價值，成為家庭主婦，這是 1950 年代女性的最佳「工作」；另一方面，另一位學生放棄讀法學院的機會，選擇當家庭主婦，而不是律師。遵守主流價值觀使得前者在婚姻中感到被奴役，而選擇家庭讓後者感到圓滿，因為她依循的是自我的價值觀。不管我們選擇什麼工作，個人價值觀能作為有意義的生活的精神支柱。這就是為何大學應該協助學生建構價值觀。

we choose, our individual values serve as an **anchor**[7] for a meaningful life, which is why universities should assist students to construct value systems.

While the two purposes mentioned in the statement are not mutually **exclusive**[8], I stand firm behind my stance that the ultimate goal of universities lies in helping students cultivate individual values, without which life is without anchor, regardless of our jobs.

題目敘述提及的兩種目的並非彼此衝突，但我仍堅持我的立場，大學的終極目標是協助學生培養個人價值觀，沒有個人價值觀的人生是沒有精神支柱的，不管我們的工作為何。

高分範文解析

關鍵句 1

On the contrary, universities are constituted by diversified departments, from sciences to humanities, indicating that the academic environment provides cultural and interdisciplinary dialogues from which professors impart their wisdom which students can imbibe to help develop personal values. （相反地，大學是由各式各樣的科系組合而成，包括各種科學和人文科系，也就意謂著學術環境提供的是文化及跨學科的交流；藉由這些交流，教授傳授他們的智慧，而學生能吸

收這些智慧以協助發展自我的價值觀。）

解析

1. 重點：on the contrary，意義相反的轉折副詞。主要動詞語態是被動語態 are constituted by，主要子句由分詞片語 indicating... 修飾。

2. indicating...中 indicate 的受詞是名詞子句 that ...，that... 包含一個形容詞子句 from which ...，which 的先行詞是 dialogues。例： On the contrary, vocational schools are composed by teachers with professional expertise and internship programs, indicating more real-life training from which students can obtain first-hand information.（相反地，職訓學校由有專業知識的老師及實習計畫組合而成，意謂著更多現實生活的訓練，從訓練中，學生能得到最新資訊。）

關鍵句 2

Conforming to the mainstream left the former feeling enslaved in her marriage, while choosing her family over being a lawyer left the latter feeling fulfilled because she followed her own value system.（遵守主流價值觀使得前者在婚姻中感到被奴役，而選擇家庭讓後者感到圓滿，因為她依循的是自我的價值觀。）

解析

1. 重點：while 連接兩個子句，主詞都是動名詞：conforming ... choosing。動詞片語：leave *Sb.* feeling *adj.*，讓人感覺……的。例：The filming process left Julia Roberts feeling tired, while winning the Oscar Award left her feeling excited.（拍攝過程讓茱莉亞·羅伯茲覺得疲倦，而贏得奧斯卡獎則讓她感到興奮。）

重要字彙與例句

① inclined *adj.* 傾向的

More and more young people are inclined to work abroad.

越來越多年輕人傾向出國工作。

② interdisciplinary *adj.* 跨學科的

Interdisciplinary programs are gaining more popularity nowadays.

當今跨學科課程正受到更多歡迎。

③ impart *v.* 傳授

Imparting knowledge is teachers' essential responsibility.

傳授知識是老師基本的責任。

④ imbibe *v.* 吸收

Whether students can imbibe most of the knowledge depends on their comprehension.

學生是否能吸收大部分的知識要看他們的理解能力。

⑤ steer *v.* 導引；控制方向

The pilot steered the course toward the destination.

駕駛朝著目的地的方向轉去。

ch.1
媒體與教育類題型

ch.2

ch.3

⑥ enslaved *adj.* **感覺被奴役的**

All work and no play might leave people feeling enslaved by their job.

只有工作沒有休閒可能讓人覺得被工作奴役。

⑦ anchor *n.* **錨；精神支柱**

Some view religion as their anchor, while others view family as their anchor.

有些人視宗教為精神支柱，而有些人視家庭為精神支柱。

⑧ exclusive *adj.* **排斥的；獨家的**

Taking care of one's family and having a career are not mutually exclusive.

照顧家庭和擁有事業並不會互相牴觸。

Unit ❺ 教育類

年輕人是否能教導長輩──搭配名人故事：史蒂夫·賈伯斯（Steve Jobs）與馬克·祖客柏（Mark Zuckerberg）

話說 iBT 新托福寫作題目與電影或名人故事
➡ 從以下題目為例，看題目與名人故事：史蒂夫·賈伯斯（Steve Jobs）及馬克·祖客柏（Mark Zuckerberg）間的關連

"Young people can hardly teach anything to older people."
Do you agree or disagree with the statement? Use specific details and examples to support your standpoint.

「年輕人幾乎不能教長輩任何事。」你同意或不同意以上敘述？請使用精準的細節和例證支持你的論點。

名人故事簡述

　　青年時期的史帝夫・賈伯斯受到 1960 年代嬉皮文化的影響，發展出自由不羈的人生觀，他的生活方式與對靈性的追求和傳統價值大相徑庭。他著迷於佛教禪宗，從大學休學後曾到印度苦行靈修。這些經歷影響了他對蘋果電腦的美學設計，他一直執著於打造個人化的產品，儘管當時大多數美國人認為電腦不可能推廣給一般民眾。而臉書創辦人馬克・祖克柏和賈伯斯有個類似點，他也看到了上一代沒發現的機會，並加以利用，開創出劃時代的產品。

此類題型重點句搶先看

❶ In fact, faced with the global vicissitudes influenced by the third industrial revolution, i.e., the digitalization of manufacturing, younger ones who grew up familiarizing themselves with computer technologies have much more to teach older ones.

事實上，面對第三次工業革命，即製造業的數位化，所影響的全球變遷，成長時已熟悉電腦科技的年輕人能教導年長者更多事物。

❷ Both Jobs and Zuckerberg seized opportunities that older people did not see, which certainly offers a lesson to learn.

賈伯斯和祖克柏都抓住年長者沒看到的機會，這的確是值得學習的。

高分範文搶先看 ▶ Track 05

Although the statement that the young can teach little to the old sounds **ostensibly**[1] plausible, I hold a contrary stance in light of the **fallacious**[2] reasoning for the statement and obvious examples that refute such an assertion.

The reason for my disagreement is that the claim is based on a **conspicuous**[3] **fallacy**[4], that is, the "all things are equal" fallacy, meaning situations remain the same in different places and times. However, the social backgrounds of two generations are rarely similar, considering the fast pace of social changes and economic fluctuations nowadays; hence, the notion of older ones teaching younger ones by drawing on personal experiences is highly **controvertible**[5]. In fact, faced with the global **vicissitudes**[6] influenced by the third industrial

雖然年輕人幾乎無法教導長輩這句話貌似合理，我持反對立場，因為此敘述是依據邏輯謬誤而成立，並有明顯的例子能反駁此敘述。

我不同意此敘述的原因是因為此敘述根據的是一個明顯的邏輯謬誤，即「一切皆同」的謬誤，指的是在不同的地方和時代，情況都相同。然而，鑒於現今社會變遷的快速步調及經濟波動，兩個世代的社會背景不盡相似。因此，年長者引用自身經驗教導年輕人的觀念是高度可議的。事實上，面對第三次工業革命，即製造業的數位化，所影響的全球變遷，成長時已熟悉電腦科技的年輕人能教導年長者更多事物。

revolution, i.e., the digitalization of manufacturing, younger ones who grew up familiarizing themselves with computer technologies have much more to teach older ones.

To support my stance, two **pronounced**[7] examples are illustrated, Steve Jobs, the founder of Apple Computers and Mark Zuckerberg, Facebook founder. Jobs' belief in creating a computer for everyone arose in his early twenties. Jobs demonstrated to his senior business partners that not only could his vision be realized, but also design and practicability could be integrated. Zuckerberg also initiated his business in his twenties. Like Jobs, Zuckerberg thinks **unconventionally**[8]. There had been social networks for university students before Facebook, yet he spotted the opportunity of turning those into a social network for the public. Both

兩個明顯的例證能支持我的立場，蘋果電腦創辦人史帝夫・賈伯斯和臉書創辦人馬克・祖克柏。賈伯斯在他二十歲初頭就有個信念，要創造每個人都能擁有的電腦。賈伯斯向年長的事業夥伴證明不但他的遠見成真，設計和實用性也能被整合。祖克柏也在二十多歲時開創他的事業。就像賈伯斯，祖克柏以非傳統的方式思考。在臉書之前，已經有給大學生使用的社交網絡，但是他看到機會並將那些網站轉變成大眾的社交網路。賈伯斯和祖克柏都抓住年長者沒看到的機會，這的確是值得學習的。

Jobs and Zuckerberg seized opportunities that older people did not see, which certainly offers a lesson to learn.

Confronted with dramatic global changes, old people have much to learn from young ones as the latter are living through those changes, thus more capable of offering insights.

面對劇烈的全球變化，年長者能從年輕人身上學習很多，因為年輕人正親身經歷那些變化，因此更能提供相關洞見。

高分範文解析

關鍵句 1

In fact, faced with the global vicissitudes influenced by the third industrial revolution, i.e., the digitalization of manufacturing, younger ones who grew up familiarizing themselves with computer technologies have much more to teach older ones. （事實上，面對第三次工業革命，即製造業的數位化，所影響的全球變遷，成長時已熟悉電腦科技的年輕人能教導年長者更多事物。）

解析

1.重點：此句由分詞片語，主要子句和形容詞子句組合而成。表被動的分詞片語 faced with ... influenced by ...，主要子句為 younger ones have much more ...，而主詞 younger ones 由限定形容詞子句 who grew up... 修飾。例：Influenced by hippie subculture in the 1960s, Steve Jobs, who already dropped out of college, travelled to India to learn eastern philosophy .（受到 1960 年代的嬉皮次文化影響，已經從大學休學的史帝夫・賈伯斯去印度學習東方哲學。）

關鍵句 2

Confronted with dramatic global changes, old people have much to learn from young ones as the latter are living through those changes, thus more capable of offering insights.（面對劇烈的全球變化，年長者能從年輕人學習很多，因為年輕人正親身經歷那些變化，因此更能提供相關洞見。）

解析

1.重點：分詞片語在句首的功能是修飾主詞。此句的過去分詞片語 confronted with 表被動語態。主動語態的語法則是 confronting N.。例：Confronted with mounting pressure, Steve Jobs are ousted from Apple Computers.（史帝夫・賈伯斯面對日益增加的壓力，被逐出蘋果電腦。）

重要字彙與例句

① ostensibly *adv.* 似乎;表面地

Narcissists behave nicely to others ostensibly only to gain benefits for themselves.

自戀人格者表面上對別人友善的目的是獲得對他們有利的益處。

② fallacious *adj.* 邏輯謬誤的

It is not uncommon to hear fallacious reasoning in public figures' critiques.

在公眾人物的評論中,聽到邏輯謬誤的推論是普遍的。

③ conspicuous *adj.* 明顯的

The conspicuous trend in our popular culture is the focus on superficial image.

在我們的流行文化中,重視膚淺的表象是明顯的趨勢。

④ fallacy *n.* 邏輯謬誤

The ability to analyze fallacies in daily life will help you gain more understanding of reality.

分析日常生活中邏輯謬誤的能力能幫助你更理解現實的狀態。

⑤ controvertible *adj.* 被爭議的;可辯駁的

Whether Steve Jobs was indifferent to his abandoned daughter, Lisa, remains controvertible.

史帝夫‧賈伯斯對被他拋棄的女兒麗莎,是否態度是冷漠的,這一點仍是被爭議的。

⑥ **vicissitude** *n.* **變遷；不定性**

The vicissitudes of scientific development in the 20ᵗʰ century laid the foundation for the giant leap of technologies in the 21ˢᵗ century.

二十世紀科學發展的變化替二十一世紀科技的大躍進奠定了基礎。

⑦ **pronounced** *adj.* **顯著的；斷言的**

The man is not afraid to air his pronounced views.

這位男士從不諱言他的觀點。

⑧ **unconventionally** *adv.* **非典型地**

Very often civilization is propelled by people who think unconventionally.

通常文明是被非典型思考者所推進的。

Unit ❻ 教育類

從人生中學習：聽取建議或親身經驗 ——搭配電影《心靈捕手》 (*Good Will Hunting*)

話說 iBT 新托福寫作題目與電影或名人故事
➡ 從以下題目為例，看題目與電影《心靈捕手》
(*Good Will Hunting*) 間的關連

"Some people learn about life by listening to the suggestions of elders or friends, while others learn about life through personal experience". Compare the advantages of these two ways and state your preference. Use specific details and examples to support your preference.

「有些人藉由聽從長輩或朋友的建議學習關於人生的事物，而其他人透過親自體驗學習人生。」請比較兩種方式的優點並提出你偏好哪一種。使用精準的細節和例證支持你的偏好。

劇情簡述

在《心靈捕手》（*Good Will Hunting*）中，二十歲的威爾‧杭汀在麻省理工學院擔任清潔工，他也是位無師自通的數學天才。數學教授藍伯為了不讓他浪費天賦，安排他去做心理輔導並媒介工作給威爾。而心理學教授西恩‧麥奎爾並不直接給威爾建議，而是輔導威爾打開心房，面對過往的心理創傷，讓他知道就算他有過人的天賦，但若不直接體驗人際關係，一切仍是徒然。當威爾面對真我後，他放棄了數學教授推薦的工作，決定追尋他的靈魂伴侶。

此類題型重點句搶先看

❶ Since children cannot provide for themselves, following suggestions from others will help protect them from undesired risks and satisfy the three levels of needs.

因為小孩無法照顧自己，遵循他人的建議能保護他們免於不必要的風險，並在基本需求的三個層次獲得滿足。

❷ Healthy adolescents should cultivate autonomy, distinctive dispositions and idiosyncrasies which cannot be achieved if they seldom experience life personally.

健康的青少年應該培養自主能力，獨特的人格和特色，而如果他們鮮少親自體驗人生，這些都達不到。

高分範文搶先看 ▶ Track 06

The two ways of learning about life as described in the statement carry various advantages depending on which stage of life we are in. I am inclined to hold the opinion that before one enters **adolescence**[1], he would explore the world more smoothly if given more advice from others, yet as one becomes a young adult, it is more beneficial to learn through personal experience.

First, it is easily comprehensible that from the moment our sense of self initially emerges in late infancy to the moment we begin forming our individual identity in late childhood, we rely on advice from not only elders but also our peers in order to develop normally both physically and mentally. Physiologically, children have the **primal**[2] instinct to cling to caretakers, seeking suggestions

題目敘述的兩種學習人生的方式都各有優點，端看我們處於哪個人生的階段。我傾向認為在少年期之前，如果多聽從他人建議，探索世界的過程會比較順利，然而當一個人成為年輕成人，透過親自體驗會比較有益處。

首先，不難理解的是從我們的自我意識在嬰兒期晚期萌芽，到兒童期晚期個人身份開始形成這段期間，我們不但依賴長輩，也依賴同儕的建議，為的是生理和心理方面都能正常發展。生理上，小孩有原始的本能要依附照顧者，為了生存而尋求關於生活基本面的建議。心理上，同儕的建議不可缺少，因為他們能幫助我們進行社交生活。因此，在成長初

regarding basic areas of life in order to survive. Psychologically, suggestions from peers are indispensable since they help us with how to socialize in groups. Thus, the advantages of imbibing and applying advice in the early stage of growth cannot be overemphasized. To **fortify**[3] my opinion, I would like to draw on the psychological theory, Maslow's hierarchy of needs, which asserts the needs for physiology, safety, and love/belonging form the fundamental levels of childhood development. Since children cannot provide for themselves, following suggestions from others will help protect them from undesired risks and satisfy the three levels of needs.

Nevertheless, as children become adolescents, I believe they should venture into the world by themselves more frequently.

期，吸收並應用忠告的優點再怎麼強調都不為過。我想引用心理學理論，馬斯洛的需求階層，來加強我的看法。此理論主張對生理，安全和愛／歸屬感的三種需求形成兒童發展的基本層次。因為小孩無法照顧自己，遵循他人的建議能保護他們免於不必要的風險，並在基本需求的三個層次獲得滿足。

然而，當小孩成長為少年，我相信他們應該更常親自探索世界。健康的青少年應該培養自主能力，獨特的人格和

Healthy adolescents should cultivate **autonomy**[4], distinctive **dispositions**[5] and **idiosyncrasies**[6] which cannot be achieved if they seldom experience life personally. My point can be **validated**[7] by taking the protagonist in the movie "Good Will Hunting" for example. Trapped mentally by his **traumatized**[8] experience, Will Hunting, a 20-year-old man and physical abuse survivor, refuses to exert his genius for math and rejects intimate relationships. It is only after a psychologist unlocks his defense that Will embraces his true self and decides to embark on a journey to follow his soul mate. Hence, experiencing both joys and sorrow directly is crucial even for adults.

As for me, I definitely find experiencing everything firsthand preferable. Occasionally, firsthand experiences might induce frustration, yet the joy of surmounting frustration is incomparable.

特色，而如果他們鮮少親自體驗人生，這些都達不到。我的論點可由《心靈捕手》的主角為例獲得證實。二十歲的威爾·杭汀是身體虐待的倖存者，他被創傷經驗侷限，拒絕發揮數學天賦並排斥親密關係。只有在一位心理學家解開他的防衛後，威爾才擁抱真我，並決定展開追尋靈魂伴侶的旅程。因此，甚至對成人而言，直接體會愉悅和悲傷都是重要的。

我本人絕對偏好親自體驗人生的一切。偶爾，直接體會可能會導致挫折感，但克服挫折感的快樂是無法比擬的。

高分範文解析

關鍵句 1 ▶

Thus, the advantages of imbibing and applying advice in the early stage of growth cannot be overemphasized.（因此，在成長初期，吸收並應用忠告的優點再怎麼強調都不為過。）

解析

1. 重點：應用慣用語 (idiom)："cannot be overemphasized" 強調此段落的主要論點。例：The theme of the quest for the true self in "Good Will Hunting" cannot be overemphasized.（《心靈捕手》中追尋真我的主題再怎麼強調都不為過。）

關鍵句 2 ▶

It is only after a psychologist unlocks his defense that Will embraces his true self and decides to embark on a journey to follow his soul mate.（只有在一位心理學家解開他的防衛後，威爾才擁抱真我，並決定展開追尋靈魂伴侶的旅程。）

解析

1. 重點：運用虛主詞 it 開頭的句子表達希望讀者特別注意的概念。基本結構是：It is only after... that S+V。介系詞 after 可視其後的受詞改成別的介系詞。例：It is only under the guidance of the counselor that Will dares to face his psychological trauma.（只有在諮商師的引導下，威爾才敢面對他的心理創傷。）

重要字彙與例句

① adolescence *n.* 少年時期

During adolescence, most people move their identification from their parents to their peers.

在少年時期，大部份人的身份認同由父母轉移到同儕。

② primal *adj.* 原始的

Young wild animals have the primal instinct to practice hunting skills through playing.

年幼的野生動物有原始本能去透過玩耍練習打獵技巧。

③ fortify *vt.* 增強；支撐

The roof of a Gothic cathedral is fortified by arch beams.

哥德式大教堂的屋頂是由拱型橫梁支撐。

④ autonomy *n.* 自治

Citizens' autonomy is one of the features of a utopian state.

公民自治是烏托邦國家的特色之一。

⑤ disposition *n.* 人格；性格

We might observe children's disposition at a very young age, maybe when they are 2 or 3.

我們可能在小孩非常小，才兩三歲時，就觀察到他們的性格。

⑥ idiosyncrasy *n.* **癖好；行為方面的特色**

Each one of us is unique because of our idiosyncrasies.

我們每個人都是因為行為特質而獨特。

⑦ validate *vt.* **證實；確認正當性**

Large-scale statistical research validated the theory.

大型統計學研究證實了這個理論。

⑧ traumatize *vt.* **造成創傷**

Many soldiers were deeply traumatized after fighting in the Iraq War.

在伊拉克戰爭後，許多士兵都深陷創傷。

Unit ❼ 環境類

正在消失的自然資源── 搭配電影：《阿凡達》（*Avatar*）

話說 iBT 新托福寫作題目與電影或名人故事 ➡ 從以下題目為例，看題目與電影《阿凡達》 （*Avatar*）間的關連

"The world is losing lots of natural resources. Choose one resource that is disappearing and explain why it's urgent to save it." Use specific details and examples to support your viewpoint.

「這個世界正在失去許多自然資源。選擇一項正在消失的自然資源並解釋為何拯救這項資源是迫切的。」請使用精準的細節和例證支持你的論點。

劇情簡述

　　3D 科幻史詩電影《阿凡達》的主軸環繞著潘朵拉星球上的人類採礦殖民地與當地原住民納美人之間的衝突。《阿凡達》的導演詹姆士·克麥隆曾表示這部電影的場景就是依據巴西的亞馬遜熱帶雨林設計的，而納美人面對的威脅事實上不是虛構的。近年來，他也積極倡導雨林保育。對熱帶雨林的原住民族群而言，他們的居住地、生活型態及文化不斷被入侵的外來者威脅。此外，熱帶雨林因為能提供各種食物、藥物、礦產及木材等等富饒的原料，雨林面積以驚人的速度被消耗。科學家預估一百年後全球的熱帶雨林將完全消失，將導致氣候及物種平衡的大浩劫。

此類題型重點句搶先看

❶ The director of *Avatar*, James Cameron, has publicly acknowledged that the setting of the movie mirrors the Brazilian rainforest and that what happens in the movie is real to numerous indigenous peoples living there.

《阿凡達》的導演詹姆士·克麥隆曾公開表示這部電影的場景呼應了巴西的雨林，而且電影裡發生的事對許多住在那裏的原住民族群而言是真實的。

❷ Worse yet, uprooting the indigenous peoples from their homeland equals destroying their culture.

更糟糕的是，將原住民族群從他們的家鄉連根拔起等同於摧毀他們的文化。

高分範文搶先看 　Track 07

Among the natural resources that are being depleted by human activities, I believe that tropical rainforests are in dire need of preservation. We should save tropical rainforests for not only ecological preservation, but also the protection of **indigenous**[1] peoples whose cultures are inseparable from the tropical rainforests.

Tropical rainforests are indispensable in stabilizing the water cycle and reducing greenhouse gases, and host over 50% of the plant and animal species on the earth, which serves a crucial function during the **Anthropocene**[2]. Since the **inception**[3] of industrialization in the 19th century, the amount of greenhouse gases has reached an **unprecedented**[4] height, indicating the urgency to save rainforests. Yet, the **deforestation**[5] of tropical

在被人類活動消耗的自然資源中，我相信熱帶雨林是需要迫切的保育。我們應該保護熱帶雨林，不只是為了生態保育，也是為了保護原住民族群，原住民族群的生活型態及文化跟熱帶雨林密不可分。

熱帶雨林在穩定水循環、減少溫室氣體是不可或缺的，它同時提供地球上超過50%的植物和動物物種的棲息地，並在人類世紀元提供關鍵的功能。自從十九世紀工業化起始，溫室氣體總量已經達到前所未有的最高點，顯示了保護雨林的急迫性。然而，熱帶雨林的砍伐以驚人的速度正在進行，也剝奪了許多地棲物種的家。沒有樹群吸收二氧化碳及產生氧氣，且 40%的氧氣是

rainforests is happening at an alarming rate, which has deprived numerous **terrestrial**[6] species of their home. <u>Without trees that absorb carbon dioxide and generate oxygen, of which 40% is generated by tropical forests, the greenhouse effect will only deteriorate drastically.</u> With fewer trees to help maintain the **equilibrium**[7] of the water cycle, humans will face more droughts.

Moreover, the destruction of tropical rainforests is as threatening as the **annihilation**[8] of species in the movie, *Avatar*. <u>The director of *Avatar*, James Cameron, has publicly acknowledged that the setting of the movie mirrors the Brazilian rainforest and that what happens in the movie is real to numerous indigenous peoples living there.</u> For example, the Brazilian government is building the world's third largest dam,

由熱帶雨林產生，溫室效應只會更劇烈惡化。能幫助維持水循環平衡的樹減少了，人類未來將面對更多旱災。

此外，熱帶雨林的破壞就如同電影《阿凡達》裡的物種滅絕一樣令人感到威脅。《阿凡達》的導演詹姆士·克麥隆曾公開表示這部電影的場景呼應了巴西的雨林，而且電影裡發生的事對許多住在那裏的原住民族群而言是真實的。例如，巴西政府正在建造世界上第三大的水壩，完成後將會淹沒亞馬遜雨林廣大的野生動物棲息地，並強迫四萬人牽移。更糟糕的是，將原住民族群從

which will flood a vast wildlife habitat in the Amazon and force 40,000 residents to relocate. Worse yet, uprooting the indigenous peoples from their homeland equals destroying their culture.

他們的家鄉連根拔起等同於摧毀他們的文化。

To conclude, tropical rainforests have been described by scientists as the lungs of the earth, and thus it is not difficult to envisage that just as dysfunctional human lungs will induce life-threatening peril, the massive destruction of tropical rainforests will cause a devastating effect on the earth.

總而言之，熱帶雨林被科學家描述為地球的肺，因此不難想像正如同功能失調的肺會導致威脅生命的危險，對熱帶雨林的大量破壞將導致地球上毀滅性的效應。

高分範文解析

關鍵句 1 ▶

Tropical rainforests are indispensable in stabilizing the water cycle and reducing greenhouse gases, and host over 50% of the plant and animal species on the earth, which serves a crucial function during the **Anthropocene**[2]. （熱帶雨林在穩定水循環，減少溫室氣體，和提供地球上超過 50%的植物和動物物種的棲息地等方面是不可或缺的，這在人類

世紀元提供關鍵的功能。）

解析

1. 重點：in 之後的受詞共二個動名詞片語：stabilizing ...、reducing ...。
關係代名詞 which 代替第一個子句，故視為單數，在此句也當作形容詞
子句的主詞，形容詞子句的主要動詞 serve 須加 s 呼應單數主詞。例：
Director James Cameron is adept in utilizing 3D technologies,
conveying the message of environmental protection, and
producing blockbuster films.（導演詹姆士‧克麥隆擅長運用 3D 科
技，傳遞環保訊息，及製作賣座鉅片。）

關鍵句 2

Without trees that absorb carbon dioxide and generate oxygen, of
which 40% is generated by tropical forests, the greenhouse effect
will only deteriorate drastically.（沒有樹群吸收二氧化碳及產生氧氣，且
40%的氧氣是由熱帶雨林產生，溫室效應只會更劇烈惡化。）

解析

1. 重點：which 的先行詞是 oxygen，of 因搭配 40%，所以不可省略。
例：Director James Cameron has dedicated his life to promoting
the preservation of tropical rainforests, of which a large
proportion has been deforested in merely one decade.（導演詹姆
士‧克麥隆致力於促進熱帶雨林的保育，熱帶雨林的一大部分在僅僅十年
中已被砍伐殆盡。）

重要字彙與例句

① indigenous *adj.* 原住民的；原生的

The relocation of indigenous peoples forced them to scatter around the city.

遷移原住民族群迫使他們散居在城市。

② Anthropocene *n.* 人類世（始於 18 世紀末人類活動開始對氣候及全球生態造成劇烈影響的時代）

The mass extinction of species due to human activities prompted scientists to popularize the word Anthropocene.

因人類活動導致物種大量滅絕，使得科學家廣泛使用人類世這個字。

③ inception *n.* 開始

The movie, *Inception*, starring Leonardo DiCaprio, introduces the idea of planting false memories into brains.

李奧納多‧狄卡皮歐主演的電影《全面啟動》介紹了在人腦植入虛假記憶的觀念。

④ unprecedented *adj.* 前所未有的

The amount of deforestation is unprecedented.

森林被砍伐的數量是前所未有的。

ch.1

ch.2

環境與人生觀類題型

ch.3

⑤ **deforestation** *n.* 砍伐森林

The deforestation of rainforests is so severe that in 100 years there will be no rainforest.

雨林的砍伐情況是如此嚴重，以至於一百年後雨林會消失殆盡。

⑥ **terrestrial** *adj.* 地棲的；地球的

Astronomers are searching for a planet that has a similar terrestrial environment like Earth.

天文學家正在尋找跟地球環境類似的行星。

⑦ **equilibrium** *n.* 平衡

The equilibrium of the worldwide ecology has been damaged over the past century.

過去一世紀以來全球生態的平衡已經被損壞。

⑧ **annihilation** *n.* 破壞；滅絕

The annihilation of most humans has become a theme for Hollywood apocalypse movies.

大部份人類滅亡這現象已經變成好萊塢末日類型電影的主題。

Unit ❽ 環境類

保育瀕臨絕種動物的環境──
搭配電影：《快樂腳》（*Happy Feet*）

話說 iBT 新托福寫作題目與電影或名人故事

➡ 從以下題目為例，看題目與電影《快樂腳》
（*Happy Feet*）間的關連

"Developing an industry is more important than saving the environmnet for endangered animals." Do you agree or disagree with the statement? Use specific details and examples to support your viewpoint.

「發展一項產業比保護瀕臨絕種動物的環境重要。」你同意或不同意以上敘述？請使用精準的細節和例證支持你的論點。

劇情簡述

　　動畫片《快樂腳》以擬人化的方式，演繹南極洲帝王企鵝求偶、繁衍及捕魚的過程。男主角波波因為不會唱歌，卻會跳踢踏舞，而被同族企鵝排擠並驅逐。之後波波踏上旅程想找出為何棲息地附近的魚群減少，經過一番波折又被人類送回到原棲息地。當一架直升機出現在牠們的棲息地上空時，波波帶領族群跳踢踏舞引起人類注意，並使人類反思漁業過度捕撈的問題。電影提供快樂的結局：人類停止捕撈南極洲海域的魚群，但在現實世界，國王企鵝和南極洲附近的海洋生態正面臨來自漁業、觀光業及石油業的多重威脅。

此類題型重點句搶先看

❶ Emperor penguins are not only deprived of their prey, fish and krill, but also are jeopardized by climate change, oil spills, and eco-tourism.

不只帝王企鵝的獵物，魚和磷蝦，被剝奪了，帝王企鵝也因氣候變遷，漏油事件和生態觀光而陷入危險。

❷ The decrease of emperor penguins did not draw public attention until the movie, *Happy Feet*, featured an emperor penguin embarking upon a journey to find out why the fish were dwindling.

直到《快樂腳》這部電影描繪一隻帝王企鵝展開旅程以找出為何魚量一直減少，帝王企鵝數量的減少才獲得大眾的注意。

高分範文搶先看 ▶ Track 08

The debate on the competition between economic development and the protection of endangered species has been going on for decades. I disagree with the view that developing an industry should take **precedence**[1] over saving the environment for endangered species as I believe that destroying the natural environment will eventually take its toll on humans in the long run.

First, the **infliction**[2] on humans due to damaging the environment for endangered animals is conspicuous, considering the **predicaments**[3] of polar bears in **the Arctic**[4] and emperor penguins in **Antarctica**[5]. Due to rapid industrialization in the past century, global warming has been **exacerbated**[6] drastically. As a result, polar bears, which spend more time at sea hunting than on land, have suffered from the melting

關於經濟發展及保護瀕臨絕種動物之爭辯已經持續了數十年。我不同意發展產業應該優先於保護瀕臨絕種動物的環境，因為我相信摧毀自然環境最終會讓人類付出代價。

首先，考慮到北極熊和南極洲帝王企鵝的困境，就能得知破壞瀕臨絕種動物的環境明顯地導致人類磨難。因為過去一世紀的急速工業化，全球暖化的現象已劇烈地惡化。因此，由於北極冰層溶化，花較多時間在海裡狩獵的北極熊備受折磨，牠們被迫覓食時游更長的距離。更糟糕的是，狩獵區域的縮減導致海豹減少，海豹是北極熊主要的獵物，而海

of Arctic ice, forcing them to swim for longer distances to search for food. What's worse, the shrinkage of the hunting area has caused the reduction of seals, polar bears' major prey, which is also affected by commercial overfishing. If industries can take more actions to alleviate global warming, not only human's condition will be relieved by the decline of air pollution, but also marine ecology will be better preserved.

Furthermore, emperor penguins in Antarctica have been threatened by the fishing industry. Emperor penguins are not only deprived of their prey, fish and krill, but also are jeopardized by climate change, oil spills, and eco-tourism. The decrease of emperor penguins did not draw public attention until the movie, *Happy Feet*, featured an emperor penguin embarking upon a journey to find out why the fish

豹減少也是受到漁業的影響。如果產業能採取更多行動減緩全球暖化，不只人類生存的狀態會因為空污減少而獲得舒緩，海洋生態也能獲得更佳的保育。

此外，南極洲帝王企鵝一直遭受漁業威脅。不只帝王企鵝的獵物，魚和磷蝦，被剝奪了，帝王企鵝也因氣候變遷，漏油事件和生態觀光而陷入危險。直到《快樂腳》這部電影描繪一隻帝王企鵝展開旅程以找出為何魚量一直減少，帝王企鵝數量的減少才獲得大眾的注意。原因就是過量捕魚。這個例子顯示上述產業傷害瀕臨絕種的動物，改變了食物鏈，

were dwindling. The reason is exactly overfishing. The example indicates that the aforementioned industry harms endangered species, altering the food chain, which will eventually harm humans as we are at the top of the food chain.

而最終將會傷害人類，因為我們處於食物鏈的最頂端。

Last but not least, since 70% of the earth is covered by oceans, if industries continue damaging marine ecology, it is not difficult to **envisage**[7] a devastating future for the human environment. If we preserve the environment for endangered animals, humans might live with them **reciprocally**[8].

最後，既然地球的 70% 的表面被海洋覆蓋，如果產業繼續損害海洋生態，不難想像出一個對人類環境而言，毀滅性的未來。如果我們保育瀕臨絕種動物的環境，人類可能與動物可以互惠共存。

高分範文解析

關鍵句 1

As a result, polar bears, which spend more time at sea hunting than on land, have suffered from the melting of Arctic ice, forcing them to swim for longer distances to search for food. （因此，由於北極冰層溶化，花較多時間在海裡狩獵的北極熊備受折磨，牠們被迫覓食時游更長的距離。）

解析

1. 重點：以形容詞子句修飾先行詞 polar bears，分詞片語 forcing them to ... 是由形容詞子句 which forces them to ... 簡化而來。

例：Emperor penguins, which feed on fish and krill, have been threatened by human activities, forcing some of them to develop anxiety reactions.（帝王企鵝的主食是魚和磷蝦，牠們持續被人類活動威脅，使得有些帝王企鵝發展出焦慮反應。）

關鍵句 2

The example indicates that the aforementioned industry harms endangered species, altering the food chain, which will eventually harm humans as we are at the top of the food chain.（這個例子顯示以上所提的產業傷害瀕臨絕種的動物，改變了食物鏈，而最終將會傷害人類，因為我們處於食物鏈的最頂端。）

解析

1. 重點：that 帶出名詞子句當作 indicates 的受詞。句中的分詞片語 altering the food chain 是由 and alters the food chain 簡化而來，簡化步驟：省略 and，動詞 alters 是主動語態，所以改成現在分詞 altering。

2. 例：The example indicates that *Happy Feet* has created positive influence, altering the audience's perception of the living condition of emperor penguins, which also raises green awareness.（這個例子顯示《快樂腳》創造了正面效應，改變了觀眾對帝王企鵝生存狀態的認知，也提升了環保意識。）

重要字彙與例句

① precedence *n.* 優先

One's health should always take precedence over one's career.

一個人的健康應該總是優先於他的事業。

② infliction *n.* 遭受折磨

The infliction of the dictatorial regime on its civilians was virtually unimaginable.

這個獨裁政權使它的人民遭受的折磨幾乎是無法想像的。

③ predicament *n.* 困境；窘境

The subprime mortgage crisis put many in a financial predicament.

次級房貸危機使得很多人陷於財務困境。

④ the Arctic *n.* 北極圈

The main tourist attraction in the Arctic is aurora borealis.

北極圈主要的觀光吸引力是北極光。

⑤ Antarctica *n.* 南極洲

The majority of residents in Antarctica are scientists.

大部分南極洲的住民是科學家。

⑥ **exacerbate** *vi* .惡化

The attack exacerbated the tense relation between Israel and Palestine.

這場攻擊讓以色列和巴勒斯坦的緊繃關係更惡化。

⑦ **envisage** *vt.* **預見；想像**

Successful entrepreneurs usually can envisage the development of their enterprises.

成功的企業家通常能預見他們企業的發展。

⑧ **reciprocally** *adv.* **互惠地**

True friendship progresses as two parties behave reciprocally.

真實的友誼隨著雙方行為互惠而展開。

Unit ❾ 環境類

人類活動是否改善環境——搭配電影《永不妥協》（*Erin Brockovich*）與名人故事：麥特・戴蒙（Matt Damon）

話說 iBT 新托福寫作題目與電影或名人故事

➡ 從以下題目為例，看題目與電影《永不妥協》（*Erin Brockovich*）及名人故事：麥特・戴蒙（Matt Damon）間的關連

"Some people believe human activities are harmful to the earth; others think human activities make the earth a better place. What is your opinion?" Use specific details and examples to support your viewpoint.

「有些人相信人類活動對地球有害；而其他人認為人類活動讓地球成為更好的地方。你的意見為何？」請使用精準的細節和例證支持你的論點。

劇情簡述

美國影星茱莉亞‧羅伯茲在《永不妥協》中扮演女主角艾琳‧波洛克維奇，並因此於西元 2000 年得到奧斯卡金像獎最佳女主角獎。《永不妥協》根據真實故事改編，波洛克維奇對抗污染地下水的 PG&E 公司，間接促成汙染地區的修復。另一影星麥特‧戴蒙成立了慈善機構 Water.org，並以他的影響力呼籲大眾關注水資源的匱乏及分配不均等問題。波洛克維奇和麥特‧戴蒙促成的活動都讓地球更好。

此類題型重點句搶先看

❶ After finding out that PG&E used carcinogenic chemicals that contaminated groundwater in Hinkley, California, Brockovich and the law firm she worked for built and won the lawsuit against PG&E, not only helping the residents receive millions in compensation, but also leading to the remediation of contaminated areas. 在發現 PG&E 使用致癌化學物質並汙染加州辛克利地區的地下水之後，艾琳‧波洛克維奇和雇用她的律師事務所提出告訴，並贏了對抗 PG&E 的官司，不只協助當地居民獲得數百萬美金的賠償，也讓汙染區域得到修復。

❷ To equalize water resource access, Matt Damon and Gary White cofounded a charity, Water.org, which builds water and sanitation facilities in destitute regions, proving that human existence can be elevated by a single act of philanthropy. 為了使水資源的取得平等化，麥特‧戴蒙和蓋瑞‧懷特共同成立了 Water.org 慈善機構，Water.org 在赤貧地區建造取水和衛生設施，證明了單一慈善行動能提升人類生存的狀態。

ch.1

ch.2
環境與人生觀類題型

ch.3

高分範文搶先看 ▶ Track 09

Never before has the earth been altered so dramatically by human activities. Yet, I believe humans are making the world a more promising place because we are capable of self-**redemption**[1].

Whereas industrialization has destroyed the wilderness, endangered numerous species, and exacerbated global warming, there is also a counterforce that strives to improve the environment. The improvement is often propelled by those with a moral conscience that assumes responsibility for the well-being of humanity, which is exemplified by the story of Erin Brockovich, an American environmental activist, who became a household name after her anti-pollution lawsuit against Pacific Gas & Electric (PG&E) was adapted into a Hollywood movie. After finding out

人類活動未曾對地球造成今日般如此劇烈的改變。但是我相信人類正使地球變成更美好的地方，因為我們有自我救贖的能力。

工業化已經摧毀了大自然，使眾多物種陷入瀕臨絕種的危機，且造成全球暖化惡化，然而，也有另一股反作用力致力於改善環境。改善環境的力量往往被擁有道德良知的人士及隨之而來對人類福祉的責任感所推動。艾琳‧波洛克維奇的故事即是例證，她是美國的環保運動人士，在她對PG&E提出的反污染官司被改編成好萊塢電影後，她成為家喻戶曉的名人。在發現 PG&E 使用致癌化學物質並汙染加州辛克利地區的地下水之後，艾琳‧波洛克維奇和雇用她的律師事務所提出告訴，並贏了對

that PG&E used **carcinogenic**[2] chemicals that contaminated groundwater in Hinkley, California, Brockovich and the law firm she worked for built and won the lawsuit against PG&E, not only helping the residents receive millions in compensation, but also leading to the **remediation**[3] of contaminated areas. As long as there are people who, like Brockovich, care about others' suffering, there is hope that human damage to the world can be amended.

While civilians' fight against **conglomerates**[4] that have conducted activities harmful to the earth might seem overwhelming, we don't have to look too far for the opportunity to make the world a better place. Taking the daily necessity, water, for example. the global water crisis is **intricately**[5] interconnected with climate

抗 PG&E 的官司，不只協助當地居民獲得數百萬美金的賠償，也讓汙染區域或得修復。只要有像波洛克維奇這樣關心他人痛苦的人士，人類對地球的損害就有被修復的希望。

平民對損害地球環境的大財團做出的抗爭可能過於吃力，然而，要使地球更好我們不用捨近求遠。以日常所需的水為例，全球水資源危機和氣候變遷，生態破壞及赤貧現象有錯綜複雜的關係。為了使水資源的取得平等化，麥特・戴蒙和蓋瑞・懷特共同成立了 Water.org 慈善機構，Water.

change, ecological destruction and extreme poverty. To equalize water resource access, Matt Damon and Gary White cofounded a charity, Water.org, which builds water and sanitation facilities in **destitute**[6] regions, proving that human existence can be elevated by a single act of **philanthropy**[7].

While it is debatable whether human activities generate positive or negative impacts, I maintain that the earth is being **meliorated**[8] with continuous philanthropic and environmental campaigns.

org 在赤貧地區建造取水和衛生設施，證明了單一慈善行動能提升人類生存的狀態。

人類活動是否造成正面或負面影響仍可辯論，但我認為隨著持續的慈善及環保運動，地球正持續被改善。

高分範文解析

關鍵句 1 ▶

Never before in history has the earth been altered so dramatically by human activities.（歷史上人類活動未曾對地球造成今日般如此劇烈的改變。）

解析

1. 重點：否定副詞 never 在句首，原本的直述句必須改成倒裝句。此句的主要動詞 has been altered 時態是現在完成式，故將助動詞 has 移到主詞 the earth 之前，形成倒裝句。例：Never had Julia Roberts won the Academy Award for Best Actress until 2000 for her performance in *Erin Brockovich*.（茱莉亞‧羅伯茲直到西元 2000 年由於她在《永不妥協》中的演出，才得到奧斯卡金像獎最佳女主角獎。）

關鍵句 2

While it is debatable whether human activities generate positive or negative impacts, I maintain that the earth is being meliorated with continuous philanthropic and environmental campaigns.（人類活動是否造成正面或負面影響仍可辯論，但我認為隨著持續的慈善及環保運動，地球正持續被改善。）

解析

1. 重點：第一個子句裡的真主詞是 whether 引導的名詞子句，當主詞的名詞子句較長時，句首以虛主詞 it 代替。例：It remains disputable whether celebrity spokespersons for charity foundations contribute substantially to destitute areas.（名人擔任慈善基金會的發言人是否對赤貧地區有實質的貢獻仍有待辯論。）

重要字彙與例句

① redemption *n.* 救贖

Redemption from God is one of the key ideas in the doctrines of Christianity.

來自上帝的救贖是基督教教義其中一項主要觀念。

② carcinogenic *adj.* 致癌的

Living in a highly industrial area exposes many to carcinogenic substances.

住在高度工業化區域使許多人暴露在致癌物質之下。

③ remediation *n.* 修復；整治

Environmentally friendly remediation measures were raised in the global conference.

在這場國際型會議裡，環保的修復措施被提出。

④ conglomerate *n.* 企業集團

Most of our daily necessities are manufactured by multinational conglomerates.

我們大部分的日用品都是由跨國企業集團生產的。

⑤ intricately *adv.* 錯綜複雜地

Physiological mechanisms and psychological mechanisms are connected intricately.

生理機能和心理機能是錯綜複雜地互為關連。

⑥ **destitute** *adj.* **赤貧的**

There is an intense debate about whether affluent nations are responsible for helping destitute third-world nations.

關於富裕國家是否有責任幫助赤貧的第三世界國家這一點仍處於激烈的辯論中。

⑦ **philanthropy** *n.* **慈善行為；慈善事業**

Mother Teresa's devotion to philanthropy has inspired many.

德雷莎修女對慈善的貢獻激勵了許多人。

⑧ **meliorate** *vt.* **改善**

Using less plastic products can help meliorate environmental damage.

少用塑膠產品能協助減緩對環境的損害。

ch.**1**

ch.**2**

環境與人生觀類題型

ch.**3**

Unit ❿ 人生觀

擁有財富即是成功？──搭配名人故事：德雷莎修女（Mother Teresa）與瑪拉拉·尤瑟夫札伊（MalalaYousafzai）

話說 iBT 新托福寫作題目與電影或名人故事

➡ 從以下題目為例，看題目與名人故事：德雷莎修女（Mother Teresa）及瑪拉拉·尤瑟夫札伊（Malala Yousafzai）間的關連

"Only people who possess a large amount of wealth are successful". Do you agree or disagree with the statement? Use specific details and examples to support your viewpoint.

「擁有許多財富的人才是成功的。」你同意或不同意以上敘述？請使用精準的細節和例證支持你的論點。

名人故事簡述

德雷莎修女（Mother Teresa）及瑪拉拉‧尤瑟夫札伊（Malala Yousafzai）在各自的領域都是普世公認的成功者。雖然他們的人生志業大不相同，但共同的是他們的成功都不是因為擁有財富，另一個類似之處是他們對自己的理念一直維持著非常堅定的信念，並以異於常人的熱誠將理念化為行動。德雷莎修女於 1979 年獲得諾貝爾和平獎，馬拉拉則是 2014 年獲頒此獎。

此類題型重點句搶先看

❶ While the examples of such figures abound, I would take two prominent figures, Mother Teresa and Malala Yousafzai as examples. It goes without saying that the former's success arose from her selfless devotion to the destitute and the ill in India, and the latter's arose from her advocacy for children's, especially girls' right of education.

這種人物的例子非常多，而我舉兩位著名人物為例，德雷莎修女和馬拉拉‧尤瑟夫札伊。無庸置疑地，前者的成功來自她在印度對貧苦及生病民眾的無私奉獻，而後者的成功來自她對兒童的，尤其是女性的受教權的倡導。

❷ Malala, the Pakistani female rights activist, is the youngest ever Nobel Peace Prize laureate, having accepted the Nobel Peace Prize at age 17 in 2014.

馬拉拉，巴基斯坦的女權運動者，是有史以來最年輕的諾貝爾和平獎得主，在 2014 年她十七歲時得到此獎。

高分範文搶先看 ▶ Track 10

In a capitalist society, owning a large amount of wealth seems to be the prime sign of success. Popular culture **exalts**[1] the rich so much so that the rich have become the new royalty. Yet, if one **delves**[2] into the constituents of success, he is likely to discover that money alone can hardly satisfy those elements, which is why I disagree with the statement.

My firm belief is that whether one has passion for what he does is the key. My opinion **resonates**[3] with Albert Schweitzer's famous saying. Albert Schweitzer, the recipient of the Nobel Peace Prize in 1952, once said, "Success is not the key to happiness. Happiness is the key to success. If you love what you are doing, you will be successful." If a person's life-long pursuit is aimed at accumulating as much wealth as possible, he is bound to lead a life

在資本主義社會，擁有大量財富似乎是成功的主要指標。流行文化是如此地推崇富裕者以至於有錢人已經變成新的貴族。然而，如果一個人深入探討成功的元素，他很可能會發現財富幾乎不可能滿足那些元素，這正是我不同意題目敘述的原因。

我確信一個人對他的所作所為是否保持熱誠才是關鍵。我的看法呼應艾伯特・史懷哲的名言。艾伯特・史懷哲是 1952 年的諾貝爾和平獎得主，他曾說「成功不是達到幸福的關鍵。幸福才是達到成功的關鍵。如果你熱愛你做的事，你就會成功」。若一個人終生追求的目標是盡量累積財富，他注定會活得像小氣財神。小氣財神是查爾斯・狄更斯的小說《聖誕頌歌》的主

like Scrooge, the protagonist in Charles Dickens' novel, *A Christmas Carol*, who is miserly and has no passion in his life. Actualizing passion into action will induce a sense of fulfillment; instead, merely owning money is no guarantee for felicity; at best, it's a **meretricious**[4] facade of success that will **disintegrate**[5] sooner or later.

Furthermore, the achievements of most public figures who are deemed successful globally are rarely **ascribed**[6] to their wealth. While the examples of such figures abound, I would take two prominent figures, Mother Teresa and Malala Yousafzai as examples. It goes without saying that the former's success arose from her selfless devotion to the destitute and the ill in India, and the latter's arose from her advocacy for children's, especially girls' right of education. Malala, the

角，他很吝嗇，而且人生中沒有熱誠。將熱誠轉化為行動能帶來成就感。反之，只有錢並不能保證幸福感；充其量這只是華而不實，遲早會崩解的成功表相。

此外，大部分在全球都被視為成功者的那些公眾人物，他們的成就很少被歸因於財富。這種人物的例子非常多，而我舉兩位著名人物為例，德雷莎修女和馬拉拉・尤瑟夫札伊。無庸置疑地，前者的成功來自她在印度對貧苦及生病民眾的無私奉獻，而後者的成功來自她對兒童的，尤其是女性的受教權的倡導。馬拉拉，巴基斯坦的女權運動者，是有史以來最年輕的諾貝爾和平獎得主，在 2014 年她十七歲時得到此獎。很明顯地，他們的成

Pakistani female rights activist, is the youngest ever Nobel Peace Prize **laureate**[7], having accepted the Nobel Peace Prize at age 17 in 2014. It is conspicuous that their success is not relevant to their possession of **opulence**[8].

The above examples demonstrate that success solely built upon wealth is hardly universally recognized. Those unquestionably acknowledged to be successful are people who are passionately committed to what they do.

功和他們擁有的財富毫無關係。

以上例證顯示只建構在財富之上的成功很難被普世認可。無疑地，被認為是成功人士的是那些對所作所為保持熱誠的人。

高分範文解析

關鍵句 1

Furthermore, the achievements of most public figures who are deemed successful globally are rarely ascribed to their wealth. （此外，大部分在全球都被視為成功者的那些公眾人物，他們的成就很少被歸因於財富。）

解析

1. 重點：形容詞子句 who are deemed successful globally 所修飾的先行詞是普通名詞 public figures，所以需使用限定形容詞子句。限定形容詞子句在關係代名詞之前不能有逗號。

2. 例：Malala Yousafzai's advocacy represents the voice which speaks for millions of young girls who are forbidden to receive education.（馬拉拉·尤瑟夫札伊的倡議代表著上百萬被禁止接受教育的年輕女性的聲音。）

關鍵句 2

The above examples demonstrate that success solely built upon wealth is hardly universally recognized.（以上例證顯示，只建構在財富之上的成功很難被普世認可。）

解析

1. 重點：分詞片語 solely built upon wealth 是由形容詞子句 which is solely built upon wealth 簡化而來。

2. 例：The fame of some Hollywood actors solely built upon PR promotion is often short-lived.（有些好萊塢演員的名聲是被公關宣傳建構的，這樣的名聲通常維持不久。）

ch.1

ch.2 環境與人生觀類題型

ch.3

重要字彙與例句

① exalt *vt.* 晉升；頌揚

The status of celebrities in the entertainment industry is overly exalted.

演藝圈名人的地位太過被提升了。

② delve *vi.* 探討

Parents need to delve into the ways to prevent their children from being addicted to 3C products.

父母需要探討避免小孩對 3C 產品上癮的方法。

③ resonate *vi.* 共鳴、回響

The stories of emotionally abused survivors resonate one another in support groups.

在支援團體裡，被情緒虐待的倖存者的故事互相引起共鳴。

④ meretricious *adj.* 華而不實的、虛誇的

It is not difficult to display meretricious images in the social media.

在社群媒體展現浮誇的形象其實不難。

⑤ disintegrate *vi.* 瓦解、分解

The Roman Empire disintegrated partially due to slaves' revolt.

羅馬帝國一部分是因為奴隸反抗而瓦解。

⑥ **ascribe** *vi.* **歸因於**

Steve Jobs' success was ascribed to his talent and perseverance.

史帝夫‧賈伯斯的成功是被歸因於他的才華和毅力。

⑦ **laureate** *n.* **獲得（某專業領域）獎項的人**

The life of the Nobel laureate, John Nash, was adapted into the movie, *A Beautiful Mind*, starring Russell Crowe.

諾貝爾獎得主約翰‧納許的人生被改編成電影《美麗心靈》，由羅素‧克洛主演。

⑧ **opulence** *n.* **奢侈、豪華**

Living in opulence can hardly compensate one's psychological emptiness.

過著奢華的生活很難彌補心靈的空虛。

Unit ⑪ 人生觀

取得成功應具備的特質——
搭配名人故事：李安（Ang Lee）
與歐普拉·溫佛瑞（Oprah Winfrey）

話說 iBT 新托福寫作題目與電影或名人故事
➡ 從以下題目為例，看題目與名人故事：李安（Ang Lee） 及歐普拉·溫佛瑞（Oprah Winfrey）間的關連

"In your opinion, what are the crucial characteristics that one must have to achieve success in life?" Use specific details and examples to support your viewpoint.

「你認為一個人要達到成功須具備哪些重要的特質？」請使用精準的細節和例證支持你的論點。

名人背景簡述

在美國，李安和歐普拉‧溫佛瑞（Oprah Winfrey）以少數族群的身份取得的成功是多數人都難以望其項背的。他們的成功絕非一蹴可及，而兩者有些共同的特質。儘管有專業上的才華，他們都曾因為少數族群的身份受到質疑，但最終仍堅持走自己的路。兩人都是自青少年時期就發展自己的興趣，並和專業結合，也在各自的領域耕耘了數十年之久，才達到今日的地位，由此可見，持之以恆的努力是成功背後最重要的因素。

此類題型重點句搶先看

❶ A renowned person who relies on positive intention as an impetus for her success is Oprah Winfrey, a billionaire and a media mogul.

歐普拉‧溫佛瑞就是依賴正向意圖驅策她成功的名人。

❷ Both Winfrey and Lee underwent experiences of invalidation, which might have swayed their determination to develop their talents, yet they believed in themselves despite others' disapproval.

溫佛瑞和李安都有不被肯定的經驗，這些經驗原本可能動搖他們發展才華的決心，但是儘管別人不認同，他們還是相信自己。

ch.1

ch.2
環境與人生觀類題型

ch.3

高分範文搶先看 ▶ Track 11

There are many motivational speakers in every country that impart the secrets of success to the public. Evidently, it is part of human nature to aspire to succeed, and personally, four characteristics stand out as indispensable traits to attain success, namely positive intention, knowing one's gift, belief in oneself, and making efforts.

Positive intention is the driving force behind success. In a materialistic society, success is often misidentified with the possession of wealth, and thus most people disregard the motivation for their pursuit. Nonetheless, I don't think that success will be **justifiable**[1] without positive intention. A renowned person who relies on positive intention as an **impetus**[2] for her success is Oprah Winfrey, a billionaire and a media **mogul**[3]. In

　　每個國家都有許多勵志演說家向大眾傳授成功的祕訣。明顯地，渴望成功是人性的一部分，就我個人而言，有四個為了取得成功不可缺少的特質，即正向意圖、瞭解自己的才華、相信自己及努力。

　　正向意圖是成功的驅策力。在物質化的社會，成功常跟擁有財富混淆，因此大部分的人忽略了追求成功的動機。然而，我認為缺乏正向意圖，成功不會有正當性。歐普拉・溫佛瑞就是依賴正向意圖驅策她成功的名人。歐普拉・溫佛瑞是億萬富翁及媒體大亨。在1990 年代，當大部分的談話性節目都製作充滿衝突的內容，溫佛瑞大膽地將她的談話性節目的風格改變成以正向意

the 1990s, while most talk shows produced **confrontational**[4] content, Winfrey boldly changed the style of her talk show to the one that was based on positive intention. Besides, Winfrey found her gift for communication early, as she started working in a radio station at 16. Knowing one's gift is one of the most **salient**[5] characteristics of successful people. Another celebrity who demonstrates this feature is Ang Lee, two-time winner of the Academy Award for Best Director, who discovered his gift for writing scripts during adolescence.

However, the aforementioned traits will not be actualized into attainment without belief in oneself and making perseverant efforts. Both Winfrey and Lee underwent experiences of **invalidation**[6] , which might have swayed their determination to

圖為出發點。此外，當溫佛瑞十六歲開始在廣播電台工作時，早就發現她對溝通的才華。瞭解自我的才華是成功人士最顯著的特色之一。另一位展現這項特色的名人是李安，他是兩次奧斯卡金像獎最佳導演獎的得主，李安在青少年時期就發現自己有寫劇本的才華。

然而，如果不相信自己和缺乏堅持不懈的努力，以上所提的特質都不會具體化為成就。溫佛瑞和李安都有不被肯定的經驗，這些經驗原本可能動搖他們發展才華的決心，但是儘管別人不認同，他們還是相信自己。李安曾經描寫他以

develop their talents, yet they believed in themselves despite others' disapproval. Ang Lee has written about his struggle of being a stay-at-home father and having his scripts constantly rejected. Winfrey described how she was invalidated because of her gender and ethnic identity. Also, they had **persevered**[7] in making endeavors for decades before acquiring their success. I believe that **endeavor**[8] is the key; without efforts, the other characteristics will hardly impel any achievement.

To sum up, among the four features, continuous endeavors should be the universally acknowledged key feature.

往當家庭主夫及劇本不斷被退回等掙扎。溫佛瑞曾描述她因性別和種族身份而不被肯定。而且，他們在獲得成功前，堅持不懈地努力，長達數十年。我相信努力是關鍵，沒有努力，其他的特質很難激發任何成就。

　　總而言之，這四個特質中，持續努力應該是普世公認的關鍵特質。

高分範文解析

關鍵句 1

Both Winfrey and Lee underwent experiences of invalidation, which might have swayed their determination to develop their talents, yet they believed in themselves despite others' disapproval. （溫佛瑞和李安都有不被肯定的經驗，這些經驗原本可能動搖他們發展才華的決心，但是儘管別人不認同，他們還是相信自己。）

解析

1. 重點：形容詞子句的關係代名詞 which 代替關代之前的主要子句，即 which 代替「溫佛瑞和李安都有不被肯定的經驗」。形容詞子句的主要動詞 might have p.p.表達與過去事實相反，即過去原本可能發生的動作，但事實上沒有發生。

2. 例：Ang Lee once considered abandoning his dream of directing movies, which might have altered his life drastically. （李安曾經考慮放棄他當導演的夢想，這原本可能劇烈地改變他的人生。）

關鍵句 2

Also, they had persevered in making endeavors for decades before acquiring their success. （而且，他們在獲得成功前，堅持不懈地努力，長達數十年。）

解析

1. 重點：句尾的分詞片語 acquiring their success 是由 they acquired their success 簡化而來。主要動詞 had persevered 時態是過去完成式，當兩個動詞的時間點互相比較，比簡單過去式更早發生的動作必須使用過去完成式。例如 acquired 是簡單過去式，persevere（堅持不懈）的時間點在獲得成功之前，故正確時態為 had persevered。

2. 例：Oprah Winfrey had been hosting her talk show for 25 years before establishing her own TV channel.（歐普拉‧溫佛瑞在成立她自己的電視頻道之前，持續主持她的談話性節目長達二十五年。）

重要字彙與例句

① justifiable *adj.* 正當的

Physical abuse on another human being is never justifiable.

對另一個人的肢體暴力從來就不是正當的。

② impetus *n.* 動力；激勵

People with resilient minds know how to turn adversity into impetus.

具有韌性心靈的人知道如何將逆境轉化為動力。

③ mogul *n.* 大人物

Oprah Winfrey is a media mogul who rose from rags to riches.

歐普拉‧溫佛瑞是白手起家的媒體業大人物。

④ **confrontational** *adj.* **對峙的、敵對的**

A confrontational relationship might be full of hostility.

一段對峙的關係可能是充滿敵意的。

⑤ **salient** *adj.* **顯著的**

One of the salient traits of celebrities is their charisma.

名人的顯著特色之一是他們的個人魅力。

⑥ **invalidation** *n.* **失效；不（被）認可**

Children who are ignored by their parents face parental invalidation.

被父母忽視的孩子面對的是不被父母認可的感覺。

⑦ **persevere** *vi.* **堅持不懈；持之以恆**

Ang Lee persevered in developing his talent during those years of unemployment.

李安在失業的那些年仍堅持不懈地發展他的才華。

⑧ **endeavor** *vi.,n.* **努力；試圖**

He endeavored for opportunities to direct movies.

他竭力想獲得執導電影的機會。

Unit ⑫ 人生觀

人們不滿足於現狀——搭配電影：《命運好好玩》（*Click*）

話說 iBT 新托福寫作題目與電影或名人故事
➡ 從以下題目為例，看題目與電影《命運好好玩》（*Click*）間的關連

"People nowadays are rarely content with the present; they always aim higher or desire more." Do you agree or disagree with the statement? Use specific details and examples to support your viewpoint.

「當今的人們很少滿足於現狀。他們總是將目標訂得更高或想要更多。」你同意或不同意以上敘述？請使用精準的細節和例證支持你的論點。

劇情簡述

亞當·山德勒（Adam Sandler）飾演《命運好好玩》（*Click*）的男主角，一位以當上公司合夥人為目標的工作狂建築師。他一直認為只要能當上合夥人，人生的一切都會圓滿。不只在工作上力爭上游，他也很在意鄰居過的物質生活比他家人的奢華，因此常常不滿意現狀。某日他意外獲得一個神奇遙控器，能讓他快轉、回溯或暫停人生。當他不斷利用遙控器操控人生，他的人生也漸漸失控。他最終成為合夥人，但失去了健康和親情。

此類題型重點句搶先看

❶ Examples abound that many men already have affectionate families, yet they still desire more power or wealth, which is portrayed in the movie, *Click*.

很多例子顯示許多人已經有摯愛他們的家人，但仍渴望更多權力或財富，電影《命運好好玩》描繪了這現象。

❷ It has become a social norm to be discontent and aspire more, which, when developed to the extreme, might place us in the predicament as symbolized by the metaphorical remote in *Click*.

不滿足並渴望更多已經變成社會常態，當這現象發展至極端時，可能會讓我們處於像《命運好好玩》裡的遙控器隱喻象徵的困境。

高分範文搶先看　▶ Track 12

Those living in a capitalist and competitive society tend to follow the path to climb the social ladder. While desiring more might induce positive or negative effects, I am inclined to agree with the statement.

First, it is part of human nature to want more. <u>Nonetheless, in a materialistic society, many people attach their individual values to material possessions due to **incessant**[1] commercials that brainwash consumers into buying more.</u> Commercials of cars and cell phones are often connected with a sense of **felicity**[2] or indication of elevated social status, implying to consumers that if they possess the products, they are one step closer to happiness or high status. However, this is only a **mirage**[3] created by marketing strategies to lure consumers into spending more, but

住在資本化和競爭激烈社會的人們都傾向要出人頭地。想要更多可能導致正面或負面的效應，但我傾向同意題目敘述。

首先，想要更多是人性的一部份。然而，在物質化的社會，許多人將他們個人的價值依附在物質財產上，因為層出不窮的廣告會洗腦消費者去做更多消費。轎車和手機的廣告常和幸福感或社會高階地位連結，向消費者暗示如果他們擁有那些產品，他們就離幸福或高社會地位更近一步。但是，這只是行銷策略創造的海市蜃樓，藉此誘惑消費者花更多錢，但消費者從不感覺滿足，因為新產品總是快速推出。因此，從物質主義尋求快樂的人們會陷於想要更多，而欲望只能暫時被滿足的惡性循環。

never feeling satisfied since new products are launched rapidly. Thus, people who seek happiness from materialism are trapped in the **vicious**[4] cycle of desiring more and having their desires satisfied only temporarily.

Secondly, as most of us belonging to the **bourgeoisie**[5] climb the social ladder, it is difficult to strike a balance between family and work. While we are constantly **swamped**[6] by work demands, we forget to pause and remind ourselves to appreciate what we already have. Examples abound that many men already have affectionate families, yet they still desire more power or wealth, which is portrayed in the movie, *Click*. The protagonist in *Click* is a workaholic who keeps ignoring his family as he strives to meet the demands from his boss and his goal to make partner in his company.

第二，當大多數屬於中產階級的我們在社會上力爭上游時，很難在家庭和工作間取得平衡。當我們不斷被工作要求淹沒時，我們會忘記暫停一下並提醒自己體會已經擁有的事物。很多例子顯示許多人已經有摯愛他們的家人，但仍渴望更多權力或財富，電影《命運好好玩》描繪了這現象。《命運好好玩》的主角是個工作狂，當他努力要達到老闆的要求及成為公司合夥人的目標時，他一直忽略他的家庭。最終，由於一個神奇遙控器掌控了他的世界，他對人生失去控制，雖然他原本想要用這遙控器將時間快轉到他升遷的時

He ultimately pays the price of losing his family as his life **spiraled**[7] out of control due to a magic remote control that overtakes his universe, though initially he intends to use the remote to fast forward the time to his promotion.

刻，他也付出失去家人的代價。

In conclusion, it has become a social norm to be discontent and aspire more, which, when developed to the extreme, might place us in the predicament as symbolized by the **metaphorical**[8] remote in *Click*.

總而言之，不滿足並渴望更多已經變成社會常態，當這現象發展至極端時，可能會讓我們處於像《命運好好玩》裡的遙控器隱喻象徵的困境。

高分範文解析

關鍵句 1

Nonetheless, in a materialistic society, many people attach their individual values to material possessions due to incessant commercials that brainwash consumers into buying more.（然而，在物質化的社會，許多人將他們個人的價值依附在物質財產上，因為層出不窮的廣告會洗腦消費者去做更多消費。）

解析

1. 重點：due to N. 是表達原因的常用片語。同義詞有 owing to，thanks to，because of，as the result of。注意這些片語之後只能搭配名詞。that brainwash consumers into buying more 是限定的形容詞子句，修飾先行詞 commercials。

2. 例：Hollywood star Adam Sandler is considered a versatile actor due to his diverse performances in various movies that include *Click, Reign over Me*, and *Men, Women & Children*.（由於他在各種電影裡的多樣化演出，包括《命運好好玩》、《從心開始》和《雲端男女》，好萊塢影星亞當·山德勒被視為多才多藝的演員，。）

關鍵句 2

In conclusion, it has become a social norm to be discontent and aspire more, which, when developed to the extreme, might place us in the predicament as symbolized by the metaphorical remote in Click.（總而言之，不滿足並渴望更多已經變成社會常態，當這現象發展至極端時，可能會讓我們處於像《命運好好玩》裡的遙控器隱喻象徵的困境。）

解析

1. 重點：關係代名詞 which 代替的是主要子句 it has become a social norm ...。此非限定的形容詞子句原本包含了兩個由 when 連接的子句：which might place us ... when it is developed to the extreme。而 when it is developed to the extreme 在此句可簡化成分詞片語。

2.例：Taking selfies has become a social norm, which, when developed to the extreme, might encourage narcissism.（自拍已經變成社會常態，當這現象發展至極端時，可能會鼓勵自戀主義。）

重要字彙與例句

① incessant *adj.* 不斷的、層出不窮的

Incessant terrorist attacks in Europe raised the tension to a new level.

在歐洲層出不窮的恐怖攻擊將緊繃的狀態提升到新的層次。

② felicity *n.* 幸福

Felicity is a state of mind, rather than material possessions.

幸福是一種心態，而不是物質財產。

③ mirage *n.* 海市蜃樓

A mirage refers to an illusion in a desert or an illusory idea.

海市蜃樓指的是沙漠裡的幻覺或妄想。

④ vicious *adj.* 惡性的、惡意的

Vicious stories sometimes become the main reports in tabloids.

惡意中傷的傳聞有時候會變成八卦媒體的主要報導。

⑤ **bourgeoisie** *n.* **中產階級**

Among all of the social strata, bourgeoisie suffered the most during the global recession.

在所有的社會階級中，中產階級在全球金融風暴中受苦最多。

⑥ **swamp** *vt.,vi.* **淹沒、陷於**

The celebrity was swamped in waves of scandals.

這位名人陷於一波波的醜聞當中。

⑦ **spiral** *vi.* **不斷升高**

The social tension spiraled in the U.S. after several African Americans were shot dead by white policemen.

美國的社會焦慮不斷升高，在幾位非裔美國人被白人警察射殺之後。

⑧ **metaphorical** *adj.* **隱喻的**

The poem abounds in metaphorical images.

這首詩充滿了隱喻的意象。

Unit ⑬
媒體類重要句型整理、解析及應用

開頭句（Openings）重要句型整理、解析及應用

1. 媒體類型題，表達個人的想法的重要句型為：
   I concede that S+V

解析 1

"I concede that...", 我認為，是比較正式的用法，其他用法還有"I believe that..."。

應用 1.1

I concede that in a democratic society with limited censorship of the media, it is rarely the duty of the media to probe further into the concepts behind those images, and that provocative images are simply indicative of the vibrant competitions in the media. (Part 1 Unit 1)

我認為在民主社會，且在有限的媒體審查制度之下，深入探討畫面背後的觀念並不是媒體的責任，而且聳動的畫面只是顯示媒體蓬勃的競爭現象。《節選自 Part 1 Unit 1》

應用 1.2

I believe that in a communist country with strict censorship on the media, it is hardly common for the media to enjoy freedom of speech, and that the media mainly serves to convey political propaganda.

我相信在有嚴格審查制度的共產國家，媒體幾乎不會有言論自由，而且媒體主要的功能是政治宣傳。

2. 表達利用電影或書籍等，支持主要論點的重要句型為：
   I would draw on N. to explain ...

解析 2

"I would draw on N. to explicate ..."，引用某事以闡述……，當題目要求引用某電影，書籍或經驗發表個人看法時，可利用此句型。類似句型有 "I would utilize N. to illustrate ..."。

應用 2.1

I would draw on the movie, "3 Idiots", to explain what I learned about current Indian society. (Part 1 Unit 2)

我將引用《三個傻瓜》這部電影闡述我從這部電影學到關於現代印度社會的某些現象。《節選自 Part 1 Unit 2》

應用 2.2

I would utilize my graduate school studying experience to illustrate that persistence is the key to success. 我將使用我在研究所讀書的經驗闡述堅持不懈是成功的關鍵。

轉承句（Transitions）重要句型整理、解析及應用

> ## 3. 表達因此或結果的重要句型為：
> Therefore, S+V.

解析 3

"Therefore"，因此，注意詞性是副詞，類似字有 **thus**、**thereby**、**hence**、**consequently**、**as a result**。

應用 3.1

Therefore, presenting provocative images has evolved into one of the fastest ways to reach consumers, though occasionally ethical questions are raised. (Part 1 Unit 1)

因此，呈現聳動的畫面已經演變成打動消費者最快速的方式，雖然偶爾道德方面的問題會被提出來。《節選自 Part 1 Unit 1》

應用 3.2

Thus, TV programs have become the means to instill political ideas, though sometimes there are entertainment programs.

因此，電視節目變成灌輸政治思想的工具，雖然偶爾會有娛樂性質的節目。

4. 表達與上一句意義相反或程度有落差，並同時舉例的重要句型為：

However, S+V, as S+V.

解析 4

"however"，然而，注意詞性是副詞，類似字有 **nevertheless**、**yet**、**contrarily**、**on the contrary**、**in contrast**。"as"，如同，或因為。在此是連接詞，串聯兩個子句。

應用 4.1

However, women face more inequality than men, as a female medical student in the film suggests that when it comes to marriage, family honor precedes a woman's individuality. (Part 1 Unit 2)

然而，女性比男性面對更多不平等現象，如同電影裡一位醫學系女學生暗示的，當面對婚姻，家族名譽比女性個人意志重要多了。《節選自 Part 1 Unit 2》

應用 4.1

However, studying in graduate school can be daunting, as one is overwhelmed by a large number of research papers that one needs to read.

然而，在研究所唸書可能是有點讓人氣餒的，學生會因為要研讀大量的研究報告而感到壓力。

論點衍伸句（Explanations）重要句型整理、解析及應用

> ## 5. 表達主要論點的重要句型為：
> I would argue that S+V

解析 5 ▶

"**I would argue that ...**"，我主張，是較普遍的句型，語氣更強烈的句型有 "**I would assert that ...**"

應用 5.1

I would argue that it is not the media's responsibility to provide deeper concepts. On the contrary, it is the viewers' responsibility to research further should they be interested. (Part 1 Unit 1)

我主張提供更深層的觀念並不是媒體的責任。相反地，做出更深入的探討應該是觀眾的責任，萬一他們有興趣的話。《節選自 Part 1 Unit 1》

應用 5.2

I would assert that it is inevitable for the media to adapt themselves to the political institution. In contrast, it is possible for viewers to decide what kind of content they want to absorb.

我主張媒體調整其內容去因應政治制度是無法避免的。相對地，觀眾是可能決定他們想吸收的是哪種內容。

6. 表達擴充論點的重要句型為：
S+V, which can be analyzed in ...

解析 6

先提出看法或論點後，利用形容詞子句擴充論點成數個小重點。

應用 6.1

Inequality and traditions seem to be intertwined in India as two sides of the same coin, which can be analyzed in two aspects: gender roles and social hierarchy. (Part 1 Unit 2)

在印度，不平等現象和傳統似乎是密不可分，一體兩面，這種關係可由兩方面分析：性別角色和社會階級。《節選自 Part 1 Unit 2》

應用 6.2

Whether a student can succeed in graduate school or not depends on his mentality, which can be analyzed in two aspects: strong will and persistence.

一個學生是否能在研究所成功，依賴的是他的心態，可由兩方面分析：強烈的意志力及恆心。

結論（Conclusions）重要句型整理、解析及應用

> ## 7. 強調自我論點的重要句型為：
> It is not ...; rather, it is ...

解析 7

"It is not...; rather, it is ..."，不是……；而是……。運用虛主詞 **it** 導引的句子將自我論點再重述一次。

應用 7.1

It is not the media's job to instill concepts into us; rather, it is the viewers' job to search for meaning. (Part 1 Unit1)

灌輸觀念給我們並不是媒體的工作；反之，追尋意義應該是觀眾的工作。

《節選自 Part 1 Unit 1》

應用 7.2

It is not the media's power to control our thoughts; rather, it is the viewer's power to do so.

媒體沒有掌控我們思考的權力；反之，觀眾才有。

8. 表達利用某事傳達訊息或概念的重要句型為：
N. conveys an important message that S+V

解析 8 ▶

"**convey**"，傳達，在此句型中，**that S+V** 功能是名詞子句，當作 **message** 的同位語。

應用 8.1

The movie conveys an important message that the younger generation in India can indeed break the shackles of traditions. (Part 1 Unit 2)

這部電影傳達一則重要的訊息，印度的年輕世代的確有可能打破傳統的枷鎖。《節選自 Part 1 Unit 2》

應用 8.2

Having succeeded in graduate school conveys an important message that one is more resistant to pressure.

在研究所能獲取成功所傳遞的訊息是學生的抗壓力較強。

Unit ⑭

媒體及教育類重要句型整理、解析及應用

主旨句（Thesis Statement）重要句型整理、解析及應用

> 1. 媒體類型題，表達個人偏好的重要句型為：
>   I prefer N1 to N2

解析 1 ▶

"I prefer N1 to N2"，注意 **to** 是介系詞，比較正式的句型有 **"My preference for N1 prevails over N2."**。

應用 1.1

I prefer movies to novels because of the diversity of angles and technologies in movies. (Part 1 Unit 3)

我偏好電影多於小說，理由是電影裡多樣化的角度和科技。《節選自 Part 1 Unit 3》

應用 1.2

My preference for sci-fi novels prevails over romance.

我偏好科幻小說多於羅曼史。

2. 教育類型題，表達個人立場的重要句型為：
I am inclined to agree/ disagree with ...

解析 2

inclined *adj.*，傾向的，是比較正式的形容詞。比較普遍的類似句型有 **I tend to agree/ disagree with ...**。

應用 2.1

I am inclined to agree with the statement. (Part 1 Unit4)

我仍傾向同意題目的敘述。《節選自 Part 1 Unit 4》

應用 2.2

I tend to read sci-fi novels when feeling depressed because imagination about the future offers a temporary escape from reality.

當我感到憂鬱時，我傾向讀科幻小說，因為關於未來的想像提供一個暫離現實的出口。

轉承句（Transitions）重要句型整理、解析及應用

3. 表達類比，同理可證的重要句型為：
Likewise, ...

解析 3

Likewise *adv.*，同樣地，類似副詞有 **similarly**、**by the same token**。

應用 3.1

Likewise, the readers' comprehension of a novel is confined by their personal background, which can be broadened by watching movies. (Part 1 Unit 3)

同樣地，讀者對小說的理解能力也會受限於個人背景，看電影可以拓展理解能力。《節選自 Part 1 Unit 3》

應用 3.2

By the same token, watching sci-fi movies help relieve our pressure.

同理可證，看科幻小說幫助舒緩壓力。

4. 補充更多細節並舉例的重要句型為：
Furthermore, ... Take N. for example. ...

解析 4

furthermore *adv.*，此外，類似副詞有 **moreover**、**besides**、**additionally**。**... such as ...**，例如。

應用 4.1

Furthermore, university education should enable us to steer our lives with personal values. Take two characters in the movie, *Mona Lisa Smile*, for example. ... (Part 1 Unit 4)

此外，大學教育應該賦予我們運用個人價值觀掌控人生方向的能力。以電影《蒙娜麗莎的微笑》的兩個角色為例…《節選自 Part 1 Unit 4》

應用 4.2

Moreover, some imagination in sci-fi novels written decades ago became realized, such as cell phones and sending probes to Mars.

此外，數十年前寫的科幻小說其中的一些想像已經被實現了，例如手機和派遣偵測器到火星。

論點衍伸句（Explanations）重要句型整理、解析及應用

5. 表達支持偏好的理由的重要句型為：
The first reason for my preference is that S+V

解析 5 ▶

此句型適合放在主文 **(main body)** 其中一個段落的第一句，當作 **topic sentence**。比較正式的句型有 **My preference arises from N.**，指肇因於、發源自。

應用 5.1

The first reason for my preference is that elements in fiction are often limited by the writer's background, while movies incorporate contemporary viewpoints and various cultural dimensions, making them more approachable to the audience. (Part 1 Unit 3)

支持我的偏好的第一個理由是，小說裡的元素常常被作者的背景限制，然而電影能融入當代觀點和豐富的文化面向，使電影對觀眾而言更容易理解。

《節選自 Part 1 Unit 3》

應用 5.2

My preference for sci-fi arose from childhood experience of watching the Hollywood sci-fi movie, *Star Wars*.

我對科幻小說偏好的理由起因於童年時觀賞好萊塢科幻片《星際大戰》。

ch.1

ch.2

6. 表達主要論點的重要句型為：

My major argument concerns N.

解析 6

類似句型有 **"My major argument is related with N."**

應用 6.1

My major argument concerns the core functions of different educational institutions. (Part 1 Unit 4)

我的主要論點是關於不同教育機構的核心功能。《節選自 Part 1 Unit 4》

應用 6.2

My major argument is related with the diversity of technologies which are applied in 4DX movies.

我的主要論點是關於被應用到 4DX 電影的豐富科技。

結論（Conclusions）重要句型整理、解析及應用

> **7. 將主文重點及偏好換句話說的重要句型為：**
>
> In sum, ... as well as..., which explains my propensity to choose N1 over N2 ...

解析 7 ▶

結論段落應利用適當的連接詞將主文重點重述一次。為避免重複使用 **preference**，改寫成 **my propensity to choose N1 over N2**。

應用 7.1

In sum, movies bridge viewers from different backgrounds and add current perspectives, without requiring viewers to possess any relevant knowledge, as well as create more thrills with technologies, which explains my propensity to choose movies over novels. (Part 1 Unit 3)

總而言之，電影縮短不同背景的觀眾間的距離，並加入當代觀點，不需要觀眾擁有相關知識，而且能運用科技創造更多刺激，以上解釋了為何我傾向偏好電影多於小說。《節選自 Part 1 Unit 3》

應用 7.2

In sum, the imagination as well as relief from pressure are the reasons which explain my propensity to choose sci-fi over romance.

總之，想像力及舒緩壓力是我傾向偏好科幻小說多於羅曼史的理由。

8. 表達強調自我立場的重要句型為：
I stand firm behind my stance that S+V

解析 8

I stand firm behind my stance that S+V，語氣較強烈，**that S+V** 的部分用類似字將贊成或反對題目敘述的立場再換句話說。

應用 8.1

I stand firm behind my stance that the ultimate goal of universities lies in helping students cultivate individual values, without which life is without anchor, regardless of our jobs. (Part 1 Unit 4)

我堅持我的立場，大學的終極目標是協助學生培養個人價值觀，沒有個人價值觀的人生是沒有精神支柱的，不管我們的工作為何。《節選自 Part 1 Unit 4》

應用 8.2

I stand firm behind my stance that the goal of vocational schools is to equip students with the most updated skills for their future jobs.

我堅持我的立場，職訓學校的目的是讓學生具備未來工作所需的最新技能。

Unit ⓯

教育類重要句型整理整理、解析及應用

開頭句（Openings）重要句型整理、解析及應用

> 1. 表達主旨句（**thesis statement**）的重要句型為：
> I hold a contrary stance in light of N.

解析 1

stance：立場，此句表達與題目敘述相反的立場，並以片語 **in light of N.**：鑒於，簡短帶出之後在主文會詳細解釋的論點。

應用 1

I hold a contrary stance in light of the fallacious reasoning for the statement and obvious examples that refute such an assertion. (Part 1 Unit 5)

我持反對立場，因為此敘述是依據邏輯謬誤而成立，並有明顯的例子能反駁此敘述。《節選自 Part 1 Unit 5》

應用 1.1

I hold a contrary stance in light of the controversial effect of corporal punishment, which has not been scientifically proven.

我持反對立場，鑒於體罰的效果具爭議性，而且還未被科學證實。

2. 另外一個表達個人立場的主旨句重要句型為：
I am inclined to hold the opinion that S+V

解析 2

be inclined to V：傾向於，類似詞有：tend to V、be prone to V。

應用 2

I am inclined to hold the opinion that before one enters adolescence, he would explore the world more smoothly if given more advice from others. (Part 1 Unit 6)

我傾向認為在少年期之前，如果多聽從他人建議，探索世界的過程會比較順利。《節選自 Part 1 Unit 6》

應用 2.1

I am inclined to hold the opinion that corporal punishment is harmful to both children's physical and psychological health.

我傾向認為體罰對小孩的生理和心理健康都是有害的。

轉承句（Transitions）重要句型整理、解析及應用

> 3. 表達與上文意義相反的重要句型為：
>
> However, ...

解析 3

however：然而，注意詞性是副詞，放在句首其後要逗號。

應用 3.1

However, the social backgrounds of two generations are rarely similar, considering the fast pace of social changes and economic fluctuations nowadays. (Part 1 Unit 5)

然而，鑒於現今社會變遷的快速步調及經濟波動，兩個世代的社會背景不盡相似。《節選自 Part 1 Unit 5》

應用 3.2

However, it is difficult to reverse the traditional mode of education.

然而，要翻轉傳統教育的模式是困難的。

4. 表達舉出例證的重要句型為：

My point can be validated by taking N for fexample.

解析 4 ▶

此句型比 **for example** 更正式及強烈；**validate**：證實。

應用 4.1

My point can be validated by taking the protagonist in the movie "Good Will Hunting" for example. (Part 1 Unit 6)

我的論點可由《心靈捕手》的主角為例獲得證實。《節選自 Part 1 Unit 6》

應用 4.2

My point can be validated by taking my experience of corporal punishment in high school for example.

我的論點可由我在高中時被體罰的經驗為例獲得證實。

論點衍伸句（Explanations）重要句型整理、解析及應用

> ### 5. 在主文中表達論點與題目敘述相反的重要句型為：
> Hence, the notion of ... is highly controvertible.

解析 5

Hence：因此，適合在主文中重申自我立場時，放在句首的轉折語，注意詞性是副詞，非連接詞。若放兩個子句中間，須補上連接詞 **and**，即 **S1+V1, and hence S2+V2**。

應用 5.1

Hence, the notion of older ones teaching younger ones by drawing on personal experiences is highly controvertible. (Part 1 Unit 5)

因此，年長者引用自身經驗教導年輕人的觀念是高度可議的。《節選自 Part 1 Unit 5》

應用 5.2

Hence, the notion of "spare the rod, spoil the child" is highly controvertible.

因此，「不打不成器」的觀念是高度可議的。

6. 將主要論點延伸出兩個細節的重要句型為：
Physiologically, ... Psychologically, ...

解析 6 ▶

意義不同的副詞放句首，表達將論點分為兩個更詳細的層次。例如此段論點是關於兒童時期的發展，故劃分為生理上和心理上。

應用 6.1

Physiologically, children have the primal instinct to cling to caretakers, seeking suggestions regarding basic areas of life in order to survive. Psychologically, suggestions from peers are indispensable since they help us with how to socialize in groups. (Part 1 Unit 6)

生理上，小孩有原始的本能要依附照顧者，為了生存而尋求關於生活基本面的建議。心理上，同儕的建議不可缺少，因為他們能幫助我們進行社交生活。《節選自 Part 1 Unit 6》

應用 6.2

Physiologically, corporal punishment might induce mild injury. Psychologically, that might leave children traumatized.

生理上，體罰可能導致輕傷。心理上，可能讓小孩留下創傷。

⫶結論（Conclusions）重要句型整理、解析及應用

> 7. 表達比較兩個世代的差異的重要句型為：
> Confronted with ... the latter ...

解析 7 ▶

結論段落句型宜精簡，故句首以分詞片語 **Confronted with...** 修飾主詞，並以 **the latter**，後者，代替主文已經重複使用過的普通名詞。

應用 7.1

Confronted with dramatic global changes, old people have much to learn from young ones as the latter are living through those changes, thus more capable of offering insights. (Part 1 Unit 5)

面對劇烈的全球變化，年長者能從年輕人身上學習很多，因為年輕人正親身經歷那些變化，因此更能提供相關洞見。《節選自 Part 1 Unit 5》

應用 7.2

Confronted with more pressure from parents, teachers have to be empathetic when teaching young children as the latter are quite sensitive.

面對來自家長的更多壓力，老師在教導小孩子時需要有同理心，因為後者非常敏感。

8. 表達個人偏好的重要句型為：

As for me, I definitely find N preferable.

解析 8

當題目要求比較兩種類型的優點，並提出個人偏好時，宜在結論段簡短陳述偏好。此句型運用副詞 **definitely**：絕對，所以語氣非常強烈。

應用 8.1

As for me, I definitely find experiencing everything firsthand preferable. (Part 1 Unit 6)

我本人絕對偏好親自體驗人生的一切。《節選自 Part 1 Unit 6》

應用 8.2

As for me, I definitely find taking suggestions from elders preferable.

至於我，我絕對偏好聽取長輩的建議。

Unit ⓰

環境類重要句型整理、解析及應用

開頭句（Openings）重要句型整理、解析及應用

> 1. 表達主旨句（**thesis statement**）的重要句型為：
> We should V. ... for not only..., but also...

解析 1 ▶

在主旨句中先簡短帶出主文的兩個論點，兩個論點以 **not only..., but also** 連接。介系詞 **for** 表達原因，注意介系詞之後只能接名詞或動名詞。

應用 1

We should save tropical rainforests for not only ecological preservation, but also the protection of indigenous peoples whose cultures are inseparable from tropical rainforests. (Part 1 Unit 7)

鑑於損害的嚴重程度，我們應該保護熱帶雨林，不只是為了生態保育，也是為了保護原住民族群，原住民族群的生活型態及文化跟熱帶雨林密不可分。

《節選自 Part 1 Unit 7》

應用 1.1

We should save tropical rainforests for not only preserving the wilderness, but also maintaining the materials humans rely on for food and medicines.

鑑於物種的多樣性，我們應該保護熱帶雨林，不只是為了保育野生生態，也是為了維護人類所依賴能做成食物和藥品的原料。

---

2. 另外一個表達個人立場的主旨句重要句型為：

I disagree with the view that S+V as I believe that S+V.

解析 2

表達立場不同意題目敘述後，以連接詞 **as** 連接第二個子句，簡短敘述不同意的原因。**as** 在學術英文中常代替 because，語氣比較正式。

應用 2.1

I disagree with the view that developing an industry should take precedence over saving the environment for endangered species as I believe that destroying the natural environment will eventually take its toll on humans in the long run. (Part 1 Unit 8)

我不同意發展產業應該優先於保護瀕臨絕種動物的環境，因為我相信摧毀自然環境最終會讓人類付出代價。《節選自 Part 1 Unit 8》

應用 2.2

I disagree with the view that a thriving economy is more important than preserving ecology as I believe that no economy can replace the intactness of ecology.

我不同意繁榮的經濟比保育生態重要，因為我相信沒有經濟能取代生態的完整性。

轉承句（Transitions）重要句型整理、解析及應用

3. 提出支持主要論點的更多理由的重要句型為：

Moreover, ...

解析 2

Moreover：此外，同義字有 **furthermore**、**besides**、**in addition**、**additionally**。詞性是副詞，放在句首其後要逗號。

應用 3.1

Moreover, the destruction of tropical rainforests is as threatening as the annihilation of species in the movie, *Avatar*. (Part 1 Unit 7)

此外，熱帶雨林的破壞就如同電影《阿凡達》裡的物種滅絕一樣令人感到威脅。《節選自 Part 1 Unit 7》

應用 3.2

Moreover, it is unavoidable to develop infrastructures at the expense of deforestation.

此外，以砍伐森林為代價去建造基礎建設是無法避免的。

4. 表達情況每下愈況的重要句型為：
   What's worse, ...

解析 4

What's worse：副詞片語。類似詞有 **Worse yet**、**To make matters worse**、**As if the situation were not bad enough**。

應用 4.1

What's worse, the shrinkage of the hunting area has caused the reduction of seals, polar bears' major prey, which is also affected by commercial overfishing. (Part 1 Unit 8)

更糟糕的是，狩獵區域的縮減導致海豹減少，海豹是北極熊主要的獵物，而海豹減少也是受到漁業的影響。《節選自 Part 1 Unit 8》

應用 4.2

What's worse, emperor penguins are affected psychologically by eco-tourism.

更糟糕的是，國王企鵝在心理方面已經被生態觀光業影響了。

論點衍伸句（Explanations）重要句型整理、解析及應用

> ### 5. 延續主文段落的 **topic sentence** 的重要句型為：
> S+V, indicating N 或 indicating that S+V

解析 5 ▶

此句型中的分詞片語 **indicating N** 是由形容詞子句 **which indicates** 簡化而來，原本的關係代名詞 **which** 的先行詞是之前的完整句。

應用 5.1

Since the inception of industrialization in the 19ᵗʰ century, the amount of greenhouse gases has reached an unprecedented height, indicating the urgency to save rainforests. (Part 1 Unit 7)

自從十九世紀工業化起始，溫室氣體總量已經達到前所未有的最高點，顯示了保護雨林的急迫性。《節選自 Part 1 Unit 7》

應用 5.2

After the construction of the world's third largest dam in Brazil is completed, tens of thousands of aborigines will be forced to relocate, indicating the urgency to save their lifestyles.

在巴西的世界第三大水壩建造完成後，上萬的原住民將被迫遷移，顯示了保留他們的生活型態的急迫性。

6. 將例證更詳細解釋的重要句型為：
The example indicates that S+V

解析 6

在主文段落描寫例證後，須在例證之後馬上解釋例證的意義或影響，或如何呼應你的立場。動詞 **indicate** 可換成 **imply**、**suggest**、**demonstrate**。

應用 6.1

The example indicates that the aforementioned industry harms endangered species, altering the food chain, which will eventually harm humans as we are at the top of the food chain. (Part 1 Unit 8)

這個例子顯示上述產業傷害瀕臨絕種的動物，改變了食物鏈，而最終將會傷害人類，因為我們處於食物鏈的最頂端。《節選自 Part 1 Unit 8》

應用 6.2

The example indicates that human intrusion into wild animal habitat affects the behaviors of wild animals.

這個例子顯示人類侵入野生動物的棲息地會影響野生動物的行為。

結論（Conclusions）重要句型整理、解析及應用

> ## 7. 總結主要論點的重要句型為：
> To conclude, ...

To conclude：總言之，普遍放在結論段開頭的轉折詞。類似詞有 **in conclusion**、**in sum**、**to sum up**。

應用 7.1

To conclude, tropical rainforests have been described by scientists as the lungs of the earth, and thus it is not difficult to envisage that just as dysfunctional human lungs will induce life-threatening peril, the massive destruction of tropical rainforests will cause a devastating effect on the earth. (Part 1 Unit 7)

總而言之，熱帶雨林被科學家描述為地球的肺，因此不難想像正如同功能失調的肺會導致威脅生命的危險，對熱帶雨林的大量破壞將導致地球上毀滅性的效應。《節選自 Part 1 Unit 7》

應用 7.2

To conclude, climate changes, saving wildlife in rainforests, and human existence are all interconnected.

總而言之，氣候變遷、保護雨林的野生生態，及人類存在的狀態全部都是互相連結的。

8. 另一個總結主要論點的重要句型為：
Last but not least, ...

解析 8

轉折副詞 **Last but not least**，適合放在結論段落開頭。結論段落須將第一段的主旨句，即同意或不同意題目敘述的立場換句話說。

應用 8.1

Last but not least, ... If we preserve the environment for endangered animals, humans might live with them reciprocally. (Part 1 Unit 8)

最後，……如果我們保育瀕臨絕種動物的環境，人類可能與動物可以互惠共存。《節選自 Part 1 Unit 8》

應用 8.2

Last but not least, human activities are transitory, yet ecology in nature is long-lasting.

最後，人類活動是一時的，但大自然生態是永久的。

Unit ⑰

環境類及人生觀類重要句型整理、解析及應用

開頭句（Openings）重要句型整理、解析及應用

> **1. 表達主旨句（thesis statement）的重要句型為：**
> Personally, I share the belief with the former/ latter in that S+V.

解析 1 ▶

在第一段介紹段落（introductory paragraph），先簡短描述某些人對題目敘述的看法（the former），及其他人的看法（the latter）。然後再提出個人看法是認同前者或後者。

應用 1.1

Personally, I share the belief with the latter in that I believe humans are capable of self-redemption, particularly amending the damage we have done to the earth. (Part 1 Unit 9)

我個人的看法與後者相同，因為我相信人類有自我救贖的能力，尤其是修復我們對地球的損害。《適用於 Part 1 Unit 9 第一段》

應用 1.2

Personally, I share the belief with the former in that **the earth has been damaged drastically in the past century.**

我個人的看法與前者相同，因為在過去一世紀地球受到劇烈的損害。

---

2. 另外一個表達個人立場的主旨句重要句型為：

S+V, which is why I agree/ disagree with the statement.

解析 2 ▶

提出同意或不同意題目敘述的主要理由後，再以形容詞子句帶出個人立場。

應用 2.1

Yet, if one delves into the constituents of success, he is likely to discover that money alone can hardly satisfy those elements, which is why I disagree with the statement. (Part 1 Unit 10)

然而，如果一個人深入探討成功的元素，他很可能會發現財富幾乎不可能滿足那些元素，這正是我不同意題目敘述的原因。《節選自 Part 1 Unit 10》

應用 2.2

The factors for success cannot be simplified to merely wealth, which is why I disagree with the statement.

成功的因素不可能簡化成只有財富，這是我不同意題目敘述的原因。

轉承句（Transitions）重要句型整理、解析及應用

3. 舉出例證的重要句型為：
S+V, which is exemplified by N.

解析 3 ▶

exemplify：以例說明。詞性是動詞，先描述某現象後，再以形容詞子句修飾這現象。關係代名詞 **which** 的先行詞是完整句時，須在完整句之後加逗號。注意此形容詞子句是被動語態。

應用 3.1

The improvement is often propelled by those with a moral conscience that assumes responsibility for the well-being of humanity, which is exemplified by the story of Erin Brockovich, an American environmental activist. (Part 1 Unit 9)

改善環境的力量往往被擁有道德良知的人士及隨之而來對人類福祉的責任感所推動。艾琳·波洛克維奇的故事即是例證。《節選自 Part 1 Unit 9》

應用 3.2

Celebrities in the entertainment industry can impact the society quite positively, which is exemplified by some movie stars' advocacy of environmental protection.

演藝圈的名人能非常正面地影響社會，某些電影明星對環保的倡導即是例證。

4. 表達相反情況的轉折語為：
   Instead, ... At best, ...

解析 4

instead 和 **at best** 詞性都是副詞。**at best**：頂多、充其量，之後的完整句更詳細解釋上文。

應用 4.1

Actualizing passion into action will induce a sense of fulfillment; instead, merely owning money is no guarantee for felicity; at best, it's a meretricious facade of success that will disintegrate sooner or later. (Part 1 Unit 10) 將熱誠轉化為行動能帶來成就感。反之，只有錢並不能保證幸福感；充其量這只是華而不實，遲早會崩解的成功表相。《節選自 Part 1 Unit 10》

應用 4.2

Helping those in need will induce a sense of happiness for us. Instead, material possessions cannot guarantee happiness; at best, wealth brings gratification temporarily. 幫助需要的人能替我們帶來快樂；反之，物質財產不能保證快樂；財富頂多暫時地帶來滿足感。

論點衍伸句（Explanations）重要句型整理、解析及應用

> ## 5. 將例證更詳細解釋的重要句型為：
> S+V, proving that S+V.

解析 5 ▶

此句型中的分詞片語 **proving that ...** 是由形容詞子句 **which proves ...** 簡化而來，原本的關係代名詞 **which** 的先行詞是之前的完整句。

應用 5.1

To equalize water resource access, Matt Damon and Gary White cofounded a charity, Water.org, which builds water and sanitation facilities in destitute regions, proving that human existence can be elevated by a single act of philanthropy. (Part 1 Unit 9)

為了使水資源的取得平等化，麥特・戴蒙和蓋瑞・懷特共同成立了 Water.org 慈善機構，Water.org 在赤貧地區建造取水和衛生設施，證明了單一慈善行動能提升人類生存的狀態。《節選自 Part 1 Unit9》

應用 5.2

Erin Brockovich was a novice when she was initially involved in the lawsuit, proving that where there's a will, there's a way.

艾琳・波洛克維奇最初接觸這場官司時，還是新手，證明有志者，事竟成。

6. 主文段落主題句（**topic sentence**）的重要句型為：

My firm belief is that S+V.

解析 6 ▶

主文段落的主題句須提出更精準的理由或想法。**firm belief** 可換成 **reason for my agreement** 或 **disagreement**。

應用 6.1

My firm belief is that whether one has passion for what he does is the key. (Part 1 Unit 10)

我確信一個人對他的所作所為是否保持熱誠才是關鍵。《節選自 Part 1 Unit 10》

應用 6.2

My firm belief is that happiness depends on how we perceive the world.

我確信幸福感是依據我們如何認知這個世界。

結論（Conclusions）重要句型整理、解析及應用

> ### 7. 重申主要論點的重要句型為：
> While it is debatable whether S+V, I maintain that S+V.

解析 7 ▶

while 引導的從屬子句裡真主詞是名詞子句 **whether S+V**，**I maintain S+V** 重申主要論點，語氣比 **I think S+V** 正式。

應用 7.1

While it is debatable whether human activities generate positive or negative impacts, I maintain that the earth is being meliorated with continuous philanthropic and environmental campaigns. (Part 1 Unit 9)

人類活動是否造成正面或負面影響仍可辯論，但我認為隨著持續的慈善及環保運動，地球正持續被改善。《節選自 Part 1 Unit 9》

應用 7.2

While it is debatable whether it is too late to reverse the effects of global warming, I maintain that everyone should contribute his share of responsibility.

反轉全球暖化的效應是否太遲仍可辯論，但我認為每個人都應該負起責任。

8. 另一個重申主要論點的重要句型為：

Those unquestionably acknowledged to be ...are people who ...

解析 8

結論段落主要的功能是濃縮主文重點並重申立場。故使用語氣強烈的副詞 **unquestionably** 修飾重述的內容。同義字有 **undoubtedly**、**undeniably**、**incontrovertibly**。

應用 8.1

Those unquestionably acknowledged to be successful are people who are passionately committed to what they do. (Part 1 Unit 10)

無疑地，被認為是成功人士的是那些對所作所為保持熱誠的人。《節選自 Part 1 Unit 10》

應用 8.2

Those unquestionably acknowledged to be successful are people who will be recorded in history.

無疑地，被認為是成功人士的是那些會被歷史記錄下的人。

Unit ⓲

人生觀類重要句型整理、解析及應用

開頭句（Openings）重要句型整理、解析及應用

> ### 1. 表達主旨句（**thesis statement**）的重要句型為：
> Evidently, ... 、Personally, ... 、namely ...

解析 1

當題型是詢問要達到某目的，需具備哪些特質或因素時，利用此句型循序漸進地寫出越來越精準的個人看法。

應用 1.1

Evidently, it is part of human nature to aspire to succeed, and personally, four characteristics stand out as indispensable traits for attaining success, namely positive intention, knowing one's gift, belief in oneself, and making efforts. (Part 1 Unit 11) 明顯地，渴望成功是人性的一部分，就我個人而言，有四個為了取得成功不可缺少的特質，即正向意圖、瞭解自己的才華、相信自己及努力。《節選自 Part 1 Unit 11》

ch.**1**

ch**2**

ch.**3** 前十二個單元句型整理、解析及應用

應用 1.2

Evidently, people have diverse concepts of happiness. Personally, three components are critical for achieving happiness, namely, having basic needs satisfied, a sense of belonging, and living with meaning. 明顯地，人們對快樂有多樣的概念。就我個人而言，有三個達到快樂的重要元素，即基本需求被滿足、歸屬感及有意義的生活。

2. 另外一個表達個人立場的主旨句重要句型為：
While S+V, I am inclined to agree/ disagree with the statement.

解析 2

先描述社會上普遍的看法後，再表明個人立場。inclined，形容詞，傾向的。

應用 2

While desiring more might induce positive or negative effects, I am inclined to agree with the statement. (Part 1 Unit 12)
想要更多可能導致正面或負面的效應，但我傾向同意題目敘述。《節選自 Part 1 Unit 12》

應用 2.1

While it is normal to climb up the social ladder, I am inclined to agree with the statement.
在社會上力爭上游是正常的，但我傾向同意題目敘述。

轉承句（Transitions）重要句型整理、解析及應用

3. 表示意義即將改變的重要句型為：

Nonetheless, ...

解析 3 ▶

nonetheless，詞性是副詞，常放句首，暗示讀者此副詞之後的下文和上文意義上相反或有落差。類似字有 **nevertheless**、**however**、 **contrarily**、 **on the contrary**。

應用 3.1

Nonetheless, I don't think that success will be justifiable without positive intention. (Part 1 Unit 11)

然而，我認為缺乏正向意圖，成功不會有正當性。《節選自 Part 1 Unit 11》

應用 3.2

Nonetheless, talent cannot sustain without continuous effort.

然而，沒有持續的努力，才華不會持久。

> 4. 舉出例證的句型為：
>
> Examples abound that S+V, … , which is portrayed in N.

解析 4

abound，不及物動詞，富於。**that** 在此是關係代名詞，引導形容詞子句修飾 **Examples**。關係代名詞 **which** 的先行詞是 **they still desire...** 這個子句。

應用 4.1

Examples abound that many men already have affectionate families, yet they still desire more power or wealth, which is portrayed in the movie, *Click*. (Part 1 Unit 12)

很多例子顯示許多人已經有摯愛他們的家人，但仍渴望更多權力或財富，電影《命運好好玩》描繪了這現象。《節選自 Part 1 Unit 12》

應用 4.2

Examples abound that hardship is an unavoidable part in life, which is portrayed in the movie, *Life of Pi*.

很多例子顯示困境是人生無法避免的一部分，電影《少年 Pi 的奇幻漂流》描繪了這現象。

論點衍伸句（Explanations）重要句型整理、解析及應用

> ## 5. 主文段落主題句（topic sentence）的重要句型為：
> The aforementioned traits will not V... without N.

解析 5

當題目要求列舉某些特質時，主文段落開頭的主題句利用雙重否定的句型，提列數個特質。**aforementioned**，形容詞，上述的；若套用此句型提出第一個特質，**aforementioned** 要省略。

應用 5.1

However, the aforementioned traits will not be actualized into attainment without belief in oneself and making perseverant efforts. (Part 1 Unit 11)

然而，如果不相信自己和缺乏堅持不懈的努力，以上所提的特質都不會具體化為成就。《節選自 Part 1 Unit 11》

應用 5.2

The aforementioned components will not be fulfilled without diligent work and perseverance.

沒有勤奮的工作和恆心，以上所提的元素都不會成真。

6. 主文段落主題句（**topic sentence**）的重要句型為：
S+V+O due to N that ...

解析 6

表達為何會產生題目敘述的現象的主題句。原因先以 **due to** 簡短舉出，再以關係代名詞 **that** 引導的限定形容詞子句詳細解釋原因。

應用 6.1

Nonetheless, in a materialistic society, many people attach their individual values to material possessions due to incessant commercials that brainwash consumers into buying more. (Part 1 Unit 12)

然而，在物質化的社會，許多人將他們個人的價值依附在物質財產上，因為層出不窮的廣告會洗腦消費者去做更多消費。《節選自 Part 1 Unit 12》

應用 6.2

Some people rely on addiction to bring them the illusion of happiness due to wrong decisions that lead their life astray.

由於做了讓人生誤入歧途的錯誤決定，有些人依賴對事物上癮，所帶來快樂的幻覺。

結論（Conclusions）重要句型整理、解析及應用

> 7. 重申主要論點的重要句型為：
>
> To sum up, ... should be the key ...

解析 7

在結論段落不一定要將所有在主文提到的特質重述，但可強調最重要的特質。

應用 7.1

To sum up, among the four features, continuous endeavor should be the universally acknowledged key feature. (Part 1 Unit 11)

總而言之，這四個特質中，持續努力應該是普世公認的關鍵特質。《節選自 Part 1 Unit 11》

應用 7.2

To sum up, among the three components, living with meaning should be the key.

總而言之，這三個元素中，有意義地生活應該是關鍵元素。

8. 另一個重申主要論點的重要句型為：

In conclusion, ...

解析 8

In conclusion：常用的結論轉折詞。一般放句首，詞性是副詞片語，其後要逗號。同義字有 **to conclude**、**to sum up**、**in a word**。

應用 8.1

In conclusion, it has become a social norm to be discontent and aspire more ... (Part 1 Unit 12)

總而言之，不滿足並渴望更多已經變成社會常態……。《節選自 Part 1 Unit 12》

應用 8.2

In conclusion, constantly feeling unsatisfied with the present might result in a vicious cycle.

總言，持續地不滿足現狀可能會導致惡性循環。

PART 2

整合題型篇

　　整合題因應不同的題目，作答方式有兩種（本書歸類為「點對點結構」[1]或「面對面結構」[2]），所以範文也有兩種架構。有的單元範文是點對點結構（著重在「Integrating 整合句型」），有的單元範文是面對面結構（著重在「Paraphrase 換句話說句型」）。但不管是哪一個結構，主文都須要換句話說，因為照抄閱讀短文和課堂講述的原句是大忌。另外，有些範文雖然是點對點結構，句型整理大部份還是偏向「Paraphrase 換句話說句型」。

註 1：「點對點結構」的寫法是主文的每一段落中兩個篇章的重點混合，即一句閱讀短文重點和另一句課堂講述重點會互相穿插在同一段落。採取點對點結構的範文有：Unit 19、22、23、24、28

註 2：「面對面結構」的寫法是主文其中一段只總結閱讀短文重點，另一段只總結課堂講述重點。採取面對面結構的範文：Unit 20、21、25、26、27、29、30

將看完的章節打個勾，搞定整合型寫作！

Unit ⑲ 美國教育類

中文學習潮 The Chinese Learning Craze in the U.S.

請先閱讀一短文與題目

Summarize the main points in the lecture, explaining how they cast doubt on those made in the reading.

With China emerging as the economic superpower in the international arena in the late 1990s, more and more students in the U.S. are eager to follow the trend of learning Mandarin Chinese. Many learners who dare to battle this notoriously difficult language hope that the ability to speak Mandarin will help them to acquire a promising job with more preponderance. The fad of learning Mandarin has reached an unprecedented climax, which is demonstrated not only by Mandarin classes offered in schools, but also by the support of Federal government policies. A government survey indicates that roughly 1,600 American public and private schools are teaching Mandarin.

While Chinese programs were mostly offered on the East and West Coasts ten years ago, Chinese lessons have surged in the heartland states in the Midwest and the South over the recent few years. The academic status of the language was formalized in 2007 when the College Board introduced the Mandarin Advanced Placement test, encouraging more high school students to learn Mandarin. The educational input is further publicized by the "1 Million Strong" initiative announced by the Obama administration in 2015, targeting the number of 1 million U.S. learners of Mandarin by 2020. Besides school and government efforts, the linguistic interest is also sparked by more Chinese movie stars appearing in Hollywood movies, such as Jackie Chan in "Shanghai Noon" and Jet Li in "the Mummy: Tomb of the Dragon Emperor".

請聽與短文相關的課堂內容　　▶ Track 13

Now listen to a lecture in a linguistics class regarding the Chinese learning phenomenon in the U.S.

(Professor) Nowadays, a lot of Americans are under the impression that being able to speak Mandarin will help lead to abundant opportunities in the world's largest economy, China. Such a notion was partially built up by the stories about the migration of business elites to affluent Chinese cities. The recurring reports illustrating China as the new superpower have motivated high school and college students to learn Chinese. However, are the U.S. students actually zealous about learning Mandarin due to the reason aforementioned?

On the contrary, students' interest in learning Mandarin is not as prevalent as some people think, and just as the heat of learning Japanese in the 1980s had faded, it's only a matter of time that the trend of learning Mandarin will fade in the American educational system. First, over the past decade, a lot of public schools had no choice but to eliminate foreign language classes owing to state budget cuts. As schools are forced to cut down on their once popular European language classes, students simply have fewer foreign languages to choose from. Meanwhile, the Chinese government has been sending more Mandarin teachers to the U.S. and partially funding their salaries, which certainly came as a relieving subsidy to many schools with tight budgets.

Secondly, the linguistic fever might be seemingly fortified by the"1 Million Strong" initiative announced by President Obama in 2015. Let's not forget that the initiative is a collaboration between the Chinese and U.S. governments, with substantial resources from China. Moreover, 1 million seems a large number, yet it barely accounts for 2% of the number of all of the U.S. students. Lastly, Hollywood movies reinforce the illusion of Chinese fever by incorporating Chinese actors, such as Jackie Chan and Jet Li, yet I seriously doubt that students are motivated to learn Mandarin by watching their performances, since they still play the stereotype of Chinese reminiscent of Bruce Lee. That is, they mainly serve to fight and kick.

高分範文搶先看 ▶ Track 14

Both the reading and the lecture describe the recent trend of acquiring Mandarin Chinese in the U.S. While the reading points out that the trend has achieved its zenith, the lecture opposes the main idea in the reading by arguing that U.S. students are not truly enthusiastic about learning Mandarin.

To begin with, the professor elaborates on the reason why more and more students in public schools begin taking Mandarin classes, which he attributes to the budget cuts that prevented schools from offering as many foreign language classes as before. During the same period, many schools accepted Mandarin teachers who were funded partly by the Chinese government so that budget cut pressure might be eased. On the

閱讀篇章及課堂演講都描述在美國近年來學習中文普通話的趨勢。雖然閱讀篇章指出此趨勢已達到近期的高峰，然而課堂演講反駁閱讀篇章的主題，且宣稱美國學生並非真的熱衷於中文學習。

首先，教授詳細闡述越來越多公立學校的學生開始上中文課的原因；他將其歸因於預算縮減，導致學校無法提供像以往那麼多的外文課程。同時間，許多學校接納了由中國政府部分資助的普通話老師，目的是舒緩預算刪減的壓力。相反地，閱讀篇章只單純描述普通話課程在許多州都持續增加。

contrary, the reading merely states that Mandarin classes are increasing in many states.

Secondly, the professor rebuts the pervasiveness of the Mandarin learning phenomenon indicated by the "1 Million Strong" initiative mentioned in the reading. He explicates that even after the number of Mandarin learners in the U.S. reaches 1 million, it will be a relatively low percentage, hardly 2% in the entire student population.

第二，教授反駁了閱讀篇章中「百萬強計畫」暗示的學習普通話流行現象。他解釋即使美國的普通話學習者達到一百萬的數量，這仍是相對低的比率，幾乎勉強達到所有學生人口的 2%。

Thirdly, the reading suggests that people are encouraged to learn Mandarin under the influence of Chinese movie stars in Hollywood, which the lecture refutes by claiming that those actors play stereotypical roles of Chinese characters.

第三，閱讀提及人們在好萊塢演出的中國電影明星影響下，會被激勵而開始學普通話。課堂演講針對此點駁斥，並主張那些演員擔任的仍是刻板印象的中國角色。

高分範文解析

關鍵句 1

While the reading points out that the trend has reached its zenith, the lecture opposes the main idea in the reading by arguing that U.S. students are not truly enthusiastic about learning Mandarin.

解析

綜合題型在第一段須開門見山地描述閱讀和聽力內容兩者間的關聯。以上這句即是此篇範文的主旨句（thesis statement）。此兩篇題目的內容為主要觀點的牴觸，因此主旨句應使用表達兩個子句大意有所落差或對照的從屬連接詞，如 while、whereas、notwithstanding……等從屬連接詞。

關鍵句 2

To begin with, the professor elaborates on the reason why more and more students in public schools begin taking Mandarin classes, which he attributes to the budget cuts that prevented schools from offering as many foreign language classes as before.

解析

作文要獲取高分必須盡量使用正式的動詞片語及複雜句。如以上範例使用動詞片語：elaborate on / attribute to / prevent ... from...，並利用形容詞子句濃縮課堂講述的重點。

◉ 閱讀短文中譯

請總結課堂講述的重點，並解釋它們如何對閱讀短文的重點提出質疑。

隨著中國以經濟強權之姿在九零年代後期的國際舞台上嶄露頭角，越來越多的美國學生渴望加入這股學習普通話中文的趨勢。許多敢挑戰這個以困難出名的語言的學習者希望的是，會說普通話的能力能幫助他們有更多優勢取得前景看好的工作。學習普通話的流行近來達到前所未有的高峰，從學校提供的普通話課程及聯邦政府政策的支持都彰顯了這趨勢。一項政府調查指出大約一千六百所美國公立及私立學校正在教普通話。

十年前大部分的中文課程是在東岸及西岸地區被提供，然而在過去幾年，中文課程在中西部和南部各州急速增加。當大學入學委員會在 2007 年開始提供普通話入學檢定考，此舉奠定了普通話正式的學術地位，並鼓勵更多高中生學這語言。當歐巴馬政府在 2015 年宣佈了「百萬強計畫」，教育界的挹注更為眾所皆知，此計畫的目標是在 2020 年之前，提升美國境內的普通話學習者數量達到一百萬人。除了學校和政府的努力，更多中國電影明星參與好萊塢電影，如成龍演出「西域威龍（"Shanghai Noon"）」及李連杰演出「神鬼傳奇 3：龍帝之墓（"the Mummy: Tomb of the Dragon Emperor"）」，他們的表演也會激發對中文的興趣。

◉ 課堂講述中譯

現在請聽一篇關於在美國中文學習現況的語言學課堂講述。

當今很多美國人都認為會說中文普通話能協助他們取得各式各樣在中國發展的機會，中國已是世界上最大的經濟體。這種觀念一部分是由商務菁英的故事建構而成，這些故事都是關於商務菁英搬移到富裕的中國城市。描繪中國為新興超級強權的報導不斷出現，且這些報導激勵了高中生和大學生學中文。然而，美國學生確實是因為以上提及的原因而熱衷於學習普通話嗎？

相反地，學生對普通話的興趣不如大多數人想的那麼普及；就如同 1980 年代美國人學日文的熱潮已經消退，在美國教育體系裡，學普通話的風潮遲早也會消退。首先，在過去十年內，由於州政府預算削減，許多公立學校不得不刪減外文課程。既然學校被迫刪減曾經備受歡迎的歐語系課程，學生對外語課程的選擇自然地隨之被限縮。同時間中國政府派遣更多普通話老師到美國，並負責提供老師們的部份薪水。對預算緊縮的學校而言，這些中國政府支援的老師和來自中國的補助的確緩解他們的預算窘況。

第二，這股語言熱潮似乎因歐巴馬總統在 2015 年宣布的「百萬強計畫」獲得加強。別忘了這個計畫是中國及美國政府的合作計畫，由中方提供大量的資源。此外，一百萬似乎是一筆很大的數字，但只幾乎佔了美國總學生數量的 2%。最後，好萊塢電影融入中國電影明星，例如成龍和李連杰，加深了中文風潮的不實印象。我嚴重懷疑學生會因為看了這些明星演出，就被激勵出學中文的興趣，因為這些演員扮演的角色，仍是好萊塢對中國人的刻板印象，讓人聯想到李小龍扮演的那種刻板印象。也就是說，他們主要的功能是展現拳腳功夫。

Unit ⑳ 美國教育類
網路教學的優點與缺點 The Advantages and Disadvantages of Online Learning

請先閱讀一短文與題目

Summarize the main points in the reading and lecture, explaining how they argue against each other.

Since the advent of the Internet in the early 1980s, the Internet has exerted powerful hold of academia. Top universities, such as M.I.T, Harvard, and Yale, have established numerous online courses for their students, while private online universities have mushroomed. The public can also take academic courses that were once confined in the scholarly circle by enrolling themselves in online programs collaborated by organizations, such as edX and Coursera, and renowned universities.

Nevertheless, newcomers in online classes might overlook the downside, or overestimate their own capability to acquire success in open courses. First, students underestimate the negative effect of little face-to-face interaction. They might find taking online classes is more like carrying out a monologue without immediate feedbacks from professors and classmates. Teachers cannot evaluate students' responses based on their facial expressions and body language, either. Secondly, even programs that utilize avatars to simulate face-to-face interactions, such as those on Second Life, might yield unexpected effects. For example, Ohio University once had to terminate its operation on Second Life when an avatar dressed as a gunman started random shooting.

Thirdly, contrary to popular impression, online courses require much more efforts than traditional ones. The amount of reading and reports usually surpasses that in conventional classes, and since students have to grapple with the reading and assignments by themselves most of the time, online courses require greater self-discipline and self-direction. For people who tend to procrastinate, they need to consider if they have adequate time-management skills to succeed. Moreover, in traditional courses, students have easier access to teachers' office hours and face-to-face meetings, which online courses have yet to achieve.

請聽與短文相關的課堂內容　▶ Track 15

Now listen to a lecture in an education class regarding online learning.

(Professor) There are numerous advantages to online learning. Today the lecture will focus on the benefits of online courses offered by higher education institutes in the U.S. The first that comes to mind is probably the worldwide access. No matter you live in Asia or Africa, as long as your qualifications meet the admission criteria, you can pursue a bachelor or master degree at the comfort of staying in your home country.

Further, with a wide variety of communication software and virtual classrooms, the interactions between students and teachers are no longer confined to plain discussion boards which can be traced to the earliest days of the Internet development. Many universities have acquired success in virtual classrooms, such as those on Second Life. In the virtual world of Second Life, users create their avatars, representative figures of their identities, and interact with one another via abundant facial expressions and gestures simulated by their avatars. Universities are able to foster a sense of community on Second Life because they build buildings and towns where avatars visit and acquaint themselves with others.

Moreover, long-distance learning is particularly appropriate for adults who have to take care of their family and work at the same time. A statistical research has indicated that the demographics of online students is very different from that in traditional classrooms. Most of them are married or divorced with children, or professionals who take part-time classes to advance their careers. For these individuals, it might be hard for them to make friends in traditional universities, yet while they take classes online, they have more access to meeting people with similar interests, careers, and experiences. Also, they can fulfill their academic pursuit while attending to their families as well as gaining internationalized vision by interacting with students from around the world in virtual classrooms.

高分範文搶先看　▶ Track 16

The reading and listening passages present contrasting views of online education, with the former focusing on disadvantages and the latter focusing on advantages.

閱讀篇章及課堂講述呈現對網路課程的相反看法，前者著重缺點而後者著重優點。

The first disadvantage of online classes is the lack of in-person interaction. Students tend to feel that their contribution to online classes is carried out in a one-way direction. The second drawback concerns the undesired effect of applying avatars in virtual classrooms. Avatars with ill intentions might cause a disturbance in online classrooms.

網路課程的第一個缺點是缺乏親身互動。學生通常覺得他們對網路課程的付出是單向的。第二個缺點是關於在虛擬教室運用替身所帶來的意料之外的效應。不懷好意的替身可能對網路教室造成困擾。第三個缺點是當人們上網路課程時，需要更多自我紀律和自我導引。

The third drawback is that more self-discipline and self-guidance are necessary when people take online courses.

The lecture refutes the reading by raising three advantages. It first points out that online courses allow students not residing in the U.S. to pursue degrees without traveling away from home. Next, the lecture draws on the example of virtual classrooms on Second Life to explain that vibrant interaction and a sense of community can be enhanced. Lastly, by raising the demographics of students, the lecture indicates that elder students are more capable of striking a balance between family and work and acquainting similar-minded friends in the online setting.

課堂講述提出三個優點駁斥閱讀篇章。它首先指出網路課程讓不住在美國的學生不須離家遠遊就能追求學位。其次，課堂講述引用位於第二人生網站的虛擬教室為例，解釋活潑的互動和社群的感覺能被加強。最後，課堂講述提出學生的人口統計數據，指出在網路情境裡，年紀較長的學生比較能取得家庭和工作的平衡，並結交興趣類似的朋友。

高分範文解析

關鍵句 1

Students tend to feel that their contribution to online classes is carried out in a one-way direction.

解析

此句的主要動詞是動詞片語 tend to V.，傾向，類似詞有 have the tendency to V.，be inclined to V.，be prone to V.。受詞是 that 導引出的名詞子句。名詞子句直到句尾，子句的動詞因為搭配主詞 their contribution，所以使用被動語態 is carried out。

關鍵句 2

Lastly, by raising the demographics of students, the lecture indicates that elder students are more capable of striking a balance between family and work and acquainting similar-minded friends in the online setting.

解析

主要動詞 indicates 的受詞是 that 導引出的名詞子句。名詞子句中，介系詞 of 之後有兩個由對等連接詞 and 連接的動名詞當受詞：striking ... 及 acquainting。

◉ 閱讀短文中譯

請總結閱讀短文和課堂講述的重點，並解釋它們如何互相駁斥。

自從在 1980 年代初期問世，網路對學術圈已產生強大的影響。頂尖大學，例如麻省理工學院、哈佛大學和耶魯大學，都為了學生設立許多網路課程，同時間私立的網路大學則迅速增加。大眾也能報名知名大學和 edX 及 Coursera 等組織合作的課程，參與以往僅限於學術圈的學術課程。

然而，網路課程的新使用者可能忽略了其負面，或高估了他們自己能在網路課程成功的能力。首先，學生低估了幾乎沒有面對面互動的負面效應。他們可能會發現上網路課程比較像是進行一場缺乏教授和同學的立即回應的獨白。老師也無法以學生的表情和肢體語言評量他們的反應。第二，即使是利用虛擬替身模擬親身互動的課程，例如在第二人生網站上的課程，可能產生意料之外的效應。例如，當一個裝扮為槍手的替身開始開槍掃射時，俄亥俄大學曾經必須中止他們在第二人生網站上的運作。

第三，與大眾印象不同的是，網路課程比傳統課程需要更多的努力。閱讀和報告的數量通常比傳統課堂多，而且既然大部份的時間學生必須單獨進行閱讀和作業，網路課程需要更多的自我紀律和自我導引。對容易拖延的人而言，他們需要考慮是否有足夠的時間管理技巧能達到成功。此外，在傳統課程，學生更容易取得老師的辦公會面時間和面對面開會的機會，而這些是網路課程仍無法比擬的。

◉ 課堂講述中譯

現在請聽一篇關於網路教學的教育學課堂講述。

網路課程有許多優點。今天的課堂講述著重於美國高等教育機構提供的網路課程所帶來的益處。第一個讓人想到的優點很可能是全球普及化。不管你住在亞洲或非洲，只要你的資格達到入學標準，你就能舒適地在自己國家追求學士或碩士文憑。

此外，運用豐富的通訊軟體和虛擬教室，學生和老師間的互動不再被限制於平淡的討論版面，討論版面在網路發展的最早期就存在了。許多大學在虛擬教室方面已獲得成功，例如那些架設在第二人生網站的教室。在第二人生的虛擬世界裡，使用者創造他們的替身，即代表他們身份的角色，並透過虛擬的豐富表情和手勢彼此互動。因為大學在第二人生網站建立建築物和城鎮，虛擬替身能造訪這些地方並認識彼此，促進社群的感覺。

另外，遠距教學特別適合必須照顧家庭及同時間工作的成年人。一項統計研究顯示網路課程學生的統計數據和傳統課堂內的學生非常不同。網路課程的學生大部份是有小孩的已婚者或離婚者，或是為了提升職涯來兼職上課的專業人士。對這些人而言，在傳統大學可能不容易交到朋友，但是當他們上網路課程，他們更有可能遇到興趣，職業及經歷類似的人。他們也能滿足對學業的追求，同時照顧家庭，並藉由在虛擬教室和來自世界各地的學生互動，增長國際觀。

Unit ㉑ 美國教育類
1960 年代的嬉皮運動 The Hippie Movement in the 1960s

請先閱讀一短文與題目

Briefly paraphrase the origin of hippies, and summarize the contradictory arguments in the reading and the lecture.

The 1960s was a period when the counterculture burgeoned in America. The most well-known lifestyle of the counterculture was hippies. Even now the hippie lifestyle is sometimes portrayed in Hollywood movies, in which hippies are presented with the image of having long hair, casual attitude, and taking drugs. Yet, if we truly understand the origin of hippies, we will understand that there were a deeper root of this lifestyle and some philosophy behind it.

The predecessors of hippies were the generation a decade earlier known as the Beats. The fundamental philosophy of the Beats includes disbelief in traditional American values, attempts to create new social standards, and rejection of materialism. At first, the Beats wanted to remain inconspicuous and keep themselves underground. However, as more and more followers of the Beats began to speak out about political issues, by 1960, the lifestyle of the Beats had transformed into the one we now call hippies.

Though hippies were sometimes criticized for their use of drugs, they indeed made significant contributions to the American society. First, in response to the U.S. involvement in the Vietnam War, the hippie lifestyle elevated itself into the movement against war. Hippies often preached love, not war, and identified themselves with the peace sign. Also, they supported the Civil Rights Movement led by Dr. Martin Luther King, and held many demonstrations against war and racial injustice, promoting equal rights for minorities. They also questioned the government's treatment of Native Americans. Last but not least, their most long-lasting legacy was raising the awareness of how humans impacted nature. Hippies' emphasis on green energy helped foster the green awareness.

請聽與短文相關的課堂內容　▶ Track 17

Now listen to a lecture in an American history class on the same topic you just read about.

(Professor) When Americans talk about the 1960s and early 1970s, two events will almost certainly be raised; one is the Vietnam War and the other is the hippie movement. The hippie movement, often seen as a symbolic rebellion of the youth at that time against the conventional values of the U.S. society, received wide media coverage due to hippies' strong anti-war sentiment and

ch.**4**
美國教育、歷史與文學類型

ch.**5**

ch.**6**

their demonstrations against the Vietnam War. Other reasons for public attention were sexual liberation and the increasing use of marijuana and other drugs. Evidently, hippies were associated with an emphasis on individualism, experimentation of sexuality, and insistence of pacifism. Some hippies did stick to their philosophy initially, yet as my argument will indicate, the reality of the hippie lifestyle was not as ideal as they had envisioned. Also, I think it is an overstatement to say that all hippies left a positive legacy.

First, the influence of hippies was magnified by the media. In fact, research has suggested that no more than 10 percent of American youths in the 1960s were hippies. Conventional lifestyles were maintained by most young Americans, who continued their parents' middle-class culture. Next, hippies' insistence on individualism paradoxically caused their preference to live in groups owing to loneliness and isolation from the mainstream society. Although the core of their philosophy is being true to oneself, they prefer living in communities known as communes where psychedelic drugs and casual sex became more available.

Finally, the idea of casual sex or free love held double standards for men and women because of the lack of birth control. Birth control pills were first sold in 1960, so they were not readily available for single women, which means that as undesired pregnancy happened, hippie women were usually the ones feeling plagued, not hippie men.

高分範文搶先看　▶ Track 18

Before hippies surfaced as a dominant part of the American counterculture in the 1960s, they were pioneered by another generation called the Beats in the 1950s. The ideas of the Beats remained with hippies except that hippies were more enthusiastic about politics.

According to the reading, the culture of the hippies left a positive legacy despite occasional criticism of their drug usage. First, as the U.S. government became more involved in the Vietnam War, the lifestyle of the hippies became more related to an antiwar movement. Secondly, the hippies allied themselves with the Civil Rights Movement and advocated racial equality. Most crucially, hippies emphasized being friendly with the Earth, and their attitude was influential in raising

在嬉皮於 1960 年代的美國反主流文化嶄露頭角之前，他們的先驅是 1950 年代的節奏世代。嬉皮維持節奏世代的理念，除了嬉皮對政治比較熱衷。

根據閱讀篇章，嬉皮文化留下正面的文化遺產，盡管偶爾有對他們使用毒品的批評。首先，當美國政府在越戰牽涉越深，嬉皮的生活方式跟反戰運動的關係就越密切。第二，嬉皮支持民權運動並倡導種族平等。最重要的是，嬉皮強調對地球友善，他們的態度對之後提升環保意識有所影響。

subsequent awareness of environmental protection.

Contrary to the main argument of the reading, the lecture casts doubt on the hippies' legacy. The professor first explains that the media at that time enlarged the influence of the hippie movement; the truth was that most American youths still followed a traditional lifestyle. Furthermore, he points out that hippies acted against their own philosophy of individualism, since they preferred living in communes where casual sex and drug usage became more prevalent. Lastly, he criticized the double standard of the hippies' attitude toward sex in that female hippies often suffered more than men when faced with unwanted pregnancy due to the lack of birth control pills.

、

課堂講述與閱讀篇章的主要論點相反，對嬉皮的文化遺產提出質疑。教授首先解釋當時的媒體將嬉皮運動的影響力放大了。事實上大部分的美國青年仍然遵循傳統生活方式。此外，他指出嬉皮的行為牴觸他們對個人主義的理念，因為他們偏好住在團體公社裡，且在公社隨意性愛和使用毒品的現象更普遍。最後，他批評嬉皮對性愛的態度的雙重標準，因為缺乏避孕藥，當被迫面對意外懷孕時，女性嬉皮受的折磨比男性多。

高分範文解析

關鍵句 1 ▶

Before hippies surfaced as a dominant part of the American counterculture in the 1960s, they were pioneered by another generation called the Beats in the 1950s. The ideas of the Beats remained with hippies except that hippies were more enthusiastic about politics.

解析

當題目有要求簡短重述閱讀篇章或課堂講述的某些知識時，此部分應構成第一段的內容，且所佔的篇幅不超過整篇文章的三分之一。

關鍵句 2 ▶

According to the reading, the culture of the hippies left a positive legacy despite occasional criticism of their drug usage. ...Contrary to the main argument of the reading, the lecture casts doubt on the hippies' legacy.

解析

此單元題目屬於 contrast 類型：課堂講述駁斥閱讀篇章的主要論點。每段的主題句（topic sentences）應該要將閱讀和聽力兩個篇章主要觀點的差異闡述清楚，如使用以下片語：contrast to N、in contrast to N、to refute N、to rebut N。當重點之間呼應的關係不明顯時（例如閱讀稱讚嬉皮對環保的影響，但課堂講述並未提及環保），可採取一段總結閱讀篇章，另一段總結課堂講述的結構。

◉ 閱讀短文中譯

請將嬉皮的起源簡短的換句話說，並總結閱讀短文和課堂講述互相駁斥的論點。

在美國 1960 年代是反主流文化急速發展的時代。反主流文化中最知名的生活方式是嬉皮。即使是現在嬉皮風格偶爾也被好萊塢電影呈現，將嬉皮呈現為留著長髮，態度隨意和吸毒的形象。但是，如果我們真的懂嬉皮的起源，我們會知道這種生活方式有較深的根基及背後有一些哲理。

嬉皮的先驅是十年前的世代，他們被稱為節奏世代。節奏世代的基本哲理包含對傳統美國價值的不信任，嘗試創造新的社會標準，及反對物質主義。最初，節奏世代想保持低調，維持地下活動的形式。然而，當越來越多節奏世代發表對政治議題的看法，到了 1960 年代，節奏世代的生活方式轉化成我們現稱的嬉皮。

雖然嬉皮有時因為使用毒品而被批評，他們的確對美國社會做出重要貢獻。首先，針對美國對越戰的干涉，嬉皮風格被提升至反戰運動。嬉皮常常宣導愛的精神，反對戰爭，並以和平圖示表達身份。另外，他們支持馬丁‧路德‧金恩博士領導的民權運動，舉辦許多反戰及反對種族不平等的示威活動，促進少數族群的平權。他們也質疑政府對待美洲原住民的方式。最後，他們對後代影響最深的貢獻是提高人類如何影響大自然的意識。嬉皮對節約能源的重視協助培養了環保意識。

● 課堂講述中譯

現在請聽一篇與閱讀篇章一樣主題的美國歷史課堂講述。

當美國人聊到 1960 年代和 1970 年代初期，兩個事件一定會被提出，一個是越戰，另一個是嬉皮運動。嬉皮運動常被視為那時年輕人對傳統美國價值的象徵性反抗，且嬉皮的強烈反戰意識及對越戰的抗議活動受到廣泛的媒體報導。性解放及大麻和其他毒品的使用增加也是引起大眾注意的原因。明顯地，嬉皮跟重視個人主義，探索性意識和堅持和平主義這些特色連結在一起。有些嬉皮最初的確遵守他們的理念，但如同我的論點會顯示的，嬉皮生活的現實面不像他們最初預想的那麼理想。而且，我認為說所有嬉皮都留下正面影響，這是誇張的說法。

首先，嬉皮的影響力被媒體誇大了。事實上，有研究顯示在 1960 年代，不到百分之十的美國青年是嬉皮。大部分美國年輕人維持了傳統的生活風格，也延續了他們父母的中產階級文化。此外，嬉皮對個人主義的堅持矛盾地導致他們偏好團體生活的形式，因為寂寞感和感到跟主流社會是疏離的。雖然他們的理念核心是忠於自我，他們偏好住在被稱為公社的社區，而迷幻藥和隨意性愛在公社更容易取得。

最後，因為缺乏避孕的關係，隨意性愛的觀念對男性和女性有雙重標準。避孕藥品在 1960 年才開始販售，所以那時單身女性無法輕易取得這種藥品，意味著當意外懷孕時，嬉皮族群的女性通常是備受折磨的，而不是男性。

Unit ㉒ 美國歷史類
美國內戰之後的重建時期 The Reconstruction Period after the Civil War

⌇請先閱讀一短文與題目

Summarize the main points in the lecture, explaining how they cast doubt on those made in the reading.

The Reconstruction period began in 1865, right after the end of the Civil War. It spanned over 12 years, ending in 1877. With the end of the Civil War, President Lincoln started to draft schemes to reunite a nation that had been separated by racism and torn apart by war. Successes had arisen from Reconstruction and they can be categorized into three aspects: political, social, and economic.

In the political aspect, the most important success was that the concept of the United States as one unified nation was finally consolidated. Reconstruction brought the Southern states back to the Union. Although many white Southerners were against the idea of reconstructing the South, political reforms were administered, notably the new constitutional amendments. The 13th Amendment to the Constitution officially ended slavery, and the 15th Amendment offered the equal right to vote to all citizens.

In the social aspect, education programs for freed slaves were initiated by the Federal government and charitable organizations, and thus literacy was greatly improved among freed slaves. Freed slaves also gained more autonomy in their cultural institutions and churches. Under the protection of the Constitution, they were able to reunite with their families and keep their personal property. Lastly, the economy in the South revitalized as the Federal government built new railroads and hospitals, and new industries, such as steel and lumber, began to prosper. A small scale of land reform was carried out, allowing freed slaves to farm on their own land.

請聽與短文相關的課堂內容　　Track 19

Now listen to a lecture in an American history class regarding the Reconstruction Period.

(Professor) Over the years, historians have debated whether the Reconstruction generated successes or failures. In my opinion, the failures undoubtedly outweigh the successes. Politically, the U.S. seemed to be one unified nation, and slaves were finally emancipated. However, that was just a façade constructed by the Federal government with legislative reforms. Deep down in the Southern states, most white people, especially the wealthy and the elites, strove to undo the reforms. It is true that slavery ended on the constitutional level, yet the legislature in every southern state passed laws, the Black Codes, to restrict most rights of African Americans, including interracial marriage, the right to serve on a jury, voting rights, and freedom of speech. As a result, African Americans could not attain true equal rights until much later during the Civil Rights Movement in the 1960s.

Some might argue that slave emancipation was improved during the Reconstruction. The truth is that such improvement happened to a relatively low proportion of emancipated slaves, no matter educationally or financially. Most freed slaves in the South remained uneducated and trapped in poverty. Their living condition was worsened by the violent threats from a racist group called the KKK, which stands for the Klu Klux Klan. Socially, freed slaves had to face a more hostile environment since the Klan resorted to extreme violence to attack and murder freed slaves and their allies.

In terms of economy, both whites and blacks suffered. Agriculture was the backbone of southern economy, yet after the Emancipation, the workers on plantations reduced. New industries, like steel, did not boost the economy since they composed a minor percentage, compared with agriculture. Land reform was not widespread, either, and lots of former slaves went back to work on plantations for their former masters under a new system, sharecropping, which tied workers to the yields of their crops on rented land. Therefore, freed slaves remained in debt and poverty.

高分範文搶先看　▶ Track 20

The lecture presents three arguments regarding the political, social and economic areas of the Reconstruction period to refute the arguments in the reading. Whereas the reading argues for the successes of Reconstruction, the lecture contends otherwise.

課堂講述呈現關於重建時期的政治，社會和經濟方面的三個論點，以反駁閱讀篇章的論點。閱讀篇章主張重建時期是成功的，然而課堂講述的主張是相反的。

First, in terms of political reforms, the reading emphasizes that Amendments to the Constitution legalized equal voting rights for all citizens and put an end to slavery. On the contrary, the lecture points out that new laws passed in the southern states, called the Black Codes, undermined the effects of the constitutional reform for freed slaves' rights were dramatically restrained.

首先，在政治改革上，閱讀篇章強調憲法修正案將所有公民的平等投票權法制化，並終結奴隸制度。相反地，課堂講述指出在南方各州通過的黑人規範新法律削弱了憲法改革的效應，因為被解放的奴隸的權力被大幅限制了。

Secondly, regarding the social aspect, the lecture contends that

第二，關於社會方面，課堂講述主張被解放的奴隸因為

freed slaves faced more hostility due to the violent intimidation from the KKK, a racist group. Although the reading mentions that education was provided for freed slaves, the lecture explains that most former slaves did not benefit from it.

Thirdly, the lecture describes that both whites and blacks went through difficult times of economic recession; in contrast, the reading merely mentions an improvement for freed slaves, a limited scale of land reform. According to the lecture, white plantation owners faced the decrease of workers, and new industries did not enhance prosperity, since they did not occupy most of the southern economy. Many emancipated slaves still returned to work for their previous owners and lived in destitution.

種族歧視團體三 K 黨的暴力威脅，而面對更多敵意。雖然閱讀篇章提到被解放的奴隸曾被提供教育，課堂講述解釋大部分的被解放奴隸並未因此獲益。

第三，課堂講述描述白人和黑人都經歷經濟蕭條的苦日子。反之，閱讀篇章只提及對被解放奴隸的改善，即小規模的土地改革。根據課堂講述，農場的白人地主面對員工減少，而且新產業並未促進繁榮，因為它們不是占了南方經濟的大部分。許多被解放的奴隸仍然回去替前主人工作且活在赤貧中。

高分範文解析

關鍵句 1 ▶

Whereas the reading argues for the successes of Reconstruction, the lecture contends otherwise.

解析

第一段的兩句都屬於此篇範文的主旨句（thesis statement）。此單元的閱讀篇章和課堂講述各提出三個相反的論點，而關鍵句 1 更精簡地闡明兩者互相駁斥的關係，otherwise（*adv.*）意近 contrarily。

關鍵句 2 ▶

On the contrary, the lecture points out that new laws passed in the southern states, called the Black Codes, undermined the effects of the constitutional reform for freed slaves' rights were dramatically restrained.

解析

轉折副詞 on the contrary 導引出與上一句意思相反的下文，that ...直到句尾是名詞子句，當作 points out 的受詞。名詞子句中的 passed 是過去分詞，修飾 new laws，表被動語態。名詞子句的主要動詞是 undermined，削弱，而 for 是表原因的連接詞，在學術文章常代替 because。

◉ 閱讀短文中譯

請總結課堂講述的重點，並解釋它們如何對閱讀短文的重點提出質疑。

重建時期在 1865 年美國內戰結束後旋即開始。它持續了十二年，於 1877 年結束。隨著內戰結束，林肯總統開始起草如何團結被種族主義和戰爭所分裂的國家的方案。重建時期獲得成功，而那些成功可被分類為三方面：政治，社會和經濟。

在政治方面，最重要的成功是美國是統一的國家這個觀念，終於受到鞏固。重建時期將南方各州和北方聯盟整合。雖然很多南方白人反對重建南方這個概念，政治改革仍被執行，值得注意的是新的憲法修正案。第十三號修正案正式終結奴隸制度，而第十五號修正案提供所有公民平等的投票權。

在社會方面，聯邦政府和慈善機構開始提供教育課程給被解放的黑奴，因此他們的識字能力大幅提升。被解放的黑奴也在他們的文化機構和教堂獲得較多的自治權。在憲法的保護之下，他們得以和家人團圓並持有私人財產。最後，隨著聯邦政府在當地興建新鐵路和醫院，南方的經濟復甦了，而且新產業，例如鋼鐵和木材業，開始發達。小規模的土地改革讓被解放的奴隸能在私有地上耕種。

◉ 課堂講述中譯

現在請聽一篇關於重建時期的美國歷史課堂講述。

多年來，歷史學家一直爭辯重建時期是導致成功，還是失敗。我認為失敗無疑地多於成功。政治上，美國似乎是統一國家了，且奴隸終於被解放。

然而，這只是聯邦政府以立法改革建構出的假象。在南方各州，大部分白人，尤其是富人和菁英人士，致力於翻轉那些改革。的確，在憲法層次，奴隸制度結束了，但南方各州通過限制非裔美國人大部份權利的法律，稱為黑人規範，這些法律對他們的限制包含跨種族婚姻，擔任陪審團成員的權力，投票權和言論自由。因此，非裔美國人直到 1960 年代的民權運動才能獲得真正的平權。

有些人可能主張在重建時期，奴隸解放的情況被改善了。事實上，改善只發生在相當少的被解放奴隸身上，不管是教育或經濟方面。大部分在南方被解放的奴隸仍未受教育且陷於貧窮。他們的生活因為暴力威脅每下愈況，威脅來自三 K 黨這個種族歧視的團體，三 K 指的是 Klu Klux Klan。在社會上，被解放的奴隸必須面對充斥更多敵意的環境，因為三 K 黨採取極端暴力的手段攻擊和謀殺被解放的奴隸及其支持者。

至於經濟上，白人和黑人都經歷痛苦。農業是南方經濟的支柱，但是奴隸被解放後，農場上的員工減少了。新產業，像是鋼鐵業，無法刺激經濟，因為跟農業相比的話，新產業只占少部分。土地改革並未普及，許多被解放的奴隸回去農場替他們的前主人工作，他們在佃農這個新制度下工作，佃農制度使他們必須在租來的土地上，依賴農作收成數量獲得收入。因此，被解放的奴隸仍陷於債務和貧窮。

Unit ㉓ 美國文學類

區域主義文學及馬克‧吐溫的《哈克歷險記》Regionalism and Mark Twain's The Adventures of Huckleberry Finn

請先閱讀一短文與題目

Summarize the main features of The Adventures of Huckleberry Finn described in the lecture, and explain why it belongs to the style of regionalism described in the reading.

Regionalism is a style of literature popular in the late 19th century American society. Famous novels that employ regionalism include Mark Twain's *The Adventures of Huckleberry Finn* and Kate Chopin's *Awakening*, and *The House of Mirth* by Edith Wharton. It also arose from the opposition to Romanticism, a previously dominant style, and sought to respond to radical social and political changes in America in the 19th century, including the end of the Civil War, the abolition of slavery, and the Industrial Revolution.

Unlike Romanticism that had emphasized stormy emotion and extravagant settings, regionalism focused on daily life and tangible details in an actual living environment. Regionalist writers tried to create a vivid sense of a time and place and experimented with dialect and slang in their narrations. Those writers also conjured up customs, conventional sayings and behaviors, as well as geography in their works. Some distinguishable features of regionalist writing include informal language of narration and description of minute details of nature. For example, *The Adventures of Huckleberry Finn* is considered the most representative of the narrator's informal language and depiction of nature, in this novel, the Mississippi River.

On the other hand, regionalism reflected Americans' new awareness after the Civil War that they formed a unified nation. Paradoxically, facing the political change, writers were eager to document traditional ways of life in response to readers' curiosity about regions that they had no opportunity to set foot on. Overall, readers can sense nostalgia in regionalist novels, for example, *The Adventures of Tom Sawyer* is a nostalgic novel of the experience of growing up in Missouri.

請聽與短文相關的課堂內容 Listening To A Lecture

Track 21

Now listen to a lecture on the topic you just read about.

(Professor) In 2010, Americans celebrated the fact that The Adventures of Huckleberry Finn turned 125. When Mark Twain published it in 1885, he probably did not envision that the novel would become an icon in American Literature, and a must-read in many middle and high schools in America. Even Earnest Hemingway claimed that The Adventures of Huckleberry Finn marked the beginning of all modern American literature. What makes this novel so quintessential in American literature?

To begin with, what probably impressed readers the most is the dialect which is so different from the Standard English we are used to nowadays. Over the past few years, the novel did stir intense controversy for its word choices, especially the word "nigger", which is considered pejorative and racist today. However, if we criticize the novel only based on word choices, we are missing the important theme that Mark Twain aimed to convey and the literary tradition that he helped to shape, a tradition we call regionalism. The novel is essentially antislavery and antiracism. I mean, we should keep the historical context and regional influence in mind. The novel was set in the pre-Civil War period, during which "nigger" was commonly used, and Mark Twain portrayed Huck as an outcast from a dysfunctional white family. Huck's language is full of slang and grammatically incorrect sentences, spoken from the perspectives of a young boy growing up in St. Petersburg, Missouri, a town on the Mississippi River. Through the wit in Huck's colloquial language and his friendship with the slave, Jim, Twain wanted to criticize the social and racial injustice at that time.

Another important element in the novel that echoes the

tradition of regionalism is the Mississippi River. Regionalist writers had the tendency to elaborate on actual geographical details which might not be directly related to the plot. Twain often digressed from the plot to describe the details of the Mississippi River, allowing readers to sense its majestic view.

高分範文搶先看　▶ Track 22

The lecture points out some characteristics of *The Adventures of Huckleberry Finn* that share the characteristics of regionalism mentioned in the reading.

課堂講述指出數個《哈克歷險記》的特色，跟閱讀篇章提到的區域主義特色是一樣的。

The first characteristic that the professor raised is the dialect and slang spoken by the characters. Mark Twain maintained the dialect used in the pre-Civil War period that forms the background of this novel. The professor used the example of the word "nigger", which is racist nowadays, yet before the Civil War, it was in common usage. In other words, it was a customary word during that period, reflecting one of the

教授提出的第一個特色是小說角色說的方言和俚語。這本小說的背景是南北戰爭之前的時期，馬克‧吐溫保留當時的方言。教授舉的例子是「黑鬼」這個字，現在這個字有種族歧視的意味，但在南北戰爭之前是普遍被使用的。換言之，這是那時的慣用字，呼應閱讀提到的特色之一，即約定俗成的說法。另外，這本小說在南北戰爭後出版，符合閱讀篇章提及的此文學風格的時

features, conventional sayings, given in the reading. Also, the novel was published after the Civil War, corresponding to the period of this literary style mentioned in the reading. The theme of the novel, that is, criticism of slavery, echoes one of the reasons that regionalism burgeoned as presented in the reading, the abolition of slavery.

期。小說的主題，即對奴隸制度的批評，呼應了閱讀篇章指出的區域主義急速發展的理由，其中之一即廢除奴隸制度。

Furthermore, another regionalist characteristic of the novel is the detailed description of the Mississippi River, which is not really relevant to the major plot. By doing so, the novelist wanted readers to have a realistic sense of the local nature. The emphasis on nature is also included in the reading.

此外，小說裡另一個區域主義的特色是對密西西比河的詳細描述，不見得跟主要劇情有關。小說家藉此讓讀者對當地自然風景有寫實的感受。閱讀篇章也提及對自然風景的重視。

The characteristics summarized above demonstrate that the novel carries regionalist style.

以上總結的特色證明這本小說屬於區域主義風格。

高分範文解析

關鍵句 1

The lecture points out some characteristics of *The Adventures of Huckleberry Finn* that share the characteristics of regionalism mentioned in the reading.

解析

此句是整篇的主旨句（thesis statement），主旨句必須闡明閱讀篇章和聽力篇章主要論點彼此間的關係。不須發表個人意見。此單元題目屬於 support 類型，即閱讀和聽力篇章的主要論點互相支持，或一方提出理論，另一方提出佐證。

關鍵句 2

Also, the novel was published after the Civil War, corresponding to the period of this literary style mentioned in the reading. The theme of the novel, that is, criticism of slavery, echoes one of the reasons that regionalism burgeoned as presented in the reading, the abolition of slavery.

解析

此句詳細整合閱讀篇章和聽力篇章互相呼應的重點，且運用分詞構句：S+V, corresponding to...及 N1 echoes N2, as presented in ...。將立場相似的重點整合的動詞有（1）呼應：reflect, echo, correspond to（2）支持：support, fortify, buttress, enhance, ally with。

● 閱讀短文中譯

請總結課堂講述對《哈克歷險記》描述的重點特色，並解釋此小說為何被歸類於閱讀短文中描述的區域主義風格。

區域主義是一種十九世紀末期在美國流行的文學風格。有名的區域主義風格小說包括馬克‧吐溫的《哈克歷險記》，凱特‧蕭邦的《覺醒》，和艾蒂斯‧霍頓的《歡樂之屋》。此風格的起源也跟反對之前流行的浪漫主義有關，並力求呼應十九世紀美國在社會及政治上劇烈的變化，包括內戰結束、廢除奴隸制度及工業革命。

區域主義不像浪漫主義重視強烈情感和奢華的背景，反而重視日常生活及生活環境的具體細節。區域主義作家嘗試創造栩栩如生的時代感和地區感，且在敘述中嘗試使用方言和俚語。這些作家也在作品中融入習俗，約定俗成的語言或行為，和地理特色。一些可辨識區域風格文章的特色包含不正式的敘述語言及對大自然的瑣碎描述。例如，《哈克歷險記》被視為敘述者使用不正式語言和描繪大自然的最佳代表作品，這本小說裡，大自然主要指的是密西西比河。

另一方面，區域主義反映的是內戰結束後，美國人對他們是統一國家的新意識形態。矛盾地，作家面對這種政治變化，反而迫切地想要紀錄傳統生活方式，也因應讀者對那些未曾造訪之地的好奇心。大致而言，讀者讀區域風格小說能感受懷舊氛圍，例如《湯姆歷險記》是本描述在密蘇里州成長的懷舊風格小說。

◉ 課堂講述中譯

現在請聽一篇與閱讀篇章一樣主題的課堂講述。

在 2010 年，美國人曾慶祝哈克歷險記出版 125 周年。當馬克・吐溫在 1885 年出版此小說時，他大概沒預想到這本小說會成為美國文學的經典作品，而且是在許多國高中必讀的書。連艾尼斯・海明威都宣稱《哈克歷險記》是所有現代美國文學的開端。是甚麼讓這本小說在美國文學深具代表性？

首先，讓讀者印象最深刻的是書中的方言，跟我們現在習慣的標準英文差異甚大。在過去幾年，這本小說的確因為用字引起激烈的爭議，尤其是「黑鬼」這個字，現在這個字是有貶抑和種族歧視意味的。然而，如果我們只依據用字就批評這本小說，我們會忽略馬克・吐溫想要傳達的重要主題，及他協助塑造的文學傳統，就是我們所稱的區域主義。這本小說本質上是反對奴隸制度及反對種族主義的。我的意思是我們應該記住當時的歷史情境和區域性的影響。這本小說的背景是設定在南北戰爭之前，當時「黑鬼」這個字普遍被使用，而且馬克・吐溫將哈克描寫成從一個功能失常的白人家庭被放逐的局外人。哈克的語言充滿俚語和文法錯誤的句子，以一位在密蘇里州的聖彼得鎮成長的男孩角度敘述，聖彼得鎮鄰近密西西比河。透過哈克充滿地方色彩的語言和他跟一位奴隸，吉姆，的友誼，吐溫想批評的是當時的社會及種族不公不義的現象。

另一個呼應地區主義的重要元素是密西西比河。區域主義作家傾向詳細地描繪實際的地理細節，而這些細節可能跟劇情沒有直接連結。吐溫常常偏離劇情去描述此河的細節，讓讀者感受到壯觀的景象。

Unit ㉔ 美國文學類
烏托邦文學及反烏托邦文學 Utopia and Dystopia

⫽⫽⫽請先閱讀一短文與題目

Summarize the main points in the reading and the lecture, explaining how they contrast one another.

The word "utopia" derived its origin from Sir Thomas More's novel, *Utopia*, written in Latin in 1516 and translated into English in 1551. More made up this word by combining the Greek words "outopos", meaning "no place" and "eutopos", meaning "good place". Although nowadays the word generally means a perfect world, some experts argue that the connotation arose from a misunderstanding about More's original intention. More intended to emphasize fictionality, and thus the title simply meant "no place".

Despite various interpretations, most agree that utopia implies a perfect world which is unattainable, ironically a nowhere place. A much earlier example of utopia is Plato's *The Republic*, in which Plato depicted an ideal society reigned by philosopher-kings. The idea of utopia continued in the 18th and 19th centuries; for example, utopian traits were illustrated in Jonathan Swift's *Gulliver's Travels* and Samuel Butler's *Erewhon*, which is an anagram of the word "nowhere".

What are the characteristics of utopia? In More's book, he described a society with economic prosperity, a peaceful government and egalitarianism for civilians, which are the most obvious traits utopian fictions share. Moreover, technologies are applied to improve human living conditions; independent thought and free flow of information are encouraged. Although the government exists, citizens are united by a set of central ideas, while abiding by moral codes. The term government in a utopia state is very different from our idea of government in the present reality. The government in a utopia is loosely composed of citizenry, without a complicated hierarchy. Furthermore, people revere nature and reverse the damage to ecology due to industrialization.

請聽與短文相關的課堂內容　　Track 23

Now listen to a lecture in a literature class regarding dystopia.

(Professor) In today's popular culture, the idea of dystopia is gaining more popularity in young adult fiction and Hollywood movies, as the success of the novels and movies of *The Hunger Games* series has demonstrated. You might know the meaning of dystopia simply from the prefix dys-, implying a negative place with conditions opposite to utopia. In fact, we can trace the origin of dystopian literature way back to 1605, to a satire in Latin called *Mundus Alter et Idem*, meaning "an old world and a new", written by Joseph Hall, Bishop of Norwich, England. *An Old World and a New* satirizes life in London and customs of the Roman Catholic Church. It also served as an inspiration to Jonathan Swift's *Gulliver's Travels*.

Speaking of Jonathan Swift's *Gulliver's Travels*, some of you might consider it utopian fiction. Well, it is both utopian and dystopian. *Gulliver's Travels* illustrates utopian and dystopian places. Or a dystopia might be disguised as a utopia, forming an ambiguous genre. One example is Samuel Butler's *Erewhon*, which consists of utopian and dystopian traits. In the 20th century, the most famous dystopian works of fiction are probably Aldous Huxley's *Brave New World*, written in 1931 and George Orwell's *1984*, written in 1949.

It is not hard to understand that the characteristics of dystopia contribute to its popularity in popular fiction and movies. Those characteristics tend to create tension and anxiety, factors that draw contemporary audience. Those include totalitarian control of citizens, a bureaucratic government, restriction of freedom and information, as well as constant surveillance on civilians with technology. Civilians' individuality and equality are abolished, while a central figurehead or bureaucracy exerts dictatorial control over society. Other traits are associated with doomsday, such as poverty, hunger, and the destruction of nature.

高分範文搶先看 ▶ Track 24

The reading and lecture delineate the contrary styles of utopian and dystopian literature by depicting the representative works and various traits of both literary genres.

First, the reading and the lecture explain the opposite definitions of these two words. Whereas utopia is a deliberately invented word with its origins in Greek, meaning an ideal place or a place that doesn't exist, a dystopia is an atrocious place contrary to a utopia.

Next, the reading traces back to the earliest utopian fiction, Plato's *The Republic*, and gives the utopian examples from British literature, which are Jonathan Swift's *Gulliver's Travels* and Samuel Butler's *Erewhon*, while

閱讀篇章及課堂講述藉由描寫烏托邦及反烏托邦兩種文學類型的代表作品和其特色，勾勒出兩種相反的風格。

首先，閱讀篇章及課堂講述解釋這兩個字的相反定義。烏托邦是一個刻意被創造出的字，源自希臘文，意為理想的地方或不存在之地，相反地，反烏托邦是個險惡之地。

其次，閱讀篇章追溯至最初的烏托邦小說，柏拉圖的《共和國》，並提出英國文學的作品為例，即強納森·斯威夫特的《格列佛遊記》和山謬·巴特勒的《烏有之鄉》，而課堂講述指出烏托邦和反烏

the lecture points out that the boundary between utopian and dystopian literature is sometimes not so definite, as both styles are present in the latter two works of fiction.

Third, in contrast to the features of a utopia, such as encouragement of independent thoughts, equal status for all citizens, and a government without obvious hierarchy, the features of a dystopia include the government's dictatorial oppression of citizens, lack of equality, and abolishment of individual freedoms.

In conclusion, the dissimilar characteristics of utopia and dystopia are discussed, supported by the renowned works from both genres.

托邦的界線有時候並非絕對，就如同兩種風格在後者兩本小説中都出現。

第三，反烏托邦的特色包含政府對公民的獨裁壓迫，缺乏平等及剝奪個人自由，這些與烏托邦的特色相反，如鼓勵獨立思考、公民均享平等，及沒有明顯階級的政府。

總而言之，烏托邦和反烏托邦的差異特色皆被討論，並以兩種文學類型的知名作品作為佐證。

高分範文解析

關鍵句 1

Next, the reading traces back to the earliest utopian fiction, Plato's *The Republic*, and gives the utopian examples from British literature, which are Jonathan Swift's *Gulliver's Travels* and Samuel Butler's *Erewhon*, while the lecture points out that the boundary between utopian and dystopian literature is sometimes not so definite, as both styles are present in the latter two works of fiction.

解析

以從屬連接詞 while 連接兩個意義相反或落差甚大的子句，而 while 前後兩個子句又各包含兩個小子句，分別由 and 及 as 連接。

關鍵句 2

In conclusion, the dissimilar characteristics of utopia and dystopia are discussed, supported by the renowned works from both genres.

解析

句尾的分詞片語 supported by ... 是由形容詞子句簡化而來，原本的完整子句：which are supported by ...，省略 which are，保留過去分詞 supported。

● 閱讀短文中譯

請總結閱讀短文和課堂講述的重點，並解釋它們如何互相駁斥。

烏托邦一詞的來源是湯瑪士‧摩爾在 1516 年以拉丁文寫的小說《烏托邦》，此著作在 1551 年被翻譯成英文。摩爾將希臘文的"outopos"（意為「不存在之地」）和"eutopos"（意為「好地方」）合併，創造出這詞。雖然現在這詞通常指的是完美世界，有些專家主張這涵義是誤解了摩爾的原意。摩爾原本是著重在虛構性，因此書名只是單純表達「不存在之地」。

儘管有不同的詮釋，大部份的專家同意烏托邦暗喻的是一個不可能達到的完美世界，諷刺地也就是一個「不存在之地」。更早期的烏托邦例子是柏拉圖的《共和國》，柏拉圖描繪了一個由哲學家國王統治的理想社會。烏托邦的概念延續到十八和十九世紀；例如，強納森‧斯威夫特的《格列佛遊記》和山謬‧巴特勒的《烏有之鄉》都描繪了烏托邦特色，《烏有之鄉》這個字是「不存在之地」的顛倒重組字。

烏托邦的特色為何？在摩爾的書裡，他描述一個擁有繁榮經濟，祥和政府和公民平等的社會，這些是烏托邦小說共有的最明顯的特色。此外，科技被應用來改善人類的生活狀態，獨立的思考和資訊自由流通是被鼓勵的。雖然政府存在，公民是被一組中心思想所團結，同時他們遵守道德規範。烏托邦的政府一詞跟我們現在對政府的概念非常不同。烏托邦政府是由公民團體鬆散地組織而成，沒有複雜的階級制度。而且，人們尊敬大自然並反轉了工業化對生態造成的損害。

◉ 課堂講述中譯

現在請聽一篇關於反烏托邦的文學課堂講述。

　　在今日的流行文化中，反烏托邦的概念在青少年小說和好萊塢電影中越來越受歡迎，如同《飢餓遊戲》的小說和電影之成功已經證明了。你們可能從字首 dys-就知道反烏托邦的意思，它暗示的是情況跟烏托邦相反的負面地方。事實上，我們能追溯反烏托邦文學的起源至 1605 年，是一本名為 *Mundus Alter et Idem* 的拉丁文諷刺小說，書名的意思是「一個舊世界和新世界」，作者是約瑟夫・霍爾，他是英國諾威治的主教。《一個舊世界和新世界》嘲諷倫敦的生活型態及羅馬天主教的習俗。這本書也啟發了強納森・斯威夫特的《格列佛遊記》。

　　提到強納森・斯威夫特的《格列佛遊記》，你們有些人可能把它視為烏托邦小說。嗯，它是烏托邦，也是反烏托邦小說。烏托邦和反烏托邦地區《格列佛遊記》都描述了。或者反烏托邦可能表面上假裝成烏托邦，形成一種模糊的文學類型。一例是在山謬・巴特勒的《烏有之鄉》裡，兩個種類的特色都並存。二十世紀最有名的反烏托邦小說應該是艾爾道斯・赫胥黎 1931 年的著作《美麗新世界》和喬治・歐威爾 1949 年的著作《1984》。

　　不難理解，反烏托邦的特色導致了這個概念在流行小說和電影中非常普遍。那些特色會創造緊繃和焦慮感，這些都是吸引當代觀眾的因素。特色包括對公民的獨裁控制，官僚化政府，對自由和資訊的限制，及不斷用科技監視人民。人民的個人特色和平等權被剝奪了，而一位中央領導或官僚體系以獨裁方式控制社會。其他特色跟末日有關聯，例如貧窮、飢餓和對大自然的破壞。

ch.**4**
美國教育、歷史與文學類型

ch.5

ch.6

Unit ㉕ 西洋藝術類

塗鴉藝術及凱斯・哈林 Graffiti Art and Keith Haring

請先閱讀一短文與題目

Summarize the main points in the lecture and Keith Haring's contributions, as described in the reading.

Keith Haring has become a worldwide icon of the 20th century Pop Art. His contribution is multifaceted, from changing our idea of street art to incorporating social and political messages in Pop Art.

In Haring's early career in the 1980s, he was fined numerous times for his graffiti drawings in the New York subway system since the police viewed his art as vandalism. Notwithstanding, Haring considered subway drawings his responsibility of communicating art to the public. While he was drawing on the blank panels, he was often surrounded and observed by commuters. Being a prolific artist, he could produce about 40 drawings a day. Yet, most of his subway drawings were not recorded, as they were either cleaned or covered by new advertisements. It was the ephemeral nature that acted as an impetus for him to reinvent themes with easily identifiable images, such as babies, dogs, and angels, all illustrated with outlines. His themes involve sexuality, war, birth, and death, often mocking the mainstream society in caricatures.

As Haring's reputation grew, he took on larger projects. His most notable work is the public mural titled, "Crack is Wack", inspired by his studio assistant who was addicted to crack and addressing the deteriorating drug issue in New York. The mural is representative of Haring's broad concerns for the American society in the 1980s. He was a social activist as well, heavily involved in socio-political movements, in which he participated in charitable support for children and fought against racial discrimination. Before his death at age 31, he established the Keith Haring Foundation and the Pop Shop; both have continued his legacy till today.

請聽與短文相關的課堂內容　▶Track 25

Now listen to a lecture in an art class regarding graffiti.

(Professor) Graffiti has existed for as long as written words have existed, with examples traced back to Ancient Greece, Ancient Egypt, and the Roman Empire. In fact, the word graffiti came from the Roman Empire. Some even consider cave drawings by cavemen in the Neolithic Age the earliest form of graffiti, and thus make it the longest existent art form. Basically, graffiti refers to writing or drawings that have been scrawled, painted, or sprayed on surfaces in public in an illicit manner. The general functions of graffiti include expressing personal emotions, recording historical events, and conveying political messages. Nevertheless, today graffiti has found its place in mainstream art, and for many graffiti artists, their works have become highly commercialized and lucrative.

Contemporary artistic graffiti has just arisen in the past twenty-five years in the inner city of New York, with street artists painting and writing illegitimately on public buildings, street signs or public transportation, more commonly on the exteriors of subway trains. These artists experimented with different styles and mediums, such as sprays and stencils. The difference between artistic graffiti and traditional graffiti is that the former has evolved from scribbling on a wall to a complex and skillful form of personal and political expression.

Graffiti artists have also branched out to collaborate with fashion designers and produce numerous products, increasing the daily and global presence of this art form. In the U. S., many graffiti artists have extended their careers to skateboard, apparel, and shoe design for companies such as DC Shoes, Adidas, and Osiris. The most famous American graffiti artist is probably Keith Haring, who brought his art into the commercial mainstream by opening his Pop Shop in New York in 1986, where the public could purchase commodities with Haring's graffiti imageries. Keith Haring viewed his Pop Shop as an extension of his subway drawings, with his philosophy of making art accessible to the public, not just to collectors.

高分範文搶先看　▶Track 26

The lecture outlines the history of graffiti from its earliest origin to its recent development in the U.S., while the reading focuses on Keith Haring's artworks and his contributions.

The lecture first points out that the history of graffiti is as long as that of written words, which can be exemplified by the origin of the word graffiti from the Roman Empire. Another view even holds that graffiti might be dated back to the Neolithic Age, to cave drawings. Then the lecture shifts to artistic graffiti which developed in New York City in the past 25 years, offering details such as locations and mediums. Besides, it describes graffiti artists that have turned their careers to the fashion industry, allowing consumers to attain their works in commercialized

課堂講述勾勒塗鴉的歷史，從最早的起源至近期在美國的發展，而閱讀篇章著重凱斯‧哈林的作品和貢獻。

課堂講述首先指出塗鴉的歷史跟文字歷史一樣久，並以塗鴉這個字發源於羅馬帝國為例。另一個看法甚至認為塗鴉可追溯到新石器時代的洞穴繪畫。接著講述轉而描述在紐約市過去 25 年間發展出的藝術性塗鴉，並提出塗鴉地點和媒介等細節。此外，講述提及塗鴉藝術家將職業轉向至流行產業，讓消費者可以透過商業型式取得他們的作品。最後，講述提出凱斯‧哈林的普普店以加強之前的敘述。

forms. Finally, Keith Haring's Pop Shop is raised to fortify the aforementioned description.

The reading not only depicts Keith Haring's major artworks, but also mentions his diverse contribution to the American society. In his early career, he was known for subway drawings, and another renowned work is a public mural that conveys an anti-drug message. His other contributions included charities for children and anti-racism campaigns.

閱讀篇章不但描述凱斯‧哈林的作品，也提到他對美國社會多方面的貢獻。在他早期的職涯，他以地鐵繪畫聞名，而另一個知名作品是一幅傳達反對毒品訊息的公共壁畫。他其他的貢獻包括兒童慈善和反對種族歧視的活動。

高分範文解析

關鍵句 1

The lecture first points out that the history of graffiti is as long as that of written words, which can be exemplified by the origin of the word graffiti from the Roman Empire.

解析

主要動詞 point out 的受詞是 that 引導的名詞子句。名詞子句互相比較兩個事物的歷史，as long as 之後的代名詞 that 是代替 history，注意代名詞 that 不可省略。形容詞子句 which ...，關係代名詞 which 的先行詞是 that 引導的名詞子句。

關鍵句 2

Besides, it describes graffiti artists that have turned their careers to the fashion industry, allowing consumers to attain their works in commercialized forms.

解析

動詞 describe 的受詞是 graffiti artists。graffiti artists 由關係代名詞的 that 導引的限定形容詞子句修飾。分詞片語 allowing... 是由形容詞子句 which allows... 簡化而來。

◉ 閱讀短文中譯

請總結課堂講述的重點及閱讀短文描述的凱斯・哈林的貢獻。

凱斯・哈林已成為二十世紀普普藝術的代表人物。他的貢獻是多方面的，從改變我們對街頭藝術的觀念到將社會及政治訊息融入普普藝術。

在 1980 年代哈林早期的職涯裡，他因為在紐約市地鐵系統塗鴉被罰款許多次，因為警察將他的藝術視為破壞公物。然而，哈林認為地鐵繪畫是他的責任，藉此他能將藝術溝通給大眾。當他在空白的長板子上繪畫時，他常常被通勤者圍觀。身為多產的藝術家，他一天可以畫大約四十幅塗鴉。但是，他大部份的地鐵繪畫沒有被記錄下來，因為它們不是被清潔掉，就是被新的廣告蓋上。正是這種稍縱即逝的本質形成他不斷重新創作主題的動力。他的塗鴉主題運用容易辨識的圖案，例如嬰兒、小狗和天使形象，而所有的圖案都只有外觀輪廓。他的主題牽涉了性意識、戰爭、出生及死亡，且經常以諷刺漫畫嘲諷主流社會。

隨著哈林的名聲提高，他進行更大型的計畫。他最值得一提的作品是名為「吸毒等同發瘋」公共壁畫，這幅壁畫的靈感來自他對毒品上癮的工作室助理，同時也針對紐約市日益惡化的毒品問題。這幅壁畫代表了哈林對 1980 年代美國社會的廣泛關注。他也是位行動主義者，深度參與社會及政治方面的活動，並支援兒童慈善活動及反對種族歧視。在他 31 歲過世前，他成立了凱斯・哈林基金會及普普店，兩者至今都延續了他的精神。

● 課堂講述中譯

現在請聽一篇關於塗鴉藝術的藝術課堂講述。

塗鴉的歷史就跟文字的歷史一樣久，塗鴉的例子可追溯到古希臘、古埃及和羅馬帝國。事實上，graffiti 這個字發源自羅馬帝國。有些人甚至將新石器時代的穴居人所畫的洞穴壁畫視為塗鴉最早的形式，使得塗鴉成為現存最久的藝術。基本上，塗鴉指的是未經法律許可在公共領域的壁面上潦草書寫，畫畫或噴漆形成的文字或圖案。塗鴉的主要功能包括表達個人情緒，記錄歷史事件，及傳達政治訊息。然而，今日塗鴉已經在主流藝術中取得一席之地，而且對許多塗鴉藝術家而言，他們的作品已經被高度商業化並帶來高度利潤。

當今的藝術性塗鴉是在過去二十五年間於紐約市中心興起的，當時街頭藝術家未經法律許可就在公共建築、馬路上的標誌或公共運輸工具上面畫畫及寫字，比較普遍的是畫在地鐵車廂的外層。這些藝術家實驗不同的風格和媒介，例如噴漆和金屬模板。藝術性塗鴉和傳統塗鴉的差異在於前者已從在牆壁上潦草畫畫進化成表達個人和政治意涵的複雜及高技術的型式。

塗鴉藝術家也和流行服飾設計師合作拓展出許多產品，提高此藝術在日常生活和全球的能見度。在美國，許多塗鴉藝術家已經將職涯延伸到滑板、服裝及鞋子設計，他們替 DC Shoes、愛迪達和 Osiris 等品牌設計。最有名的美國塗鴉藝術家可能是凱斯‧哈林。他在 1986 年於紐約開了他的普普店，將他的藝術帶入商業主流。在這間店大眾可以買到印有哈林的塗鴉圖案的商品。哈林視普普店為他的地鐵繪畫的延伸，這間店蘊含他對藝術的哲學，即藝術應該讓大眾輕易取得，而不是只針對收藏家。

Unit ㉖ 西洋藝術類
現代主義建築及貝聿銘 Modern Architecture and I. M. Pei

⫶⫶⫶ 請先閱讀一短文與題目

Summarize the main points in the reading and listening, with an emphasis on the features of I. M. Pei's architectures.

"Modern architecture" is an overarching term, which generally is applied to architectures emerging at the end of the 19th century under the influence of modernism and to those that shared similar characteristics throughout the 20th century. Compared with previous architectures, modern architectures focus more on geometric forms, harmony with location, and function over ornament.

Modern architectures exhibit certain characteristics, including simplicity in design, merging of nature and buildings, rectangular forms and linear structures. In the U.S., the most quintessential buildings are those designed by Frank Lloyd Wright, such as the Robie House and Fallingwater. Frank Lloyd Wright was referred to as "the greatest American architect of all time" by the American Institute of Architects, for he cultivated the original American architectural philosophy called "organic architecture", which means that architectures should be incorporated into their natural environment. Wright's buildings are characterized by linear elements. Numerous components, such as beams, posts, staircases and windows, are utilized to construct a linear space. The interior space also extends to the exterior, forming another feature, that is, blurring the boundary between indoor space and outdoor space. To achieve that, floor-to-ceiling glass windows are employed. Large expanses of glass not only bring in natural light, but also generate a magnificent view. Another iconic example that demonstrates the dramatic function of glass windows is the glass pyramid designed by I. M. Pei at the Louvre Museum in Paris.

In the 1960s, waves of criticism arose in reaction to modern architecture, and since the 1960s, the mainstream architectural philosophy has embraced postmodernism, gradually replacing modernism.

請聽與短文相關的課堂內容　▶ Track 27

Now listen to a lecture in an art class regarding I. M. Pei, a renowned Chinese-American architect.

(Professor) Ieoh Ming Pei, commonly known as I. M. Pei, is often referred to as the master of modern architecture. He was born in Guangzhou, China in 1917, and spent his childhood and adolescence in Hong Kong and Shanghai, where he was profoundly influenced by Hollywood movies and the style of colonial architecture.

As Pei's secondary education in Shanghai drew near an end, he decided to enter an American university, a decision which he once admitted was made under the influence of Bing Crosby movies, in which college life in America seemed full of fun. Though he soon found out that the rigorous academic life differed drastically from the portrayal in movies, he excelled in the architecture school of the Massachusetts Institute of Technology (MIT). Particularly, he was drawn to the school of modern architecture, featuring simplicity and the utilization of glass and steel materials, and influenced by architect Frank Lloyd Wright.

Throughout his career, Pei has designed numerous notable buildings. In 1961, he began designing the Mesa Laboratory for the National Center for Atmospheric Research in Colorado. The Mesa Laboratory embodied his philosophy akin to Organic Architecture. The building rests harmoniously in the Rocky Mountains, as if sculpted out of rocks. Then, after President John F. Kennedy's assassination in 1963, Pei was chosen by Ms. Kennedy to design the John F. Kennedy Presidential Library and Museum, which includes a large square glass-enclosed courtyard with a triangular tower and a circular walkway. Following some remarkable architectures in the U.S., such as Dallas City Hall, the Hancock Tower in Boston and the

National Gallery East Building in Washington, D.C., Pei executed the most challenging project in his career in the 1980s, the renovation of the Louvre Museum in Paris. His decision to build a huge glass and steel pyramid at the center of the courtyard initially ignited controversy, yet since its completion, the glass pyramid has become a famous landmark in Paris and Pei's most representative work.

高分範文搶先看　▶ Track 28

The reading passage depicts the school of modern architecture, with a focus on its development in the U.S., and the listening passage features I.M. Pei, the master of modern architecture.

閱讀篇章描述現代建築學派，特別是這個學派在美國的發展，而聽力篇章著重現代建築大師，貝聿銘。

Modern architecture is a comprehensive genre that includes architecture influenced by modernism, with traits such as functionality, simplicity, geometric shapes, and a harmonious relationship with the surrounding environment. The most representative architect of this genre is Frank Lloyd Wright, whose

現代建築是一個廣泛的類型，包括被現代主義影響的建築，這個類型的特色有功能性、極簡風、幾何形狀和建築與周遭環境的和諧關係。此類型最具代表性的建築師是法蘭克・洛伊・萊特，他的學派被稱為有機建築。有機建築的特色包括線性設計、缺乏室內與室外間明確的界線及巨大的玻

school is termed organic architecture. Organic architecture is characterized by linear design, lack of the definite boundary between interior and exterior and huge glass windows.

I. M. Pei's philosophy of design is also under the influence of Frank Lloyd Wright. One of his works of architecture in the Rocky Mountains in Colorado fits in with the natural environment seamlessly, echoing the feature mentioned in the reading. His design of the John F. Kennedy Presidential Library and Museum exhibits geometric forms and carries historic significance. Pei's most well-known building is the glass and steel pyramid at the Louvre Museum in Paris.

璃窗戶。

貝聿銘的設計理念也被法蘭克‧洛伊‧萊特影響。他設計的其中一棟建築位於科羅拉多州洛磯山脈，這棟建築和自然環境無縫地接合，呼應了閱讀篇章提到的特色。他對甘迺迪總統圖書館及紀念館的設計展現了幾何型式，並蘊含歷史意義。貝聿銘最知名的建築是位於巴黎羅浮宮博物館的玻璃及鋼鐵結構的金字塔。

高分範文解析

關鍵句 1

Modern architecture is a comprehensive genre that includes architecture influenced by modernism, with identifiable traits such as functionality, simplicity, geometric shapes, and a harmonious relationship with surrounding environment.

解析

形容詞子句 that ... with surrounding environment. 是限定形容詞子句，關係代名詞 that 的先行詞是 genre；that 在此也是形容詞子句的主詞。副詞片語 with ... 強調形容詞子句提及的 architecture 的特色。

關鍵句 2

One of his works of architecture in the Rocky Mountains in Colorado fits in with the natural environment seamlessly, echoing the feature mentioned in the reading.

解析

句尾的分詞片語 echoing... 是由形容詞子句 which echoes... 簡化而來。which 的先行詞是之前的完整子句 One of his works of archiectures... seamlessly。

● 閱讀短文中譯

請總結閱讀短文和課堂講述的重點，並著重於貝聿銘建築的特色。

現代建築是一個廣泛的稱呼，通常被套用在受到現代主義影響，於十九世紀末出現的建築，及那些有類似特色的二十世紀建築。跟之前的建築比起來，現代建築比較重視幾何型式、與地點的和諧關係和功能性超越裝飾性。

現代建築展現了某些特色，包括極簡設計、自然與建築融合及長方形和線性結構。在美國，最具代表性的是法蘭克‧洛伊‧萊特的建築，例如羅比屋和瀑布屋。法蘭克‧洛伊‧萊特被美國建築師學院稱為「歷史上最偉大的美國建築師」，因為他發展了「有機建築」這個美國原創的建築哲學，此哲學的意義在於建築應該融入自然環境當中。萊特的建築特色是直線元素。許多元素，例如橫梁、柱子、樓梯間和窗戶，都被利用來建構直線型空間。室內空間也延伸到戶外，形成另一個特色，即模糊了室內空間和戶外空間的界線。為了達到這種模糊界線，玻璃落地窗被使用。大片的玻璃不但引進自然光，也創造出莊嚴的視野。另一個示範玻璃窗能產生強大功能的經典例子是貝聿銘設計的玻璃金字塔，玻璃金字塔位於巴黎羅浮宮博物館。

1960 年代興起了一波波對現代建築的批評，自從 1960 年代，建築哲學的主流擁抱了後現代主義，現代主義就逐漸被取代了。

課堂講述中譯

現在請聽一篇關於知名華裔美籍建築師貝聿銘的藝術課堂講述。

貝聿銘常被稱為現代建築大師。他於 1917 年在中國的廣州出生，童年及青少年時期在香港和上海度過，他在這兩個城市受到好萊塢電影和殖民式建築風格的深遠影響。

貝聿銘從在上海就讀的高中快畢業時，他決定到美國念大學。他曾承認這個決定是受到賓‧克洛斯比的電影影響，在那些電影裡，美國的大學生活似乎是充滿了歡樂。雖然他很快就發現嚴格的學術生活和電影的描繪相差甚多，他就讀於麻省理工學院的建築系時表現得非常優秀。他尤其被現代建築吸引，現代建築的特色是極簡風和運用玻璃及鋼鐵素材，他也被法蘭克‧洛伊‧萊特影響。

在他的職業生涯中，貝聿銘設計了許多值得一提的建築。在 1961，他開始替位於科羅拉多州的國家大氣研究中心設計麥莎實驗室大樓。麥莎實驗室大樓展現了類似有機建築的哲學。這棟建築物和諧地和洛磯山脈並存，看起來像是直接從岩石雕鑿出來的。之後，在 1963 年甘迺迪總統被刺殺後，甘迺迪夫人選擇貝聿銘為甘迺迪總統圖書館及紀念館做設計。此圖書館及紀念館包含一大片被玻璃環繞的方形中庭、三角錐狀的高塔和圓形的走道。在美國完成一些知名建築之後，例如達拉斯市政廳、波士頓的漢考克大廈和首府華盛頓的國家美術館東側大樓，貝聿銘於 1980 年代執行了職業生涯中最具挑戰性的案子，就是巴黎羅浮宮博物館的翻新工程。他決定在羅浮宮中庭的中央建造一座巨型玻璃和鋼鐵金字塔，這個決定最初引起爭議，但是玻璃金字塔完成後，它成為巴黎知名的地標，也是貝聿銘最具代表性的作品。

Unit ㉗ 西洋藝術類
伍迪・艾倫對戲劇的貢獻 Woody Allen's Contribution to Cinema

請先閱讀一短文與題目

Summarize the main points in the reading and the lecture.

Woody Allen is undeniably one of the greatest American auteurs; his films carry a unique signature that makes his comic personae easily distinguishable from those in other Hollywood movies. In most of his films, the major personae exhibit neurotic disposition, and are frequently anxiety-ridden. Very often, those characters behave like schlemiels who undergo some sort of spiritual awakening or personal transformation through entanglements in relationships. With this comic portrayal, Allen presents philosophical issues in humorous ways, a theatrical scheme that he has developed since his early career as a stand-up comedian in Broadway in the 1960s.

Performing as stand-up comedian has exerted a substantial influence on his films, many of which are seemingly autobiographic, the most quintessential being *Annie Hall* (1977), which won 4 Academy Awards in 1978, including Best Actress for Diane Keaton,

Best Script, Best Director and Best Picture, and was voted the funniest screenplay ever written by the Writers Guild of America in 2015. Although often categorized as a romantic comedy, *Annie Hall* actually breaks many traditions of this genre due to the experimental style, non-linear narrative akin to stream of consciousness, and the lack of a felicitous ending. As the story about the neurotic couple, Alvy and Annie, unfolds, viewers learn that it's not really about Alvy's lament on why the relationship ends, but on the perpetual loneliness of human existence.

Regarding the experimental nature of *Annie Hall*, Allen employed several unconventional visual techniques, such as split screens, animation, subtitles indicating the main characters' thoughts to contradict the onscreen dialogues, and the protagonist's direct address to the audience.

請聽與短文相關的課堂內容　▶ Track 29

Now listen to a lecture in a movie appreciation class regarding Woody Allen.

(Professor) Renowned American director and comedian, Woody Allen, became an octogenarian in 2015, meaning he is in his 80s. The younger generation of audiences might not be so familiar with his early career, although many have acquainted themselves with Woody Allen's more recent movies set in major European cities, such as *Match Point*, set in London and released in 2005, *Midnight in Paris*, released in 2011, and *To Rome with Love*, released in 2012. It is true that the highly-acclaimed director made a major comeback to the cinema with those movies, particularly with *Midnight in Paris*, which not only won him the Academy Award for Best Original Screenplay and the Golden Globe Award for Best Screenplay, but also attained the highest box office revenue in North America among all of Woody Allen's movies.

It is fair to say that Woody Allen is a natural born comedian. His involvement in comedy started very early at the age of 15 when he began writing jokes for comedians performing on Broadway, and at age 20 in 1955, he was hired by The NBC Comedy Hour on Los Angeles as a full-time writer for many comedy shows. Since then, he has remained a prolific writer, having written numerous TV show scripts, short stories, works of comic fiction, and screenplays. He extended his caliber to stand-up comedy in the 1960s, performing as a stand-up comedian in nightclubs in Manhattan. Allen became well-known nationwide in 1965, when he had his own TV show, "The Woody Allen Show".

The common theme of Allen's films, that is, the satirical reflection of the absurdity of life, can be traced to his early works. His jokes were based on daily incidents that everyone could relate to, but were performed with very serious and neurotic expressions. The neurotic persona later became a trademark in his movies. In his stand-up comedies, he often satirized intellectuals and turned monologues into ironic remarks on contemporary cultural phenomena.

高分範文搶先看　▶ Track 30

Both the reading and the lecture describe the features of the main characters in Woody Allen's movies. The reading emphasizes *Annie Hall*, and the listening elaborates on Allen's successful career.

According to the reading, Woody Allen's films carry a distinctive style that distinguishes his movies easily from the rest of the Hollywood movies. The major characters are usually angst-ridden people who behave clumsily and undergo changes in life when dealing with relationships. The comic elements are heavily influenced by Allen's early experiences of performing as a

閱讀篇章和課堂講述都描述了伍迪‧艾倫的電影裡主要角色的特點。閱讀篇章著重在《安妮‧霍爾》這部電影，而課堂講述詳細闡述艾倫成功的職業生涯。

根據閱讀篇章，伍迪‧艾倫的電影有獨特的風格，使得他的電影容易和其他好萊塢電影區分開來。他的主要角色通常是感覺十分焦慮的人，而他們的行為笨拙，並在處理人際關係時經歷人生的變化。艾倫早期身為單人脫口秀表演者的經歷深遠地影響這種喜劇元素。在他豐富的作品中，《安妮‧霍爾》得到最多讚賞。《安妮‧霍爾》被視為一部浪

stand-up comedian. The film, *Annie Hall*, has received the most accolades among his abundant works. Regarded as a romantic comedy, *Annie Hall* was actually highly experimental because of its non-linear narrative, the lack of a happy ending, and various new filming techniques.

The lecture first raises the success of Allen's more recent films set in Europe, and then traces back to his budding career as a writer, stand-up comedian, and TV show host in the 1950s and 1960s. The protagonists in his comedies are characterized by a neurotic nature, and the prevalent theme is the absurdness of life expressed in satirical ways. Also, intellectuals and contemporary culture often become targets of his sarcasm.

漫喜劇,而事實上由於它非線性的敘述,缺少快樂的結局,及各式各樣新的拍片技巧,《安妮‧霍爾》是高度實驗性質的電影。

課堂講述首先指出艾倫將場景設在歐洲的近期電影及其成功,接著回溯至他早期的職業,他在 1950 和 1960 年代身為作家,單人脫口秀表演者及電視節目主持人。他的喜劇裡的主角有神經質特色,而常見的主題是以諷刺的方式表現出人生的荒謬。此外,知識份子和當代文化常成為他諷刺的對象。

高分範文解析

關鍵句 1 ▶

The major characters are usually angst-ridden people who behave clumsily and undergo changes in life when dealing with relationships.

解析

此例句中的形容詞子句包含了一個分詞片語 when dealing with relationships，此分詞片語是由副詞子句 when they deal with relationships 簡化而來。代名詞 they 和關係代名詞 who 指的先行詞都是 angst-ridden people，兩個代名詞的指涉對象相同時，此副詞子句中的 they 才能省略，並將副詞子句簡化成分詞片語。

關鍵句 2 ▶

Regarded as a romantic comedy, *Annie Hall* was actually highly experimental because of its non-linear narrative, the lack of a happy ending, and various new techniques.

解析

分詞片語在句首一定是修飾主詞，因為主詞是電影名稱 *Annie Hall*，所以分詞片語以過去分詞 regarded 表達被動，意思是：被視為。

◉ 閱讀短文中譯

請總結閱讀短文和課堂講述的重點。

伍迪‧艾倫無疑是美國導演中，個人風格強烈的最偉大導演之一。他的電影有獨特風格，使他的喜劇角色能輕易地和其他好萊塢喜劇角色區分。在他的大部份電影裡，主要角色展現神經質的特色，而且常常感到焦慮。那些角色常表現笨拙，並透過人際關係的牽扯，經歷某種靈性覺醒或個人蛻變。艾倫運用這種喜劇手法的描繪，以幽默的方式提出哲學議題，自從他的早期職業，即 1960 年代在百老匯表演單人脫口秀時，他就已經發展這種戲劇手法。

單人脫口秀表演對他的電影有深厚的影響，他的許多電影似乎都具備自傳性質，最具代表性的是《安妮‧霍爾》（1977），這部電影在 1978 年得到四座奧斯卡金像獎，包括黛安‧基頓贏得最佳女主角獎，最佳劇本獎，最佳導演獎及最佳影片獎，並在 2015 年由美國作家協會投票選為史上最有趣的劇本。雖然《安妮‧霍爾》常被歸類在浪漫喜劇，由於這部電影的實驗風格，類似意識流的非線性敘述，及缺乏幸福結局，它其實打破許多這個類型的傳統。隨著電影裡阿飛和安妮這對神經質情侶的故事展開，觀眾漸漸知道電影內容並不是真的關於阿飛在悼念為何這段感情結束，而是關於人類生存的持續寂寞狀態。

關於《安妮‧霍爾》的實驗性質，艾倫運用了幾個非典型的視覺技巧，例如分割螢幕畫面、動畫、字幕顯示的是主要角色的想法，和他們對話的內容是相反的，及主角直接向觀眾說話。

● 課堂講述中譯

現在請聽一篇關於伍迪‧艾倫的電影賞析課堂講述。

知名的美國導演及喜劇演員，伍迪‧艾倫，在 2015 年已經八十歲了。較年輕的觀眾可能對他早期的職涯不是很熟悉，雖然很多人熟悉伍迪‧艾倫近年來將場景設在歐洲主要城市的電影，例如場景在倫敦並於 2005 年上映的《愛情決勝點》、2011 年上映的《午夜巴黎》及 2012 年上映的《愛上羅馬》。的確，這位備受讚賞的導演以這些電影成功地重返大螢幕，尤其是他不但因《午夜巴黎》得到奧斯卡金像獎最佳原創劇本獎及金球獎最佳劇本獎，而且《午夜巴黎》在北美洲的票房獲利是伍迪‧艾倫所有的電影裡最高的。

若說伍迪‧艾倫是天生的喜劇演員應該不為過。他和喜劇的關係早在 15 歲就開始了，他那時開始替在百老匯表演的喜劇演員寫笑話，在 1955 年他 20 歲時，洛杉磯 NBC 電視台的喜劇節目雇用他為全職作家，他為許多喜劇秀寫劇本。自此之後，他一直是位多產的作家，寫下眾多電視節目腳本，短篇故事，喜劇小說和電影劇本。在 1960 年代，他的才華延伸到單人脫口秀，他在曼哈頓的夜間俱樂部表演。在 1965 年，艾倫有了他個人的電視節目：伍迪‧艾倫秀，此時他成為全國知名的人物。

艾倫的電影的普遍主題，即諷刺地反映人生的荒謬之處，可以追溯至他早期的作品。他的笑話是依據每個人都能感同身受的日常事件，但是以非常嚴肅和神經質的表達方式演出。神經質的角色之後成為他電影的特色。在他的單人脫口秀，他經常諷刺知識份子，並將獨白轉化成對當代文化現象的嘲諷批評。

ch.4

ch.5
西洋藝術與科學類型

ch.6

Unit ㉘ 科學類

火星真的適合居住嗎？Is Mars Really Habitable?

請先閱讀一短文與題目

Summarize the main points in the reading and the lecture, indicating how the reading casts doubt on the lecture.

The public's interest in Mars was revived in 2015, with the release of the sci-fi movie, *The Martian*, starring Matt Damon. The technologies the protagonist utilized on Mars are highly endorsed by the scientific community, thus leaving many viewers convinced of prospective human habitation on Mars. At least, NASA is optimistic of sending astronauts to Mars in the 2030s at the earliest.

There is a high probability that during our grandchildren's era, humans will have developed sufficient technologies to begin a colony on Mars. The most exciting discovery is that lots of water exist on Mars. The terrain on Mars looks like a desert, yet it's not. The soil there comprises about 60% of water, and ice abound in lots of craters, as well as underground water. Thus, the water is sufficient for developing the first human colony; we just need to find the alternative energy and develop new technologies to obtain it.

Furthermore, there is the fundamental issue of how humans will acquire oxygen. In fact, a technology called electrolysis is already applicable to generating oxygen on Mars. According to NASA, the rover they will send to Mars in 2020 will carry a device that carries out electrolysis — absorbing Martian air and separating oxygen from carbon dioxide. Moreover, scientists have devised terraforming methods to thicken the Martian atmosphere in order to protect humans from radiation. NASA is conducting a project on a solar sail, which functions as gigantic mirrors to reflect solar radiation to heat up dry ice on Mars, subliming it, releasing carbon dioxide, and thickening the atmosphere.

請聽與短文相關的課堂內容　▶ Track 31

Now listen to a lecture in an astronomy class regarding Mars.

(Professor)There has been a consensus in the astronomers' community that eventually humans will have to move off the planet perhaps in the next 200 years, if not in the next 100 years. Sci-fi films in recent years, such as *The Martian* and *Interstellar*, seem to boost the public's confidence in interstellar exploration. However, is it realistic to envisage a rosy picture of life on Mars? Are we too sanguine about the prospect of migrating to Mars? In my opinion,

Mars is not habitable for humans, which is not hard to grasp if one takes into account the relevant scientific facts.

First, consider the essential element for our survival, that is, oxygen. The air on Mars is simply poisonous for humans. Carbon dioxide makes up an extremely high ratio of the atmosphere on Mars; in fact, it is as high as 95%. Secondly, although water has been found, remember that one of the main energy sources on the Earth comes from photosynthesis, meaning that sunlight is indispensable if our survival there is based on the hypothesis that future scientific technologies will be capable of transforming Mars into an earth-like planet. Nevertheless, liquid water is found only underground, definitely indicating that there is no sunlight for photosynthesis, and hence there is the lack of this crucial energy source. This is not to say that no life would possibly exist on Mars. In fact, primitive organisms that do not rely on photosynthesis might very well exist on Mars.

Thirdly, even if future technologies allow us to utilize other sources of energy, for instance, hydrogen gas, humans still have to tackle the harsh fact of little or even no ozone layer. It goes without saying that without the protection of an ozone layer, the level of radiation on Mars is lethal. Therefore, given the present technologies, I believe that human survival on Mars is a far-fetched idea, which only remains in the realm of sci-fi fiction.

高分範文搶先看　▶ Track 32

The major points in the reading and listening passages contradict one another in terms of the fundamental issues humans will need to tackle with considering prospective habitation on Mars.

First, the critical issue of how to attain oxygen is addressed in both passages. The reading points out that NASA has already devised a process called electrolysis that breaks down carbon dioxide and emits oxygen. On the contrary, the lecture simply describes that the atmosphere on Mars consists of a high proportion of carbon dioxide.

Next, as for how humans will obtain water, the reading describes various sources of water, from water in soil, underground water, to ice in craters. In contrast, the lecture merely focuses on

閱讀篇章和聽力講述篇章的重點互相駁斥，這些重點是關於人類未來居住在火星上必須處理的基本議題。

首先，兩個篇章都針對如何取得氧氣這個重要議題做出描述。閱讀篇章指出 NASA 已經研發出一個稱為電解的程序，能分解二氧化碳並排放氧氣。相反地，課堂講述只是描述火星的大氣層包含高比率的二氧化碳。

此外，關於人類如何取得水，閱讀篇章描述各式各樣的水資源，包括土壤裡的水，地下水和火山口的冰。反之，課堂講述僅著重地下液態水，且另外指出由於液態水的地質位

underground liquid water, adding that due to its geological location, photosynthesis will not be possible, and thus there will be no energy from photosynthesis.

Lastly, whereas the lecture states that humans will not survive on Mars due to the lack of an ozone layer, the reading raises a new technology called solar sail, which will thicken the ozone layer and protect humans from solar radiation.

置，不可能進行光合作用，因此就不會有來自光合作用的能源。

最後，課堂講述提出因為缺少臭氧層，人類無法在火星生存，而閱讀篇章提出一個稱為太陽帆的新科技，能增加臭氧層厚度，並保護人類不被陽光輻射傷害。

高分範文解析

關鍵句 1 ▶

In contrast, the lecture merely focuses on underground liquid water, adding that due to its location, photosynthesis will not be possible, and thus there will be no energy from photosynthesis.

解析

此例句中的分詞片語 adding that... from photosynthesis 是由對等子句 and (the lecture) adds that ... 簡化而來。動詞 add 的受詞是 that 引導的名詞子句。

關鍵句 2

Lastly, whereas the lecture states that humans will not survive on Mars due to the lack of an ozone layer, the reading raises a new technology called solar sail, which will thicken the ozone layer and protect humans from solar radiation.

解析

whereas 是連接兩句意義相反的子句的連接詞，此單元的閱讀篇章和課堂講述篇章各有三個互相駁斥的重點，故採取點對點的答題結構。例句整合兩個篇章的重點之一：火星臭氧層對人類造成的影響。第一個子句的主要動詞 state 的受詞是 that 引導的名詞子句；第二個子句包含非限定形容詞子句，修飾先行詞 solar sail。因為 solar sail 是專有名詞，不須要限定，非限定形容詞子句的關係代名詞不能使用 that，且在關係代名詞之前要逗號。

● 閱讀短文中譯

　　請總結閱讀短文和課堂講述的重點，並解釋閱讀短文如何駁斥課堂講述。

　　隨著麥特・戴蒙主演的科幻片《火星救援》在 2015 年上映，大眾又興起了對火星的興趣。此片主角在火星上使用的科技受到科學家社群肯定，讓許多觀眾相信人類未來能移居火星。至少 NASA 對派遣太空人到火星是樂觀的，他們最快於 2030 年代能成行。

　　很有可能在我們的孫子的年代，人類就已經發展足夠的科技能開始在火星殖民。最讓人興奮的發現是火星上有很多水。火星的地形看似沙漠，事實上不是。那裏的土壤成分有 60%是水，而且火山口充滿著冰，那裏也有地下水。因此，有足夠的水能讓我們建立第一個人類殖民地。我們只是需要另外找尋能源及發展新科技去取得那些水。

此外，基本的議題是人類如何獲得氧氣。事實上，稱為電解的科技已經能被應用在火星上產生氧氣。根據 NASA 的說法，他們在 2020 年要送到火星的探測車將裝載進行電解的設備一能吸收火星上的空氣並將氧氣從二氧化碳分離。而且，科學家已經研發出將火星環境地球化的方法，能加厚火星的大氣層以保護人類不被輻射線傷害。NASA 正進行一項陽光帆（又譯：陽光反射器）的計畫，它的作用像巨大的鏡子，能反射太陽輻射以加熱火星上的冰，使冰昇華，釋放二氧化碳，並加厚大氣層。

◉ 課堂講述中譯

現在請聽一篇關於火星的天文學課堂講述。

在天文學家的社群已經有共識，最終人類必須離開地球，這可能在未來兩百年內發生，就算不是在未來一百年內。近年來的科幻片，例如《火星救援》和《星際效應》，似乎加強了大眾對星際探險的信心。但是，將未來在火星的生活想像成美好的是實際的嗎？我們對遷移到火星是否太過樂觀？我認為火星不適合人類居住，如果一個人考慮相關的科學事實，就知道這不難理解。

首先，考慮我們生存所需的基本元素：氧氣。火星上的空氣基本上對人類是有毒的。二氧化碳佔了大氣層極高的比率，事實上，高達 95%。第二，雖然已經發現水了，記得地球上主要的能源之一是來自光合作用，意即陽光是不可缺少的，如果我們在火星能生存是根據未來科技的假説，那種科技能將火星轉化成類似地球的星球。然而，液態水只存在於地表下，當然那裏沒有陽光能進行光合作用，因此就缺乏了這項重要的能源。這並不是説生命在火星不可能存在。事實上，不須依賴光合作用的原始生物很有可能存在於火星。

第三，就算未來科技能讓我們利用其他能源，例如氫氣，人類仍需要處理稀薄的臭氧層，甚至缺乏臭氧層的嚴重問題。可想見沒有臭氧層的保護，火星上的輻射程度是致命的。因此，考慮到目前的科技，我相信人類在火星上生存是太過牽強的想法，而且這個想法只存在於科幻小説的領域。

Unit ㉙ 科學類
CRISPR 基因剪輯技術和其爭議 CRISPR Technology and Its Controversy

請先閱讀一短文與題目

Summarize the main points in the reading and the lecture, indicating how the lecture casts doubt on the reading.

CRISPR-Cas9 is a revolutionary genetic engineering technology that allows scientists to edit genomes with high precision and efficiency. The technology was co-invented in the early 2010s by Jennifer Doudna and Emmanuelle Charpentier, the former a professor of chemistry and cell biology at the University of California, Berkeley and the latter a French microbiologist. CRISPR, which is pronounced as "crisper", and stands for "Clustered Regularly Interspaced Short Palindromic Repeats", basically refers to a group of molecules that scientists can use to edit DNA. Cas-9 is an enzyme that functions as scissors. Simply put, the ground-breaking technology works like the cut and paste functions in word processing software, allowing scientists to cut a strand of DNA and insert another strand of DNA to replace the original one. Equally unprecedented as the technology is the fact that when it is applied on embryos, the genetic changes will be inherited, meaning that scientists now have the technology to change an entire germline.

The exciting technology sheds light on prospective improvement of human genome. The most positive application of CRISPR is medical. With CRISPR, fixing a defective gene is fast and easy. For example, patients with cystic fibrosis, a genetic disease that affects lungs and other organs, might be treated by having their defective gene repaired. Theoretically, cancer can also be treated with the same process. Likewise, genes that cause dementia or obesity can be taken out or modified. If the application is realized, millions of patients will be spared from suffering and billions of dollars of medical costs will be saved.

請聽與短文相關的課堂內容　▶ Track 33

Now listen to a lecture in a biology class regarding CRISPR.

(Professor)When scientists Jennifer Doudna and Emmanuelle Charpentier published their study on gene editing using CRISPR-Cas9 in the journal Science in 2012, their invention overwhelmed the genetic engineering community. There is virtually no organism that scientists cannot apply CRISPR to; so far, there have been experiments on rats, monkeys, flies, and baker's yeast. In 2015, some Chinese scientists used it on non-viable human embryos, with an attempt to edit a gene which caused certain mutation.

It's not hard to imagine that waves of controversies soon arose, especially those concerning ethical issues. Unlike any preceding genetic engineering technology, using CRISPR-Cas9 to edit genes in embryos will generate a long-lasting and unprecedented impact on a whole species, since altered genes will be inherited through generations. I would foresee that CRISPR-Cas9 will open up a Pandora's box of unexpected consequences should scientists modify the genes of human embryos disregarding ethical codes.

The controversies and lack of a global ethical protocol led the co-inventor, Doudna, to urge a pause worldwide on experimenting with alternation on human embryos with CRISPR. So, what is the main controversy in terms of bioethics? Notice that CRISPR-Cas9 not only can repair defective genes, but also strengthen genes. Even if the technology is utilized to fix genes that cause genetic disorders, we must ask who will have access to the therapeutic treatment. The possibility cannot be ruled out that only the wealthy will afford this treatment, and will that make our society more stratified when the health of our offspring becomes a privilege? On the other hand, the technology will very likely be utilized to enhance genes, which presents huge profits for the biotech industry, so in the future, "designer babies" might be created. For instance, parents will demand that their unborn children be designed for certain talents by enhancing related genes, such as those influencing athletic capability and linguistic ability. Or gene editing might be used to design appearances, for example, eye color and hair color.

高分範文搶先看 ▶ Track 34

Both the reading and the lecture discuss the various applications of the revolutionary gene-editing technology, CRISPR-Cas9. While the reading focuses on the positive application, the lecture raises doubts regarding this technology from an ethical perspective.

The reading first gives an introduction to the background of the invention of CRISPR-Cas9. Working like the cut and paste functions in word processing software, CRISPR-Cas9 enables scientists to edit genes precisely and efficiently. Besides, the reading describes how the medical application of this technology will benefit patients with genetic diseases and other illness, though it still remains at a theoretical level.

閱讀篇章和課堂講述都討論革命性技術 CRISPR-Cas9 的多重應用。閱讀篇章著重正面應用，然而課堂講述從倫理觀點提出對這項技術的質疑。

閱讀篇章首先介紹發明 CRISPR-Cas9 的背景。就像文書處理軟體的剪下及貼上功能，CRISPR-Cas9 讓科學家能精準地，有效率地編輯基因。此外，閱讀篇章描述醫學方面的應用將如何使有遺傳疾病及其他疾病的病人獲益，雖然醫學應用仍處於理論層次。

Contrary to the reading, the lecture emphasizes the controversies concerning ethical issues. Since edited genes in embryos will be inherited, the professor thinks that in the future, the consequences might be outside of scientific expectations. Even if CRISPR-Cas9 is used to treat genetic diseases, another social issue might arise regarding who will gain access to such treatment. Moreover, using gene editing to strengthen genes might lead to the so-called "designer babies".

與閱讀篇章相反的是，課堂講述著重關於倫理議題的爭議。因為胚胎中被編輯過的基因會遺傳，教授認為在未來，後果可能超出科學家的期待。就算 CRISPR-Cas9 被用來治療遺傳疾病，關於誰能取得這種治療可能引起另一個社會議題。此外，使用基因編輯去加強基因可能導致所謂的「設計師嬰兒」。

高分範文解析

關鍵句 1

Working like the cut and paste functions in word processing software, CRISPR-Cas9 enables scientists to edit genes precisely and efficiently.

解析

句首的分詞片語 Working like ... 修飾主詞 CRISPR-Cas9。主要動詞片語 enable Sb. to V.，讓某人能去做，類似詞：allow Sb. to V.，這兩個片語的語氣都比使役動詞 make Sb. V.正式。

關鍵句 2

Even if CRISPR-Cas9 is used to treat genetic diseases, another social issue might arise regarding who will gain access to such treatment.

解析

此句包括由連接詞 if 導引的從屬子句和主要子句。主要動詞 arise，興起或升起，regarding 在此是介系詞，也可換成 concerning 或 in respect to，語氣比 about 正式。

◉ 閱讀短文中譯

　　請總結閱讀短文和課堂講述的重點，並解釋課堂講述如何對閱讀短文提出質疑。

　　CRISPR-Cas9 基因編輯技術是項革命性的基因工程技術，能讓科學家以高度精準度和效率編輯基因組。這項技術在 2010 年代初期由珍妮佛‧多得娜和伊曼紐‧夏龐蒂埃共同研發，前者是加州大學柏克萊分校的化學及細胞生物學的教授，後者是法裔的微生物學家。CRISPR 發音成 crisper，是「規律成簇的間隔短回文重複」的縮寫，CRISPR 基本上指的是科學家可以用來編輯 DNA 的一組分子。Cas-9 是作用類似剪刀的酵素。簡單來說，這項開創性技術的功能類似文書處理軟體的剪下及貼上功能，能讓科學家剪下一段 DNA 並插入另一段 DNA 以取代之。像這個技術一樣前所未有的是，當它被應用至胚胎，基因改變將會被遺傳，也就是說科學家現在有了技術能改變一整個生殖系。

這項讓人興奮的技術揭示了未來對人類基因組的改善。CRISPR 最正面的應用是醫療方面的應用。利用 CRISPR 修復有瑕疵的基因是快速且簡單的。例如，針對囊性纖維化這種會影響肺部和其他器官的遺傳疾病，可能藉由修復瑕疵基因治療病人。理論上，癌症也能以同樣的過程治療。類似地，導致癡呆症和肥胖症的基因可以被剪下或修改。如果未來醫療應用成真，上百萬的病人將可免於痛苦，且幾十億的醫療成本將能被省下。

◉ 課堂講述中譯

現在請聽一篇關於 CRISPR 的生物學課堂講述。

當科學家珍妮佛‧多得娜和伊曼紐‧夏龐蒂埃在《科學》這份期刊發表他們以 CRISPR-Cas9 進行基因編輯的研究時，他們的發明震撼了基因工程界。幾乎沒有生物是科學家不能應用 CRISPR 這項技術的。目前已經有針對大鼠、猴子、蒼蠅和麵包酵母的實驗。在 2015 年，一些中國科學家將這項技術應用至不能存活的人類胚胎，嘗試修改會導致某種突變的基因。

不難想像一波波的爭議很快興起，尤其是關於倫理議題的爭議。不像任何之前的基因工程技術，使用 CRISPR-Cas9 編輯胚胎的基因將會對一整個物種產生長遠且前所未有的效應，因為被變更的基因將會被世代遺傳。我能預想 CRISPR-Cas9 將來就像打開了潘朵拉的盒子，導致了預期之外的後果，萬一科學家不顧倫理規範修改人類胚胎的基因。

　　這些爭議和缺乏全球化的倫理規範使得共同發明人多得娜呼籲全球暫停使用 CRISPR 進行變更人類胚胎的實驗。所以，關於生物倫理的主要爭議是甚麼呢？要注意的是 CRISPR-Cas9 不只能修復瑕疵基因，也能增強基因。就算這項技術被用來修復導致遺傳疾病的基因，我們必須問誰有管道取得這種療程。只有富人能負擔這種療程的可能性不能被排除，當我們後代的健康變成一種特權，這會讓我們將來的社會階級更分化嗎？另一方面，這項技術很可能被用來增強基因，意謂著將替生物技術產業帶來巨大利潤，所以在未來可能創造出「設計師嬰兒」。例如，父母會要求藉由加強相關基因，替他們未出世的孩子設計某方面的才華，例如那些影響運動能力和語言能力的基因。或者基因編輯可能被用來設計外表，例如眼睛的顏色和髮色。

ch.4

ch.5
西洋藝術與科學類型

ch.6

Unit ㉚ 科學類

玩耍對動物的重要性 The Importance of Play for Animals

請先閱讀一短文與題目

Summarize the main points in the reading and the lecture.

People who have puppies or kittens know very well that they spend significant amount of time on playing. How do we distinguish nonhuman animals' play from actual fighting? How do animals communicate to their playmates so that their partners know their intent is to play?

To answer the above questions, the meaning of play should be clarified first. Basically, play refers to behaviors of mimicking actual hunting, fighting and mating carried out by adults. One way to distinguish play from the aforementioned adult behaviors is to observe that when young animals engage in play, their mimicking behaviors do not exhibit fixed sequences; in other words, they are performed and combined randomly. Another sign of play is that these behaviors are less intense compared with adult behaviors.

As for communicating to their partners to initiate play, animals use facial expressions and gestures to send out signals. Take dogs for example, dogs are in the mood for play when their facial expressions are placid and mild, with their mouths slightly open, which many dog owners describe as a "smile". Canines, including dogs, wolves, and coyotes, all employ the gesture of "play bow" to signal to their playmates. It is worth noting that "play bow" is exclusive to canines. Their front limbs stand firm, heads duck quickly, and hind limbs kick up. Besides facial expressions and gestures, dogs even signal verbally. The verbal signal is their panting noise in play, which has a different frequency from the frequency of panting when they are not playing.

請聽與短文相關的課堂內容　▶ Track 35

Now listen to a lecture in a biology class regarding animal play.

(Professor)In today's lecture, we are going to cover more details concerning the play of young animals. In particular, how many types of animal play have biologists discerned so far? And what are the benefits? The first type is locomotor play. As the word locomotor implies, this type of play strengthens muscle and physical coordination. The second type is predatory play, in which animals stalk and swoop upon playmates to mimic hunting behaviors. Even birds, such as falcons, crows, and swallows, engage in predatory play; they drop tiny objects from above and descend rapidly to catch those objects.

The third type is object play, which is often played solitarily and combined with predatory play, though not always. For instance, primates, due to their adroitness, play with various objects in a similar way as human children do. Primates have been proven to demonstrate their imagination in object play. In research, a chimpanzee having been trained to use sign language placed a purse on his foot, and gave the sign for "shoe". The fourth type is social play, which allows animals to form friendship, learn cooperation, and mimic adult competitive behaviors without acting violent.

Regarding the benefits of play, I would like to focus on the effects on the brain, since you already know that play is crucial in developing muscle and coordination. Emotionally, play just makes animals feel relaxed and less stressed. They touch one another the most when playing, and touching stimulates a chemical in the brain called opiate, which generates a soothing feeling. Moreover, play enhances neuron connections in the brain. The stronger neuron connections are, the more efficiently brains function, which makes animals more intelligent. For mammals, play even helps remove superfluous brain cells, and prepares their brains to function more efficiently during adulthood. To sum up, there are at least four areas that play exerts positive effects on: physical, social, emotional, and intelligent areas.

高分範文搶先看　▶ Track 36

Both the reading and the lecture concern the theme of animal play. The reading gives the definition of play and describes how animals communicate to one another about their intent to play, and the lecture provides more details regarding the types and benefits of play.

The reading defines animal play as mimicking a variety of adult behaviors. Unlike adult behaviors, young animals' play does not follow any order, and is less violent. Facial expressions and gestures are utilized to communicate to partners to begin playing. Canines are used as an example to illustrate signals of communication. Dogs have a smile-like expression, and all canines display "play bow". A different frequency of panting is

閱讀篇章和課堂講述都是關於動物玩耍的主題。閱讀篇章給了玩耍的定義及描述動物如何彼此溝通關於他們想玩的意圖，而課堂講述提供更多關於玩耍的類型和益處等細節。

閱讀篇章將動物玩耍定義為模仿各式各樣成年行為。不像成年行為，年輕動物的玩耍不按照任何順序，而且比較不暴力。表情和肢體動作被用來向玩伴溝通以開始玩耍。犬類被使用為例子，描繪溝通的訊號。狗有一種類似微笑的表情，而所有犬類都展現「玩耍敬禮」。喘息的不同頻率也是一個跡象。

also an indicator.

The lecture first lists four kinds of plays: locomotor, predatory, object, and social plays. Locomotor play enhances muscular and coordinative movements. Predatory play imitates hunting. Object play, for primates particularly, is similar to human children's play of objects. Social play builds animals' socializing skills. Finally, the benefit of how play stimulates the brain by reinforcing a certain chemical and neuron connections is explained.

課堂講述先列舉四種玩耍：運動、捕食、物體和社交玩耍。運動玩耍加強肌肉和協調動作。捕食玩耍模仿打獵。物體玩耍，尤其對靈長類而言，類似人類小孩玩物體的行為。社交玩耍建立動物的社交技巧。最後解釋玩耍如何藉由增強某種化學物質及神經細胞連結，以刺激頭腦的這個益處。

高分範文解析

關鍵句 1

Facial expressions and gestures are utilized to communicate to partners to begin playing.

解析

句型的豐富度是評分重點之一，應輪流使用主動和被動語態的句型。此句是被動語態，動詞 utilize 比 use 語氣更正式。被動語態的主要動詞是 be 動詞搭配過去分詞 is explained。

關鍵句 2

Finally, the benefit of how play stimulates the brain by reinforcing a certain chemical and neuron connections is explained.

解析

此句是被動語態句型，介系詞 of 之後的受詞是由 how 引導的名詞子句。reinforcing 是動名詞，以搭配介系詞 by。

◉ 閱讀短文中譯

請總結閱讀短文和課堂講述的重點。

有養幼犬或幼貓的人一定知道他們花很多時間玩耍。我們要如何區分非人類的動物是在玩耍，還是實際在打架呢？動物是如何跟玩伴們溝通，讓玩伴知道他們想玩耍的意圖呢？

要回答以上的問題，玩耍的定義應該先被釐清。基本上，玩耍指的是模仿成年動物實際打獵、打鬥和交配的行為。一個區分上述成年行為和玩耍的方式是去觀察當幼年動物玩耍，他們的模仿行為沒有固定的順序；也就是說他們是任意地表現和結合這些行為。另一個跡象是這些行為比起成年行為沒那麼激烈。

關於如何和玩伴們溝通以開始玩耍，動物利用表情和肢體動作傳送訊息。以狗為例，當他們的表情冷靜溫和，嘴巴稍微張開，就是準備好玩耍，許多狗主人將這個表情描述為「微笑」。犬類，包括狗、狼和郊狼，都使用「玩耍敬禮」這個肢體動作傳送訊息給玩伴。值得注意的是「玩耍敬禮」是犬類獨特有的行為。他們的前腿穩穩地站著，縮頸躬身且快速地點頭，後腿向上踢。除了表情和肢體動作，狗甚至會傳送口語訊號。口語訊號指的是他們玩耍時發出的喘氣聲，這種喘氣聲的頻率和不是在玩耍時的喘氣聲的頻率是不同的。

◉ 課堂講述中譯

現在請聽一篇關於動物玩耍的生物學課堂講述。

今天的講課，我們將涵蓋更多關於年輕動物玩耍的細節。尤其，科學家至目前分析了多少種動物玩耍的類型？玩耍的好處有哪些？第一種類型是運動玩耍。就像運動這個字暗示的，這個類型加強肌肉和身體協調能力。第二種類型是捕食玩耍，玩耍當中動物會尾隨並突然襲擊玩伴，這是在模仿打獵行為。甚至鳥類，例如獵鷹、烏鴉和燕子，也會進行捕食玩耍。他們會從高處丟下小型物體，然後快速下降去抓那些物體。

　　第三個類型是物體玩耍，常常是獨自進行並和捕食玩耍合併，雖然不見得總是這樣。例如，由於靈長類的肢體靈巧，他們玩各種物體的方式和人類小孩玩耍的方式是類似的。在進行物體玩耍時，靈長類已經被證實會展現想像力。在一個研究中，一隻曾受過手語訓練的黑猩猩將一個皮包放在腳上，並比出「鞋子」的手語。第四個類型是社交玩耍，讓動物建立友誼，學習合作，並模仿成年競爭性的行為，但不會展現暴力。

　　關於玩耍的益處，我想專注在對頭腦的影響，既然你們已經知道玩耍對肌肉發展和協調是重要的。情緒上，玩耍就是讓動物覺得放鬆，比較沒壓力。當玩耍時，他們碰觸彼此最多，而碰觸會刺激腦內一種稱為鴉片類物質的化學物質，這化學物質會產生放鬆的感覺。此外，玩耍加強腦內神經細胞的連結。神經細胞連結越強，頭腦運作地更有效率，這讓動物更聰明。對哺乳類而言，玩耍甚至會幫助清除多餘的腦細胞，讓他們的頭腦為成年時期更高效率的運作做準備。總之，玩耍至少在四個方面發揮正面效應：生理、社交、情緒和智能方面。

Unit ㉛

美國教育類重要句型整理、解析及應用

闡明兩個篇章關係的主旨句（Thesis Statement）重要句型、解析及應用

使用說明

Unit 19 的範文採取點對點結構的寫法，Unit 20 的範文採取面對面結構，但不管是哪一個結構，主文都須要換句話說，所以句型重點都在 **"Paraphrase 換句話說句型"**。個別段落開頭的主題句（**topic sentence**）不如整篇文章的主旨句（**thesis statement**）及換句話說（**paraphrase**）重要，所以只有這個單元有加入主題句的句型討論。

1. 指出兩篇章的關係為論點相反的重要句型為：

   While the reading points out that S+V, the lecture opposes the main idea in the reading by arguing that S+V

解析 1

此句型表達閱讀篇章和課堂講述的論點如何互相抵觸。也可套用在每一段開頭的 **topic sentence**。

應用 1.1

While the reading points out that **the trend has reached its zenith,** the lecture opposes the main idea in the reading by arguing that **U.S. students are not truly enthusiastic about learning Mandarin.** (Part 2 Unit 19)

雖然閱讀篇章指出此趨勢已達到近期的高峰，然而課堂演講反駁閱讀篇章的主題，且宣稱美國學生並非真的熱衷於中文學習。《節選自 Part 2 Unit 19》

應用 1.2

While the reading points out that **more and more American students select Chinese courses,** the lecture opposes the main idea in the reading by arguing that **they are simply restricted by budget cuts on other language courses.**

雖然閱讀篇章指出越來越多美國學生選修中文，然而課堂演講反駁閱讀篇章的主題，宣稱他們只是被別的語言課程預算減縮限制住了。

2. 指出兩篇章的關係為論點相反的重要句型為：

The reading and listening passages present contrasting views of N., with the former focusing on disadvantages and the latter focusing on advantages.

解析 2

此主旨句句型可套用在任何閱讀篇章及課堂講述分別闡述優點及缺點的考

題，唯 **advantages** 及 **disadvantages** 需視情況對調。句尾是 **with** 導引的分詞片語。

應用 2.1

The reading and listening passages present contrasting views of online education, with the former focusing on disadvantages and the latter focusing on advantages. (Part 2 Unit 20)

閱讀篇章及課堂講述呈現對網路課程的相反看法，前者著重缺點而後者著重優點。《節選自 Part 2 Unit 20》

應用 2.2

The reading and listening passages present contrasting views of using avatars in online classroom settings, with the former focusing on disadvantages and the latter focusing on advantages.

閱讀篇章及課堂演講呈現對在網路教室情境中使用虛擬替身的相反看法，前者著重缺點而後者著重優點。

閱讀篇章主要論點──換句話說（Paraphrase）的重要句型、解析及應用

解析 1

考生能否避免抄襲題目篇章裡的單字和句型是整合題型的考試重點之一。應盡量以類似字（**synonyms**）和跟不同的句型結構將主要論點重述。

論點原句

The fad of learning Mandarin has reached an unprecedented climax.

(Part 2 Unit 19)

學習普通話的流行近來達到前所未有的高峰。《節選自 Part 2 Unit 19》

應用-換句話說 1.1

The reading points out that the trend has achieved its zenith. (Part 2 Unit 19)

閱讀篇章指出此趨勢已經達到高峰。《節選自 Part 2 Unit 19》

應用-換句話說 1.2

According to the reading, a peak of Chinese learning craze has been observed.

根據閱讀篇章，中文學習熱潮的高峰近期被注意到。

解析 2

利用詞性轉換將論點原句重述，例如動名詞 **carrying out** 變化成被動語態的動詞 **is carried out**。

論點原句

They might find taking online classes is more like carrying out a monologue without immediate feedbacks from professors and classmates. (Part 2 Unit 20)

他們可能會發現上網路課程比較像是進行一場缺乏教授和同學的立即回應的獨白。《節選自 Part 2 Unit 20》

應用-換句話說 2.1

Students tend to feel that their contribution to online classes is carried out in a one-way direction. (Part 2 Unit 20)

學生通常覺得他們對網路課程的付出是單向的。《節選自 Part 2 Unit 20》

應用-換句話說 2.2

Participating in online classes seems making unilateral efforts.

參與網路課程似乎是做出單方面的付出。

闡明兩個篇章關係的主題句（Topic Sentence）重要句型、解析及應用

3. 詳細解釋兩篇章的論點如何互斥的重要句型為：

The professor rebuts N. mentioned in the reading. He explicates that S+V.

解析 3

與主旨句（**thesis statement**）不同的是，主文每一段開頭的主題句（**topic sentence**）須更詳細解釋兩篇章論點的差異。

應用 3.1

Secondly, the professor rebuts the pervasiveness of the Mandarin learning phenomenon indicated by the "1 Million Strong" initiative mentioned in the reading. He explicates that even after the number of Mandarin learners in the U.S. reaches 1 million, it will be a relatively low percentage, hardly 2% in the entire student population. (Part 2 Unit 19)

第二，教授反駁了閱讀篇章中「百萬強計畫」暗示的學習普通話流行現象。他解釋即使美國的普通話學習者達到一百萬的數量，這仍是相對低的比率，

幾乎勉強達到所有學生人口的 2%。《節選自 Part 2 Unit 19》

應用 3.2

The professor rebuts the high figure of Mandarin learners. He explicates that 2% remains a relatively low figure in the whole student population.

教授反駁了中文學習者的高數據。他解釋 2% 仍是所有學生人口中相對低的數據。

---

4. 解釋兩篇章的論點如何互斥的重要句型為：

The lecture refutes the reading by raising ... It first points out that S+V.

解析 4

先簡短提出主題句（**topic sentence**），再將課堂講述之論點逐一列出。**refute，vt.，**反駁，類似詞有：**rebut**、**contravene**、**dispute**、**argue against**。

應用 4.1

The lecture refutes the reading by raising three advantages. It first points out that online courses allow students not residing in the U.S. to pursue degrees without traveling away from home. (Part 2 Unit 20)

課堂講述提出三個優點駁斥閱讀篇章。它首先指出網路課程讓不住在美國的學生不須離家遠遊就能追求學位。《節選自 Part 2 Unit 20》

應用 4.2

The lecture refutes the reading by raising **three disadvantages.** It first points out that **the accreditation of online universities is difficult to verify.** 課堂講述提出三個缺點駁斥閱讀篇章。它首先指出網路大學的認證是很難去核實的。

課堂講述主要論點──換句話說（Paraphrase）的重要句型、解析及應用

解析 1

整合題型的答題文章類型是 **summary**，因此只須將主要論點重述，應省略次要細節，如人名。

論點原句

Lastly, Hollywood movies reinforce the illusion of Chinese fever by incorporating Chinese actors, such as Jackie Chan and Jet Li, yet I seriously doubt that students are motivated to learn Mandarin by watching their performances, since they still play the stereotype of Chinese reminiscent of Bruce Lee. (Part 2 Unit 19) 最後，好萊塢電影融入中國電影明星，例如成龍和李連杰，加深了中文風潮的不實印象。我嚴重懷疑學生會因為看了這些明星演出，就被激勵出學中文的興趣，因為這些演員扮演的角色，仍是好萊塢對中國人的刻板印象，讓人聯想到李小龍扮演的那種刻板印象。《節選自 Part 2 Unit 19》

應用-換句話說 1.1

The lecture refutes by claiming that those actors play stereotypical roles of Chinese characters. (Part 2 Unit 19)　課堂演講駁斥並主張那些演員擔任的仍是刻板印象的中國角色。《節選自 Part 2 Unit 19》

應用-換句話說 1.2

The lecture offers rebuttal that only stereotypes of Chinese are presented in movies.　課堂講述提供駁斥指出只有華人的刻板印象被電影呈現。

解析 2 ▶

論點原句裡瑣碎的細節應省略，如 **facial expressions and gestures**。

論點原句

In the virtual world of Second Life, users create their avatars, representative figures of their identities, and interact with one another via abundant facial expressions and gestures simulated by their avatars. (Part 2 Unit 20)　在第二人生的虛擬世界裡，使用者創造他們的替身，即代表他們身份的角色，並透過虛擬出的豐富表情和手勢彼此互動。《節選自 Part 2 Unit 20》

應用-換句話說 2.1

Next, the lecture draws on the example of virtual classrooms on Second Life to explain that vibrant interaction ... can be enhanced. (Part 2 Unit 20)　其次，課堂講述引用位於第二人生的虛擬教室為例，解釋活潑的互動能被加強。《節選自 Part 2 Unit 20》

應用-換句話說 2.2

Interactions that are close to real life can be achieved by using avatars.　近似現實生活的互動可利用替身達成。

Unit **32**

美國歷史類重要句型整理、解析及應用

將閱讀篇章的主要論點換句話說（Paraphrase）的重要句型、解析及應用

使用說明

Unit 21 的範文採取面對面結構，以及 **Unit 22** 的範文採取點對點結構，但不管是哪一個結構，主文都須要換句話說，所以句型重點都在 **"Paraphrase 換句話說句型"**。

解析 1

除了以類似字（**synonyms**）將主要論點重述。最佳的 **paraphrase** 應變化原句的結構，且保留大部分的原意。例如 **although S+V** 轉換為 **despite N** 或 **in spite of N**。

論點原句

Though hippies were sometimes criticized for their use of drugs, they indeed made significant contributions to the American society. (Part 2 Unit 21)

雖然嬉皮有時因為使用毒品而被批評，他們的確對美國社會做出重要貢獻。

《節選自 Part 2 Unit 21》

應用-換句話說 1.1

The culture of the hippies left a positive legacy despite occasional criticism of their drug usage. (Part 2 Unit 21) 嬉皮文化留下正面的文化遺產，儘管偶爾有對他們使用毒品的批評。《節選自 Part 2 Unit 21》

應用-換句話說 1.2

In spite of some comments on their taking drugs, the hippies influenced the American society in critical ways. 儘管有些針對他們吸食毒品的評論，嬉皮對美國社會產生重大影響。

解析 2

考生能否辨別關鍵資訊（主要論點）和次要資訊（瑣碎細節）是整合題型的考點之一。次要資訊，如數字，答題時可省略。技巧：同一個字的詞性轉換。例如 end 是動詞也是名詞，原句 ended N. 轉換成 put an end to N。

論點原句

Political reforms were administered, notably the new constitutional amendments. The 13th Amendment to the Constitution officially ended slavery, and the 15th Amendment offered the equal right to vote to all citizens. (Part 2 Unit 22)

政治改革被執行，值得注意的是新的憲法修正案。第十三號修正案正式終結奴隸制度，而第十五號修正案提供所有公民平等的投票權。《節選自 Part 2 Unit 22》

應用-換句話說 2.1

In terms of political reforms, the reading emphasizes that

Amendments to the Constitution legalized equal voting rights for all citizens and put an end to slavery. (Part 2 Unit 22) 在政治改革上，閱讀篇章強調憲法修正案將所有公民的平等投票權法制化，並終結奴隸制度。《節選自 Part 2 Unit 22》

應用-換句話說 2.2

Politically, the new constitutional amendments outlawed slavery and affirmed all citizens' equity of voting rights.

政治上，新的憲法修正案明文制定奴隸制度為非法，並確認所有公民投票權的平等狀態。

解析 3

技巧：同時使用詞性轉換和類似詞換句話說。例如 **helped foster...** 改寫為 **was influential in raising...**。動詞轉換成 **be** 動詞 + 形容詞。

論點原句

Last but not least, their most long-lasting legacy was raising the awareness of how humans impacted nature. Hippies' emphasis on green energy helped foster the green awareness. (Part 2 Unit 21) 最後，他們對後代影響最深的貢獻是提高人類如何影響大自然的意識。嬉皮對節約能源的重視協助培養了環保意識。《節選自 Part 2 Unit 21》

應用-換句話說 3.1

Most crucially, hippies emphasized being friendly with the Earth, and their attitude was influential in raising subsequent awareness of environmental protection. (Part 2 Unit 21)

最重要的是，嬉皮強調對地球友善，他們的態度對之後提升環保意識有所影響。《節選自 Part 2 Unit 21》

應用-換句話說 3.2

Hippies' profound influence is helping to publicize the consciousness of protecting the Earth.

嬉皮深遠的影響是協助讓環保意識普及化。

解析 4

原句的重點字是 **education**，所以省略次要資訊，例如 **the Federal government and charitable organizations**。

論點原句

Education programs for freed slaves were initiated by the Federal government and charitable organizations. (Part 2 Unit 22)

聯邦政府和慈善機構開始提供教育課程給被解放的黑奴。《節選自 Part 2 Unit 22》

應用-換句話說 4.1

The reading mentions that education was provided for freed slaves. (Part 2 Unit 22)

閱讀篇章提到被解放的奴隸曾被提供教育。《節選自 Part 2 Unit 22》

應用-換句話說 4.2

Emancipated slaves attended classes especially designed for them。

被解放的奴隸參加特別為他們設計的課程。

將課堂講述的主要論點換句話說（Paraphrase）的重要句型整理、解析及應用

解析 1

技巧：主動語態和被動語態互相轉換。例如 **... were maintained by...** 改寫成 **... followed ...**。

論點原句

The influence of hippies was magnified by the media. ... Conventional lifestyles were maintained by most young Americans, who continued their parents' middle-class culture. (Part 2 Unit 21)

嬉皮的影響力被媒體誇大了。……大部分美國年輕人維持了傳統的生活風格，也延續了他們父母的中產階級文化。《節選自 Part 2 Unit 21》

應用-換句話說 1.1

The media at that time enlarged the influence of the hippie movement; the truth was that most American youths still followed a traditional lifestyle.

當時的媒體將嬉皮運動的影響力放大了；事實上大部分的美國青年仍然遵循傳統生活方式。(Part 2 Unit 21)。《節選自 Part 2 Unit 21》

應用-換句話說 1.2

Hippies' influence was exaggerated by the media. Traditions and bourgeois culture were observed by most young Americans. 嬉皮的影響被媒體誇大了。傳統及中產階級文化被大部分年輕美國人遵循。

解析 2

threat 的類似字：**intimidation**。並轉換詞性，例如 **a more hostile environment** 改寫成 **more hostility**。

論點原句

Their living condition was worsened by the violent threats from a racist group called the KKK ... Socially, freed slaves had to face a more hostile environment ... (Part 2 Unit 22) 他們的生活因為暴力威脅每下愈況，威脅來自三 K 黨這個種族歧視的團體。在社會上，被解放的奴隸必須面對充斥更多敵意的環境。《節選自 Part 2 Unit 22》

應用-換句話說 2.1

The lecture contends that freed slaves faced more hostility due to the violent intimidation from the KKK, a racist group. (Part 2 Unit 22) 課堂講述主張被解放的奴隸因為種族歧視團體三 K 黨的暴力威脅，而面對更多敵意。《節選自 Part 2 Unit 22》

應用-換句話說 2.2

Threatened by the KKK, emancipated slaves confronted more animosity. 被三 K 黨威脅之下，被解放的奴隸面對更多敵意。

解析 3

運用詞性轉換將關鍵字換句話說，如 **being true to oneself** 改寫為 **individualism**。類似詞：**prevalent** 及 **popular**。

論點原句

Hippies' insistence on individualism paradoxically caused their preference to live in groups ... Although the core of their philosophy is being true to oneself, they prefer living in communities known as communes where psychedelic drugs and casual sex became more available. (Part 2 Unit 21)

嬉皮對個人主義的堅持矛盾地導致他們偏好團體生活的形式…雖然他們的理念核心是忠於自我，他們偏好住在被稱為公社的社區，而迷幻藥和隨意性愛在公社更容易取得。《節選自 Part 2 Unit 21》

應用-換句話說 3.1

Hippies acted against their own philosophy of individualism, since they preferred living in communes where casual sex and drug usage became more prevalent. (Part 2 Unit 21)

嬉皮的行為牴觸他們對個人主義的理念，因為他們偏好住在團體公社裡，且在公社隨意性愛和使用毒品的現象更普遍。《節選自 Part 2 Unit 21》

應用-換句話說 3.2

Although hippies insisted on individualism, their preference of residence was communes where drugs and casual sex became more popular. 雖然嬉皮堅持個人主義，他們居住的偏好卻是集體公社，在那裡隨意性愛和毒品更流行。

解析 4

類 似 詞：**boost the economy**、**enhance prosperity** 及 **thrive**。
compose、**constitute** 及 **occupy**。

論點原句

New industries, like steel, did not boost the economy since they composed a minor percentage, compared with agriculture. (Part 2 Unit 22)

新產業，像是鋼鐵業，無法刺激經濟，因為跟農業相比的話，新產業只占少部分。《節選自 Part 2 Unit 22》

應用-換句話說 4.1

New industries did not enhance prosperity, since they did not occupy most of the southern economy. (Part 2 Unit 22) 新產業並未促進繁榮，因為它們不是占了南方經濟的大部分。《節選自 Part 2 Unit 22》

應用-換句話說 4.2

The economy didn't thrive with the emergence of new industries which constituted a small portion of the economy. 經濟並未隨著新產業出現而繁榮，新產業只佔經濟的一小部分。

Unit ㉝

美國文學類重要句型整理、解析及應用

闡明兩個篇章關係的主旨句（Thesis Statement）重要句型、解析及應用

使用說明

Unit 23、24 的範文都採取點對點結構的寫法，所以句型重點都在 **Integrating** 整合句。**Conclusion** 在整合題型比起 **Paraphrase** 沒那麼重要，其實是可有可無，不是主要的評分重點，所以只有這個單元有。

---

1. 指出兩篇章的關聯性為論點類似的重要句型為：

The lecture points out ... that share the characteristics of ... in the reading.

解析 1

主要動詞 **points out** 之後的受詞可視文章重點改為 **arguments**、**viewpoints** 或 **features**。注意整合題的兩篇章會各提出至少三個論點，因此受詞應該是複數。

應用 1.1

The lecture points out some characteristics of *The Adventures of Huckleberry Finn* that share the characteristics of regionalism mentioned in the reading. (Part 2 Unit 23)

課堂講述指出數個《哈克歷險記》的特色，跟閱讀篇章提到的區域主義特色是一樣的。《節選自 Part 2 Unit 23》

應用 1.2

The main points raised by the professor are similar to the main features of regionalism in the reading.

教授提出的重點跟閱讀篇章提到的區域主義主要特色是類似的。

---

2. 指出兩篇章主要論點相反的重要句型為：

The reading and lecture delineate the contrary styles of N1 and N2.

解析 2 ▶

在第一段開門見山指出閱讀篇章和課堂講述提到的兩種文體特色是相反的。若閱讀篇章和課堂講述的內容是相反意見或不同的理論，則將 **styles** 改寫為 **opinions** 或 **theories**。

應用 2

The reading and lecture delineate the contrary styles of utopian and dystopian literature by depicting the representative works and various traits of both literary genres. (Part 2 Unit 24)

閱讀篇章及課堂講述藉由描寫烏托邦及反烏托邦兩種文學類型的代表作品和其特色，勾勒出兩種相反的風格。《節選自 Part 2 Unit 24》

應用 2.1

The reading and lecture delineate the contrary opinions of Darwinism and Catholic theology regarding the evolution of creatures.

閱讀篇章及課堂講述描寫達爾文理論和天主教神學對生物演化的相反看法。

整合句（Integrating）重要句型、解析及應用

> 1. 在主文（**main body**）中，詳細整合兩個篇章類似的次要論點的重要句型為：
> S+V, corresponding to N.

解析 1 ▶

表呼應或符合的動詞片語 **correspond to**。或視上下文套用以下片語：**the same as..., share similar features, which is the same ...**

應用 1

Also, the novel was published after the Civil War, corresponding to the period of this literary style mentioned in the reading. (Part 2 Unit 23)

此外，這本小說在南北戰爭後出版，符合閱讀篇章提及的此文學風格的時期。《節選自 Part 2 Unit 23》

應用 1.1

The novel was published in the late 19ᵗʰ century, which was the same period when regionalist novels became popular as pointed out in the reading.

這本小說在十九世紀末期出版，跟閱讀篇章指出的區域主義小說流行的時期是一致的。

2. 在主文（main body）中，將相反的細節整合的重要句型為：
Whereas S1+V1, S2+V2.

解析 2

Whereas *conj.*，反之，連接意義相反的兩個子句。可放句首或兩個子句中間。

應用 2

Whereas utopia is a deliberately invented word with its origins in Greek, meaning an ideal place or a place that doesn't exist, a dystopia is an atrocious place contrary to utopia. (Part 2 Unit 24)

烏托邦是一個刻意被創造出的字，源自希臘文，意為理想的地方或不存在之地，相反地，反烏托邦是個險惡之地。《節選自 Part 2 Unit 24》

應用 2.1

Whereas scientists believe in evolution, Catholics believe in the Genesis in the Bible.

科學家相信演化論，反之，天主教徒相信聖經裡的創世紀。

整合句（Integrating）重要句型、解析及應用

> **3. 整合兩個篇章類似的次要論點的重要句型為**
> The theme... echoes...as presented in the reading

解析 3

表呼應的動詞：**reflect**、**echo** 及 **correspond to**。注意此句型的分詞片語是以過去分詞 **presented** 表達被動，如同在閱讀中呈現。

應用 3.1

The theme of the novel, that is, criticism of slavery, echoes one of the reasons that regionalism burgeoned as presented in the reading, the abolition of slavery. (Part 2 Unit 23)

小說的主題，即對奴隸制度的批評，呼應了閱讀篇章指出的區域主義急速發展的理由，其中之一即廢除奴隸制度。《節選自 Part 2 Unit 23》

應用 3.2

The theme of the novel reflects people's anxiety in response to the Industrial Revolution as presented in the reading.

這本小說的主題呼應了人們對工業革命的焦慮，如同閱讀篇章呈現的。

4. 整合相反細節的重要句型為：

In contrast to the features of N1, the features of N2 include...

解析 4

In contrast to 類似片語有 **on the contrary to**、**as opposed to**。**features** 視篇章細節可改寫為 **details**、**theories**，或 **phenomena** 等。

應用 4.1

Third, in contrast to the features of a utopia, such as encouragement of independent thoughts, equal status for all citizens, and a government without obvious hierarchy, the features of a dystopia include the government's dictatorial oppression of citizens, lack of equality, and abolishment of individual freedom. (Part 2 Unit 24)

第三，反烏托邦的特色包含政府對公民的獨裁壓迫，缺乏平等及剝奪個人自由，這些與烏托邦的特色相反，如鼓勵獨立思考、公民均享平等，及沒有明顯階級的政府。《節選自 Part 2 Unit 24》

應用 4.2

In contrast to millions of years of evolution, the Genesis states that God created the world in seven days.

相較於數百萬年的演化，創世紀宣稱上帝在七天內創造世界。

結論（Conclusions）重要句型、解析及應用

> ## 1. 表達總結兩篇章互相支持關係的重要句型為：
> The characteristics summarized above demonstrate that S+V

解析 1

整合題型不一定要寫結論句，結論句只需重述兩篇章的關係是互相支持或反對，類似主旨句。或換句話說：**The features explained above prove that S+V**

應用 1.1

The characteristics summarized above demonstrate that the novel carries regionalist style. (Part 2 Unit 23)

以上總結的特色證明這本小說屬於區域主義風格。《節選自 Part 2 Unit 23》

應用 1.2

The features explained above prove that the novel belongs to the genre of postmodernism.

以上解釋的特色證明這本小說屬於後現代主義類型。

2. 表達兩個篇章的主要論點有明顯差異的結論句重要句型為：

In conclusion, the dissimilar characteristics of N1 and N2 are discussed.

解析 2

dissimilar 可換成類似字 **discrepant** 或 **divergent**。若兩個篇章都有舉出例證，句尾再加上分詞片語 **supported by the examples of N.**

應用 2.1

In conclusion, the dissimilar characteristics of utopia and dystopia are discussed, supported by the renowned works from both genres. (Part 2 Unit 24)

總而言之，烏托邦和反烏托邦的差異特色皆被討論，並以兩種文學類型的知名作品作為佐證。《節選自 Part 2 Unit 24》

應用 2.2

In conclusion, the dissimilar characteristics of evolution and the Genesis are discussed.

總而言之，演化論和創世紀的差異特色皆被討論。

Unit ㉞

西洋藝術類重要句型整理、解析及應用

闡明兩個篇章關係的主旨句（Thesis Statement）重要句型、解析及應用

使用說明

Unit 25、26 的範文都採取面對面結構，所以句型重點都在**"Paraphrase 換句話說句型"**。

---

1. **指出兩篇章的主題為學說及相關佐證的重要句型為：**

   The lecture outlines N, while the reading focuses on N.

解析 1

當閱讀和聽力兩個篇章的內容並非主要論點互相支持或反對，而是其中一個篇章介紹某一理論或學派，另一個篇章舉出相關的例證或知名人物時，可在答題第一段套用此句型。

應用 1.1

The lecture outlines the history of graffiti from its earliest origin to its recent development in the U.S., while the reading focuses on Keith Haring's artworks and his contributions. (Part 2 Unit 25) 課堂講述勾勒塗鴉的歷史，從最早的起源至近期在美國的發展，而閱讀篇章著重凱斯‧哈林的作品和貢獻。《節選自 Part 2 Unit 25》

應用 1.2

The lecture outlines the Renaissance, while the reading focuses on Leonardo da Vinci's versatile talents. 課堂講述勾勒文藝復興時期，而閱讀篇章著重李奧納多‧達文西的多樣才華。

2. 另一指出兩篇章的主題為學說及相關佐證的重要句型為：
The reading passage depicts N, and the listening passage features N.

解析 2

當閱讀和聽力兩個篇章其中一個篇章介紹某一理論或學派，另一個篇章舉出相關的例證或知名人物時，可套用此句型。**depict**，描述，類似詞有**describe**、**illustrate**、**portray**。

應用 2.1

The reading passage depicts the school of modern architecture, with a focus on its development in the U.S., and the listening passage features I.M. Pei, the master of modern architecture. (Part 2 Unit 26) 閱讀篇章描述現代建築學派，特別是這個學派在美國的發展，而聽力篇章著重現代建築大師，貝聿銘。《節選自 Part 2 Unit 26》

應用 2.2

The reading passage depicts the school of organic architecture, and the listening passage features Frank Lloyd Wright. 閱讀篇章描述有機建築學派，而聽力篇章著重於法蘭克‧洛伊‧萊特。

課堂講述與閱讀篇章主要論點──換句話說（Paraphrase）的重要句型、解析及應用

解析 1

除了以類似字（**synonyms**）將主要論點重述，論點原句是主動語態時，可轉換成被動語態。

論點原句

Some even consider cave drawings by cavemen in the Neolithic Age the earliest form of graffiti, and thus make it the longest existent art form. (Part 2 Unit 25) 有些人甚至將新石器時代的穴居人所畫的洞穴壁畫視為塗鴉最早的形式，使得塗鴉成為現存最久的藝術。《節選自 Part 2 Unit 25》

應用-換句話說 1.1

Another view even holds that graffiti might be dated back to the Neolithic Age, to cave drawings. (Part 2 Unit 25) 另一個看法甚至認為塗鴉可追溯到新石器時代的洞穴繪畫。《節選自 Part 2 Unit 25》

應用-換句話說 1.2

Graffiti is viewed as the earliest art, if cave drawings in the Neolithic Age are included in the genre.

塗鴉被視為最早的藝術，如果新石器時代的洞穴繪畫被包括在這個類型。

解析 2

利用句尾的分詞片語 **echoing ...** 強調兩個篇章都提到的類似特色，**echo**，呼應，類似詞有 **correspond to N**、**refer back to N**。

論點原句

The Mesa Laboratory embodied his philosophy akin to Organic Architecture. The building rests harmoniously in the Rocky Mountains, as if sculpted out of rocks. (Part 2 Unit 26) 麥莎實驗室大樓展現了類似有機建築的哲學。這棟建築物和諧地和洛磯山脈並存，看起來像是直接從岩石雕鑿出來的。《節選自 Part 2 Unit 26》

應用-換句話說 2.1

One of his works of architecture in the Rocky Mountains in Colorado fits in with the natural environment seamlessly, echoing the feature mentioned in the reading. (Part 2 Unit 26) 他設計的其中一棟建築位於科羅拉多州洛磯山脈，這棟建築和自然環境無縫地接合，呼應了閱讀篇章提到的特色。《節選自 Part 2 Unit 26》

應用-換句話說 2.2

His design of the building in the Rocky Mountains in Colorado demonstrates the idea of organic architecture, corresponding to the school mentioned in the reading. 他設計的位於科羅拉多州洛磯山脈的那棟建築展現了有機建築的理念，呼應了閱讀篇章提到的學派。

解析 3

換句話說時常須要使用間接引述（**reported speech**）的句型，例如 **The lecture describes that S+V**、**The professor explains that S+V**。

論點原句

Graffiti artists have also branched out to collaborate with fashion designers and produce numerous products, increasing the daily and global presence of this art form. (Part 2 Unit 25)

塗鴉藝術家也和流行服飾設計師合作拓展出許多產品，提高此藝術在日常生活和全球的能見度。《節選自 Part 2 Unit 25》

應用-換句話說 3.1

Besides, the lecture describes graffiti artists that have turned their careers to the fashion industry, allowing consumers to attain their works in commercialized forms. (Part 2 Unit 25)

此外，講述提及塗鴉藝術家將職業轉向至流行產業，讓消費者可以透過商業型式取得他們的作品。。《節選自 Part 2 Unit 25》

應用-換句話說 3.2

Graffiti artists and fashion designers cooperated on their works so that their works are accessible to consumers. 塗鴉藝術家和流行服飾設計師合作，使消費者能輕易取得他們的作品。

解析 4

答題時只需挑選與主題關係最密切的重點換句話說，例如主題是現代建築，雖然課堂講述提到了甘迺迪夫人，但答題時應該省略。

論點原句

Pei was chosen by Ms. Kennedy to design the John F. Kennedy Presidential Library and Museum, which includes a large square glass-enclosed courtyard with a triangular tower and a circular walkway. (Part 2 Unit 26)

甘迺迪夫人選擇貝聿銘為甘迺迪總統圖書館及紀念館做設計。此圖書館及紀念館包含一大片被玻璃環繞的方形中庭、三角錐狀的高塔和圓形的走道。《節選自 Part 2 Unit 26》

應用-換句話說 4.1

His design of the John F. Kennedy Presidential Library and Museum exhibits geometric forms and carries historic significance. (Part 2 Unit 26) 他對甘迺迪總統圖書館及紀念館的設計展現了幾何形式，並蘊含歷史意義。《節選自 Part 2 Unit 26》

應用-換句話說 4.2

Geometric forms and historic significance are embodied in his design of the John F. Kennedy Presidential Library and Museum. 幾何形式及歷史意義都被包含在他對甘迺迪總統圖書館及紀念館的設計。

解析 5

以類似詞和不同詞性轉換論點原句的結構，但仍須保留原意。

論點原句

He was a social activist as well, heavily involved in socio-political movements, in which he participated in charitable support for children and fought against racial discrimination. (Part 2 Unit 25) 他也是位行動主義者，深度參與社會及政治方面的活動，並支援兒童慈善活動及反對種族歧視。《節選自 Part 2 Unit 25》

應用-換句話說 6.1

His other contributions included charities for children and anti-racism campaigns. (Part 2 Unit 25) 他其他的貢獻包括兒童慈善和反對種族歧視的活動。《節選自 Part 2U25》

應用-換句話說 6.2

Charities for children and campaigns against racism were among his concerns. 兒童慈善和反對種族歧視的活動都在他的關注範圍內。

解析 6 ▶

類似詞替換，例如 **blurring the boundary ...** 改寫成 **lack of definite boundary ...**。

論點原句

Wright's buildings are characterized by linear elements. ... The interior space also extends to the exterior, forming another feature, that is, blurring the boundary between indoor space and outdoor space. To achieve that, floor-to-ceiling glass windows are employed. (Part 2 Unit 26) 萊特的建築特色是直線元素。…室內空間也延伸到戶外，形成另一個特色，即模糊了室內空間和戶外空間的界線。為了達到這種模糊界線，玻璃落地窗被使用。《節選自 Part 2 Unit 26》

應用-換句話說 6.1

Organic architecture is characterized by linear design, lack of definite boundary between interior and exterior and huge glass windows. (Part 2 Unit 26) 有機建築的特色包括線性設計、缺乏室內與室外間明確的界線及巨大的玻璃窗戶。《節選自 Part 2 Unit 26》

應用-換句話說 6.2

Linear components, lacking absolute dividing lines, and large glass windows are all features of organic architecture. 線性元素、缺乏室內與室外明確的界線及巨大的玻璃窗戶都是有機建築的特色。

Unit 35

西洋藝術類及科學類重要句型整理、解析及應用

闡明兩個篇章關係的主旨句（Thesis Statement）重要句型、解析及應用

使用說明

Unit 27 的範文採取面對面結構、Unit 28 的範文採取點對點結構，但不管是哪一個結構，主文都須要換句話說，所以句型重點都在 **"Paraphrase 換句話說句型"**。

---

1. 指出兩篇章主要論點類似的重要句型為：

   Both the reading and the lecture describe...The reading emphasizes ... , and the listening elaborates on ...

解析 1

動詞片語 **elaborate on**，詳細闡述，適合搭配細節較多的篇章。

應用 1.1

Both the reading and the lecture describe the features of the main characters in Woody Allen's movies. The reading emphasizes *Annie Hall,* and the listening elaborates on Allen's successful career. (Part 2 Unit 27)

閱讀篇章和課堂講述都描述了伍迪·艾倫的電影裡主要角色的特點。閱讀篇章著重在《安妮·霍爾》這部電影，而課堂講述詳細闡述艾倫成功的職業生涯。《節選自 Part 2 Unit 27》

應用 1.2

Both the reading and the lecture describe the features of Woody Allen's comic performance. The reading emphasizes his movies, and the listening elaborates on his stand-up comedy.

閱讀篇章和課堂講述都描述了伍迪·艾倫的喜劇表演特色。閱讀篇章著重他的電影，而課堂講述詳細闡述他的單人脫口秀。

2. 指出兩篇章主要論點相反的重要句型為：

The major points in the reading and listening passages contradict one another in terms of ...

解析 2

contradict，牴觸，駁斥。類似詞有 **oppose**、**dispute**、**contravene**。

應用 2.1

The major points in the reading and listening passages contradict one another in terms of the fundamental issues humans will need to tackle with considering prospective habitation on Mars. (Part 2 Unit 28)。

閱讀篇章和聽力講述篇章的重點互相駁斥，這些重點是關於人類未來居住在火星上必須處理的基本議題。《節選自 Part 2 Unit 28》

應用 2.2

The major points in the reading and listening passages contradict one another in terms of the possibilities for humans to build a colony on Mars.

閱讀篇章和聽力講述篇章的重點互相駁斥，這些重點是關於人類在火星建立殖民地的可能性。

閱讀篇章主要論點——換句話說（Paraphrase）的重要句型、解析及應用

解析 1

換句話說及濃縮重點是寫作整合題型的主要考點。以詞性轉換和形容詞子句將兩個長句濃縮為一個短句。

論點原句

In most of his films, the major personae exhibit neurotic disposition, and are frequently anxiety-ridden. Very often, those characters behave like schlemiels who undergo some sort of spiritual awakening or personal transformation through entanglements in relationships. (Part 2 Unit 27)

在他的大部份電影裡，主要角色展現神經質的特色，而且常常感到焦慮。那些角色常表現笨拙，並透過人際關係的牽扯，經歷某種靈性覺醒或個人蛻變。《節選自 Part 2 Unit 27》

應用-換句話說 1.1

The major characters are usually angst-ridden people who behave clumsily and undergo changes in life when dealing with relationships. (Part 2 Unit 27)

他的主要角色通常是感覺十分焦慮的人，而他們的行為笨拙，並在處理人際關係時經歷人生的變化。《節選自 Part 2 Unit 27》

應用-換句話說 1.2

The protagonists are often anxious people who act clumsily and gain life lessons through relationships. 主角們通常是焦慮的人，他們行動笨拙，透過人際關係學習關於人生的事物。

解析 2

利用類似詞重述重點，如 **generating oxygen** 轉換成 **emit oxygen**、**separating oxygen from carbon dioxide** 轉換成 **break down carbon dioxide**。

論點原句

In fact, a technology called electrolysis is already applicable to generating oxygen on Mars....absorbing Martian air and separating oxygen from carbon dioxide. (Part 2 Unit 28) 事實上，稱為電解的科技已經能被應用在火星上產生氧氣…能吸收火星上的空氣並將氧氣從二氧化碳分離。《節選自 Part 2 Unit 28》

應用-換句話說 2.1

The reading points out that NASA has already devised a process called electrolysis that breaks down carbon dioxide and emits oxygen. (Part 2 Unit 28) 閱讀篇章指出 NASA 已經研發出一個稱為電解的程序,能分解二氧化碳並排放氧氣。《節選自 Part 2 Unit 28》

應用-換句話說 2.2

Electrolysis, which generates oxygen by breaking down carbon dioxide, will be used on Mars.

電解藉由分解二氧化碳,產生氧氣,將被應用在火星。

課堂講述主要論點──換句話說(Paraphrase)的重要句型、解析及應用

解析 1

將論點原句主動語態句型轉換成被動語態句型。如 **become a trademark** 改成 **are characterized by**。

論點原句

The common theme of Allen's films, that is, the satirical reflection of the absurdity of life, can be traced to his early works....The neurotic persona later became a trademark in his movies. (Part 2 Unit 27)

艾倫的電影的普遍主題,即諷刺地反映人生的荒謬之處,可以追溯至他早期的作品。……神經質的角色之後成為他電影的特色。《節選自 Part 2 Unit 27》

應用-換句話說 1.1

The protagonists in his comedies are characterized by a neurotic nature, and the prevalent theme is the absurdity of life expressed in satirical ways. (Part 2 Unit 27)

他的喜劇裡的主角有神經質特色，而常見的主題是以諷刺的方式表現出人生的荒謬。《節選自 Part 2 Unit 27》

應用-換句話說 1.2

The ironic portrayal of folly in life is prevalent in Allen's movies, and the main characters are usually anxious.

艾倫的電影中，對人生的荒謬以諷刺的方式描繪是普遍的，且主角常感覺焦慮。

解析 2

take up，佔據，類似詞有 **consist of**、**constitute**、**occupy**、**account for**。

論點原句

Carbon dioxide makes up an extremely high ratio of the atmosphere on Mars. (Part 2 Unit 28)

二氧化碳佔了大氣層極高的比率。《節選自 Part 2 Unit 28》

應用-換句話說 2.1

The lecture simply describes that the atmosphere on Mars consists of high proportion of carbon dioxide. (Part 2 Unit 28)

課堂講述只是描述火星的大氣層包含高比率的二氧化碳。《節選自 Part 2 Unit 28》

應用-換句話說 2.2

Carbon dioxide accounts for a very large percentage of the

atmosphere on Mars. 二氧化碳佔了火星大氣層的一大比率。

解析 3

將論點原句的兩個子句濃縮成一個短句。原句的類似詞 **satirize** 和 **turn...into ironic remarks** 重述為 **become targets of his sarcasm**。

論點原句

In his stand-up comedies, he often satirized intellectuals and turned monologues into ironic remarks on contemporary cultural phenomena. (Part 2 Unit 27)。在他的單人脫口秀，他經常諷刺知識份子，並將獨白轉化成對當代文化現象的嘲諷批評。《節選自 Part 2 Unit 27》

應用-換句話說 3.1

Also, intellectuals and contemporary culture often become targets of his sarcasm. (Part 2 Unit 27) 此外，知識份子和當代文化常成為他諷刺的對象。《節選自 Part 2 Unit 27》

應用-換句話說 3.2

Highly educated people and contemporary culture tend to become the subject of his irony. 知識份子和當代文化常成為他諷刺的主題。

解析 4

將論點原句的兩個長句濃縮成一個短句。**lethal** 轉換成 **will not survive**。

論點原句

Thirdly, even if future technologies allow us to utilize other sources of energy, for instance, hydrogen gas, humans still have to tackle the harsh fact of little or even no ozone layer. It goes without saying that without the protection of an ozone layer, the level of radiation on Mars is lethal. (Part 2 Unit 28) 第三，就算未來科技能讓我們利用其他能源，例如氫氣，人類仍需要處理稀薄的臭氧層，甚至缺乏臭氧層的嚴重問題。可想見沒有臭氧層的保護，火星上的輻射程度是致命的。《節選自 Part 2 Unit 28》

應用-換句話說 4.1

The lecture states that humans will not survive on Mars due to the lack of an ozone layer. (Part 2 Unit 28) 課堂講述提出因為缺少臭氧層，人類無法在火星生存。《節選自 Part 2 Unit 28》

應用-換句話說 4.2

Human survival is not possible on Mars because of thin or no ozone layer on Mars. 人類在火星上生存是不可能的，因為火星上的臭氧層是稀薄的，或沒有臭氧層。

Unit 36

科學類重要句型整理、解析及應用

闡明兩個篇章關係的主旨句（Thesis Statement）重要句型、解析及應用

使用說明

Unit 29、30 的範文都採取面對面結構，所以句型重點都在 **"Paraphrase 換句話說句型"**。

---

1. 指出兩篇章主要論點相反的重要句型為：

   While the reading focuses on ..., the lecture raises doubts regarding...

解析 1

raise doubts regarding...，提出關於……的質疑。類似詞有 **cast doubts on**、**remain skeptical about...**。

應用 1.1

While the reading focuses on the positive application, the lecture raises doubts regarding this technology from an ethical perspective.

(Part 2 Unit 29) 閱讀篇章著重正面應用，然而課堂講述從倫理觀點提出對這項技術的質疑。《節選自 Part 2 Unit 29》

應用 1.2

While the reading focuses on the negative influence of this technology, the lecture raises doubts regarding the main points in the reading. 閱讀篇章著重這科技的負面影響，而課堂講述對閱讀篇章的重點提出質疑。

2. 指出兩篇章針對同一主題發表各種研究成果的重要句型為：
The reading gives the definition of...and the lecture provides more details regarding...

解析 2

整合題型考題設計：①兩篇章的主要論點類似、②兩篇章的主要論點互相質疑、駁斥，或③一個篇章提出定義或理論，另一篇章描述相關研究成果或實驗。此句型即回答第三種設計的主旨句。

應用 2.1

The reading gives the definition of play and describes how animals communicate to one another about their intent to play, and the lecture provides more details regarding the types and benefits of play. (Part 2 Unit 30)。
閱讀篇章給了玩耍的定義及描述動物如何彼此溝通關於他們想玩的意圖，而

課堂講述提供更多關於玩耍的類型和益處等細節。《節選自 Part 2 Unit 30》

應用 2.2

The reading gives the definition of nebula, and the lecture provides more details regarding the nebular hypothesis.

閱讀篇章給了星雲的定義，而課堂講述提供更多關於星雲假說的細節。

將閱讀篇章的主要論點換句話說（Paraphrase）的重要句型整理、解析及應用

解析 1

濃縮重點時各種疾病的專有名詞可省略。以連接詞 **though** 將兩個完整句濃縮為一完整句。

論點原句

The most positive application of CRISPR is medical ... For example, patients with cystic fibrosis, a genetic disease that affects lungs and other organs, might be treated by having their defective gene repaired. Theoretically, cancer can also be treated with the same process. (Part 2 Unit 29)

CRISPR 最正面的應用是醫療方面的應用。…例如，針對囊性纖維化這種會影響肺部和其他器官的遺傳疾病，可能藉由修復瑕疵基因治療病人。理論上，癌症也能以同樣的過程治療。《節選自 Part 2 Unit 29》

應用-換句話說 1.1

Besides, the reading describes how the medical application of this technology will benefit patients with genetic diseases and other illness, though it still remains at a theoretical level. (Part 2 Unit 29) 此外，閱讀篇章描述醫學方面的應用將如何使有遺傳疾病及其他疾病的病人獲益，雖然醫學應用仍處於理論層次。《節選自 Part 2 Unit 29》

應用-換句話說 1.2

This technology will be beneficial to patients with genetic and other diseases, though clinical treatment remains theoretical. 這科技對有遺傳疾病和其他疾病的病人是有益的，雖然臨床治療仍屬理論階段。

解析 2

do not exhibit fixed sequences 以類似詞 **does not follow any order** 重述。

論點原句

One way to distinguish play from the aforementioned adult behaviors is to observe that when young animals engage in play, their mimicking behaviors do not exhibit fixed sequences; ... Another sign of play is that these behaviors are less intense compared with adult behaviors. (Part 2 Unit 30) 一個區分上述成年行為和玩耍的方式是去觀察當幼年動物玩耍，他們的模仿行為沒有固定的順序；…另一個跡象是這些行為比起成年行為沒那麼激烈。《節選自 Part 2 Unit 30》

應用-換句話說 2.1

Unlike adult behaviors, young animals' play does not follow any order, and is less violent. (Part 2 Unit 30)

不像成年行為，年輕動物的玩耍不按照任何順序，而且比較不暴力。《節選自 Part 2 Unit 30》

應用-換句話說 2.2

Young animals play with less intensity, and their mimicking behaviors are performed randomly. 年輕動物玩耍比較不激烈，而且他們是隨意表現模仿行為。

將課堂講述的主要論點換句話說（Paraphrase）的重要句型、整理及應用

解析 1

將論點原句主動語態句型轉換成被動語態句型。如 **become a trademark** 改成 **are characterized by**。

論點原句

Using CRISPR-Cas9 to edit genes in embryos will generate long-lasting and unprecedented impact on a whole species, since altered genes will be inherited through generations. I would foresee that CRISPR-Cas9 will open up a Pandora's box ... (Part 2 Unit 29)

使用 CRISPR-Cas9 編輯胚胎的基因將會對一整個物種產生長遠且前所未有的效應，因為被變更的基因將會被世代遺傳。我能預想 CRISPR-Cas9 將來就像打開了潘朵拉的盒子……《節選自 Part 2 Unit 29》

應用-換句話說 1.1

Since edited genes in embryos will be inherited, the professor thinks that in the future, the consequences might be outside of scentific expectaitons. (Part 2 Unit 29)

因為胚胎中被編輯過的基因會遺傳，教授認為在未來，後果可能超出科學家的期待。《節選自 Part 2 Unit 29》

應用-換句話說 1.2

If CRISPR-Cas9 is used to edit genes in embryo, the aftermath might be beyond scientists' expectation.

若 CRISPR-Cas9 被用來編輯胚胎的基因，後果可能超出科學家的期待。

解析 2

論點原句 **play ... in the similar way that S+V 轉換成 Object play ... is similar to N**。

論點原句

The third type is object play,... For instance, primates, due to their adroitness, play with various objects in a similar way as human children do. (Part 2 Unit 30)

第三個類型是物體玩耍…例如，由於靈長類的肢體靈巧，他們玩各種物體的方式和人類小孩玩耍的方式是類似的。《節選自 Part 2 Unit 30》

應用-換句話說 2.1

Object play, for primates particularly, is similar to human children's play of objects. (Part 2 Unit 30) 物體玩耍，尤其對靈長類而言，類似人類小孩玩物體的行為。《節選自 Part 2 Unit 30》

應用-換句話說 2.2

Primates and human children play objects in the similar mode.

靈長類和人類小孩玩物體的模式是類似的。

解析 3

論點原句是被動語態句型,轉換成主動語態。

論點原句

On the other hand, the technology will very likely be utilized to enhance genes, ... so in the future, "designer babies" might be created. (Part 2 Unit 29)。

另一方面,這項技術很可能被用來增強基因,……所以在未來可能創造出「設計師嬰兒」。《節選自 Part 2 Unit 29》

應用-換句話說 3.1

Moreover, using gene editing to strengthen genes might lead to the so-called "designer babies". (Part 2 Unit 29)

此外,使用基因編輯去加強基因可能導致所謂的「設計師嬰兒」。《節選自 Part 2 Unit 29》

應用-換句話說 3.2

"Designer babies" might become part of reality with this technology.

利用這科技,「設計師嬰兒」可能變成真實的一部分。

解析 4

enhance,加強,類似字有 **reinforce**、**enrich**、**strengthen**。

論點原句

... touching stimulates a chemical in the brain called opiate, which generates a soothing feeling. Moreover, play enhances neuron connections in the brain. (Part 2 Unit 30)

碰觸會刺激腦內一種稱為鴉片類物質的化學物質，這化學物質會產生放鬆的感覺。此外，玩耍加強腦內神經細胞的連結。《節選自 Part 2 Unit 30》

應用-換句話說 4.1

Finally, the benefit of how play stimulates the brain by reinforcing a certain chemical and neuron connections is explained. (Part 2 Unit 30)

最後，玩耍如何藉由增強某種化學物質及神經細胞連結，以刺激頭腦這個益處被解釋。《節選自 Part 2 Unit 30》

應用-換句話說 4.2

A chemical in the brain that builds up a relaxing feeling is stimulated, and neuron connections are strengthened by play.

會產生放鬆感覺的化學物質被玩耍刺激分泌，而且神經細胞連結被玩耍加強。

Learn Smart! 070

iBT 新托福寫作：獨立＋整合題型拿高分 （附 MP3）

作　　者	莊琬君
發 行 人	周瑞德
執行總監	齊心瑀
企劃編輯	饒美君
校　　對	編輯部
封面構成	高鍾琪

內頁構成	菩薩蠻數位文化有限公司
印　　製	大亞彩色印刷製版股份有限公司
初　　版	2016 年 12 月
定　　價	新台幣 399 元
出　　版	倍斯特出版事業有限公司
電　　話	(02) 2351-2007
傳　　真	(02) 2351-0887
地　　址	100 台北市中正區福州街 1 號 10 樓之 2
E - m a i l	best.books.service@gmail.com
網　　址	www.bestbookstw.com

港澳地區總經銷	泛華發行代理有限公司
地　　　　址	香港新界將軍澳工業邨駿昌街 7 號 2 樓
電　　　　話	(852) 2798-2323
傳　　　　真	(852) 2796-5471

國家圖書館出版品預行編目資料

iBT 新托福寫作：獨立+整合題型拿高分
/ 莊琬君著. -- 初版. -- 臺北市：倍
斯特，2016.12
　　面 ； 公分. -- (Learn smart! ; 70)
ISBN 978-986-93766-2-4 （平裝附光碟
片）

1.托福考試 2.寫作法

805.1894　　　　　　　　105021007